Praise for *The Ad*

"A bright and poignant coming-of-age story t.
ing, 'I hope Bronwyn Fischer writes more!'"

—Emily Austin, author of *Everyone in
This Room Will Someday Be Dead*

"A powerful, queer coming-of-age story about a young woman in the throes of first love . . . This gripping novel has the distinct pang of nostalgia mixed with the discomfort of growing up."　　—Buzzfeed

"Natalie's voice—restrained, lyrical, and precise—transported me back to the exquisite desperation of first love. Fischer's debut novel is like a visit from your younger self—even as you worry about Natalie, you won't be able to look away."

—Alyssa Songsiridej, author of *Little Rabbit*, short listed
for the Center for Fiction First Novel Prize

"Insightful . . . a page-turning novel that explores the emotionally revelatory nature of sexual awakenings. This is a surprising, engrossing story of innocence, obsession, and desire."　　—*Bay Area Reporter*

"A haunting tale of love, heartbreak, and deceit. In precise, lyrical prose, Bronwyn Fischer captures Natalie's growing pains in all their hilarity, devastation, and piercing tenderness This is an electric debut."

—Antonia Angress, author of *Sirens & Muses*

"[An] engrossing debut . . . Fischer paints Natalie with care, exploring the depths of her spinning, developing mind. Full of heart, this perfectly captures the lonely messiness of youth."　　—*Publishers Weekly*

"A compelling and quietly disturbing coming-of-age novel . . . Fischer expertly captures the intensity of a first relationship and the constant self-questioning of an insecure young woman."　　—*Booklist*

"Bronwyn Fischer's *The Adult* is a gorgeous daydream of a novel. In her immersive and lyrical prose, Fischer unravels a stunning portrait of a young woman's queer sexual awakening. A tender and sometimes heartbreaking coming-of-age story, *The Adult* nevertheless shows us how profoundly we can grow when we move past shame and allow ourselves to be vulnerable to love and desire. I adore this book!"

—Jennifer Savran Kelly, author of *Endpapers*

"Brilliant, a true original."

—Souvankham Thammavongsa, winner of the 2020 Scotiabank Giller Prize

"This insightful novel is alive with vibrant prose, emotional acuity, and complex female characters. A meditation on what it means to step into your authentic self—with all the subsequent confusion and pain laid bare." —*Kirkus Reviews*

"A masterful debut . . . confident, perceptive . . . intoxicating—I'm reminded of the emotional command of Brandon Taylor['s] debut novel, *Real Life* . . . Fischer is a new talent to watch—a young fiction writer with a poet's ears and eyes, whose understanding of queer heads and hearts is already compelling and indispensable." —*Xtra* magazine

"Fischer perfectly captures that enraptured feeling of first love, especially with someone older and more experienced. There are parts of this book that are also deeply melancholy; bits and pieces that made me exhale and set the book aside for a minute or two. A little bit heart-wrenching, this one will be perfect for Sally Rooney fans and sad gay people alike." —*Southern Review of Books*

"A beautiful and beguiling world, in which Fischer's sentences do what the best writing does: alter my way of seeing. The novel offers a deeply embodied sense of being eighteen in a new place, even as the narrator longs simultaneously to step into a new self. The unexpected perils and complexities of her journey are rendered with utmost specificity, offered to the reader with verve, heartbreak, and comedy. This is the debut of an utterly original new voice."

—Catherine Bush, author of *Blaze Island*

"Deftly capturing the awkward loneliness of early adulthood, Bronwyn Fischer's debut novel *The Adult* is an affecting queer coming-of-age story. . . . A very strong debut." —*Winnipeg Free Press* the adult

the adult

Bronwyn Fischer

ALGONQUIN BOOKS OF CHAPEL HILL   2024

Published by
ALGONQUIN BOOKS OF CHAPEL HILL
Post Office Box 2225
Chapel Hill, North Carolina 27515-2225

an imprint of Workman Publishing
a division of Hachette Book Group, Inc.
1290 Avenue of the Americas,
New York, NY 10104

Library of Congress Cataloging-in-Publication Data

Names: Fischer, Bronwyn, author.
Title: The adult / Bronwyn Fischer.
Description: First edition. | Chapel Hill, North Carolina : Algonquin Books of
   Chapel Hill, 2023. | Summary: "Natalie, a college freshman from a remote
   small town, is drawn into an all-consuming affair with an older woman"—
   Provided by publisher.
Identifiers: LCCN 2022061903 | ISBN 9781643752723 (hardcover) |
   ISBN 9781643755113 (ebook)
Subjects: LCGFT: Lesbian fiction. | Novels.
Classification: LCC PR9199.4.F5626 A67 2023 | DDC 813/.6—dc23/eng/20230113
LC record available at https://lccn.loc.gov/2022061903

ISBN 978-1-64375-629-5 (paperback)

10 9 8 7 6 5 4 3 2 1
First Paperback Edition

For Emma, and for my parents.

the adult

Soon, but not yet, Nora will look up and she will see me, sitting at a distance. In the wet grass, the imprints of Nora's shoes will fill back slowly, and I won't suspect that she is walking toward me.

After Nora meets me on the bench, it will be difficult to recall that in the beginning there were moments so plain and unconsumed that I felt I could watch them like a distant view. Like hills rolling away.

Once she holds out her hand and asks, *Do you mind if I sit,* no other memory will exist without brushing backward or forward over the moment her eyes looked down at me. The soft and penetrable skull of the world will suddenly harden and everything will be seen through the damp and wilful light of our first meeting.

one

At first, the trees behind the McKinnon dorm had looked like a real woods. The leaves were facing up as though it might rain. I stood by the bedroom window, my nose accidentally touching the glass, and I watched my parents walk down the path toward their car.

On the drive, the car window hadn't been shut all the way. The wind had buffeted as we drove, killed all conversation. My mother, a few times, looked over her shoulder at me. Arm pressing against the back of my father's seat so that she could crane her neck to see. I wanted her to ask if I would be all right. I wanted her to turn to my father, say, "Are we really going to leave her?"—the beginning of a tearful conversation. But the next time my mother turned, she met my eyes and she mouthed, *That's making a lot of noise,* and I realized, she hadn't been looking back at me, but at the sound of the wind rushing by.

I felt like I'd had a terrible day even though I hadn't. The day had been long, not terrible. But, being alone, everything I thought was true, so I thought, *What a terrible day,* and I sat in my room.

My suitcase was still open. Before they'd left, my parents had made the bed for me. I thought of them pulling the sheets up, patting the duvet. I'd noticed the wrinkles on their hands as they smoothed out the sheets. Tight gold rings around their fingers, were they old? I'd wanted to lie down and have them make the bed over me as though I were a child. But I'd stayed standing. Watching unhelpfully as they worked.

It didn't take long before everything was made, unpacked. My parents had looked around the dorm room and then they'd looked at me. The walls around us were white and bare, absolute possibility. When I met their eyes, I felt like promising them something, but what to promise eluded me, and with the bed already pressed so flat, my father said, "Okay, we should leave."

In the afternoon there were a lot of introductions. We stood in circles all over campus. We found a landmark, played a get-to-know-you game. The grass had been wet and soft, like washed hair. At four o'clock we stood under the arch of an old tower and our guide, a girl a few years older, said, "At some point you'll hear the carillon." We nodded. "That's fifty-one bronze bells." I looked at all the heavy stones that had been placed, one onto the other, to reach the height of the tower. "It's pretty cool," the guide said. I accidentally met her eyes. She smiled at me assuredly, and I suddenly wished that she would take me aside and tell me that I should stick with her. That we should hang out. But before I could smile back, or consider another more compelling expression, she and the rest of the group had started to walk away.

Near the dorms, we played another game. As instructed, I said my name and then a hobby, and then two truths and a lie. Everyone guessed the lie correctly, and I wondered how I could be transparent already. It had been a bright day. We wore matching red shirts that said *Frosh*. They smelled like vinegar and by evening the printing had already started to peel, making some of us *rosh* and *F osh*.

We ate in a big group, arranged by dorm floor. We kept talking and talking. I watched the girl across from me chew, while the girl beside her asked, "Where did you go to high school?"

A slipstream of questions and answers. Was it Ashley who had gone to Oakwood? Was it Fiona sitting across from me, and was it rude to ask, and how often was it rude to ask, if that was in fact her name?

I wanted something unequivocal to bond us. But all together, our voices chattered and choired, indistinct. I wished that one of our voices would catch. I thought a couple good, hard words could maybe start a fire. That was all we needed. Smoke underneath us, the table crackling—at first, we would all be slow to react, but then we would get going. Nothing to blow the fire out with, we would have to use our breaths. As we stood over the table, smoke would billow to the high ceiling of the dining hall, and the flames would go out. We would all be red-faced and tired, so bonded and accomplished that we would probably be able to leave school without degrees. Our one meal, life-long—

"Do you guys want to go out?"

It was a warm night. Everyone's makeup was darker than their skin. Our shoes sounded wet against the ground. We moved off-campus toward a bar.

Inside, we sat at a table near the wall. A girl named Clara raised an arm over her head to get our attention. She wore a strapless shirt and I felt like I'd looked at her armpit for too long, and that she noticed. She told us to make sure we knew our birthdays if we were using fakes. She was already nineteen.

"Do you have a fake?" I shook my head at the girl beside me, who showed me an ID that belonged to her cousin but that she thought would work because their eyes were similar. She thought their differently styled hair would actually play to her advantage, because changing your haircut could really affect the look of your face. She went ahead of me and didn't have any problems. I had an underage wristband put around my wrist.

Everyone ordered beers because no one wanted to order what their mothers ordered, and we'd seen men order beer. The girl who looked like her cousin poured some of hers into an empty water glass and I drank from it. The tabletop was sticky. On the walls there were string lights and bicycle parts. It looked as though someone's garage had been turned into an art installation.

"You said you're from up north?"

"Yeah, you said you had two sisters?"

"Where up north are you from?"

"Are you close with your sisters?"

"What do your parents do?"

The girl across from me had a tattoo. A snake coming down her arm. I thought if I ever got a tattoo, it would be of a husband telling his wife that he wanted to move from their nice house to live in the wilderness. And then on the opposite arm I'd get his wife, her eyes held in the longest blink.

I said, "My parents own a lodge—"

It was actually called Lakeside Inn and Resort. But I thought calling it a resort would give the wrong impression. I could have said *inn*, but I thought *lodge* sounded more wooden. My parents had renamed it Lakeside Inn and Resort when they bought it. Before, it had been called Timothy's Lodgings. The place was a cluster of five cabins. There was a main house with a front desk and a dining room, and there was an outdoor firepit where people cooked packs of hot dogs, and just-caught fish.

If you were to enter our town from the left side, coming north to south, you would find one grocery store, one restaurant, and four churches. The day before I left, one of the church marquees said, *If you got arrested for being a Christian would there be enough evidence to prove it?* I'd heard my dad say once that the only thing the town could really support was people praying for money, and the room had laughed. I thought of repeating this to the girl on my left, Annie.

"That's cool," she said.

"Yeah," I said. "It's on Lake Temagami."

Annie shook her head. "I haven't heard of it."

"It's really small," I said. "Not the lake, but the town."

She gave me a small laugh and looked down at the table. I couldn't tell if she was laughing because I was embarrassing myself or if she was laughing because we were at a bar and drinking and we didn't know each other.

We all swapped beers. We were deciding what we should like. I was tempted to say that I liked the one that was dark

brown, the one the bartender had said was hoppy. But it wouldn't
be true, and I thought everyone would be able to tell.

The girl with that tattoo rubbed her hand against her knee
and said, "I think I like the dark one."

We all looked at her. She shifted in her chair and then drank
another sip. As everyone went on talking, I watched her eyes slip
from the conversation to her glass. And for a moment I felt steady,
right to have said nothing.

On the way home from the bar, the group separated. A few girls
went to a second bar and some went to a frat house. For the rest
of us, the way back to the dorm seemed long.

"You know, just because we're going back to the dorm doesn't
mean we have to go to sleep," Clara said.

When we got up to our floor, I left the group quietly and sat
back in my room. I felt like a remnant. The pressure of eyes
looking at me had been lifted, but my throat was hot from drinking and when I went over to the window, I could still see the soft
bends of my parents' backs as they walked away.

I could hear talking through a vent. Laughter intermittently.
I felt stupid for leaving myself out. I sat on my bed. I watched a
video called "crunchy chicken cooked in the middle of the forest
(NO TALKING)." The man builds a fire, runs his hand
through a nearby stream, pets a cat that's been following him.
Then he brings out his heavy cast iron pan, shows us his salt and
oil. The only sounds are of the stream, the fire, and the chicken
crackling. When the chicken is almost brown, the man crouches
and starts cutting basil on the flat of a tree stump. He cuts with
a slow, smug rhythm that seems self-aware, and suddenly the

natural calm of the brown forest floor and of the moss and weeds that surround the firepit feels inflicted. I stopped the video. And then I noticed that the dorm had gotten quiet.

I stepped out of my room. I wanted to go outside to the trees beyond the window, they reminded me of Temagami. I wondered if standing among them would make me feel sad or happy about leaving. If I felt happy, then it was simple. It would mean that I didn't have to worry, and that the choice to come to school was justified, already good for me. If I felt sad, well, it wouldn't mean the opposite, necessarily. I decided to expect to feel sad. And then I also decided that neither feeling should mean very much at this stage.

Annie was sitting in the common room. She held a book open against her chest. She was wearing a little toque that made her look cold. It occurred to me that if I asked her to come outside with me, we might have the kind of moment that makes people friends. We might both stare at the trees, unusually gray, unable to think of a color brighter. Our steps would be louder than usual on the sidewalk, and for a moment we would mistake ourselves as the only two people alive and this would bring a sudden gladness. It would vanish every question we had about our possible futures, and we would become suddenly strong, and purposeful.

Annie smiled. "Are you going back out?" she asked.

"Yeah, I think so," I said. A finality that made her nod politely. I opened my mouth as though the space between roof of mouth and tongue might give more conversation, but because I said nothing, Annie just looked at me, and I had to whistle until the elevator arrived.

Down by the trees, the black sky seemed more distant without stars. Behind the dipping branches, the city was easy to see.

The light from high windows made burrows of white and yellow through the night. I tried to look into the blackest row of trees. A place where they had been planted narrowly together, a thicket where the needles of their branches overlapped. But between each tree, there was a space where the darkness fell away, not like Temagami. I could look and look but the darkness would never look back at me. I waited a minute for realization. For the assurance of some resounding feeling, but all I could think was that the trees here did not make a real woods, although, with the sound of the street nearby, people's voices and cars, there was the same sense of unknown company.

two

I got lost on the way to my first class because my dot on the map kept swiveling. I was late and the lecture hall was full. I stood looking through the small window in the door. The professor was all the way down at the bottom of the amphitheater. There were rows of people flipping their laptops open.

"Excuse me."

I moved to the side and a guy behind me pulled the door out of his way. When it closed, it made a loud sound, which a few people turned to look at, and suddenly I felt the impossibility of going in after him. I watched the guy find a seat, shuffling by people into the middle of a row. I imagined myself, legs bumping against all the desks. Trying to crouch out of the way, but unable to become small enough to cause no inconvenience.

I looked down at my shoes. I thought of my parents who had bought me my shoes, and who had bought me all the shoes I'd ever had in my life. And I wondered if it would disappoint them if I didn't go in and sit down. Or, if it was exactly the thing they expected I would do. Spend a few weeks in the city before coming home. Return to the lodge, no smarter, but smartened up. My mother had said, *Sometimes you have to go away for a while to find a new appreciation for—*

I could go back. Look after the cabins, strip the beds, and then make them. Bring plates of eggs around the dining room, talk about whether or not the biggest fish bite in the early morning, or in the evening, in the last dregs of light.

I didn't get any braver thinking these thoughts. I would lie when my parents asked me how my first day had gone. Pretend that I hadn't just stared at the door, pretend that I'd gone inside.

I walked back to my dorm room, the sun on the back of my head. I passed a hot dog stand and a noodle shop, and both smelled red and yellow. I tried to look into some of the faces I was passing to see if they looked worried, to see if any of them were also wondering if they'd gotten everything all wrong. But everyone seemed all right. They were talking to the person beside them, or they were walking at a meaningful clip, listening to something.

In the dorm, Clara hung a small whiteboard on the back of her door. When I walked past her, she was deciding what to write. She looked over her shoulder and called to my back, "Natalie, right?"

"Yeah," I said, and tried to smile nicely.

"Want to come inside?"

Clara sat on her bed. I sat on the chair by her desk. She had a purple duvet, and a black-and-white map on her wall. Her blond bangs looked like a tuft of fur.

"So, Natalie. Who gave you that name?"

"I don't know, I think my mom chose it."

"You mean, you've never asked?"

I shook my head. She looked at me as though I also might never have looked at myself in the mirror.

"My grandmother named me after her sister who died in an accident when she was little."

"Oh—"

"That's why it might sound old-fashioned."

I was sure that my name didn't have a story. I knew no one had died for me to have it.

"We should exchange schedules so that we know when we're both off class."

"I'm supposed to be in class right now," I said.

She smiled at me. "You're kind of cool, Natalie."

I looked down at my legs but couldn't stop myself from smiling too. Which proved my uncoolness to myself and I thought, probably to Clara as well.

"Sarah said you were quiet, but I don't think so. You're not quiet, are you?"

I couldn't imagine Sarah, but I said, "Sarah said that?"

Clara smiled again. She had the kind of blond hair that would fade easily into white. She would be the kind of old woman that people still found beautiful.

"Yeah," Clara said. "But don't pay any attention to her."

She asked me if I wanted to go to the dining hall with her. We lined up outside. Clara spoke quickly to me, and the girls in front of us, about what kind of meal plan she had. And then she told us excitedly about the pasta station. She said, "I'll probably eat pasta every single night."

The pasta station had the biggest crowd around it. Clara went over, but then met me near the toasters, bowl empty.

"It looked very soft," she said. "And I honestly can't stand when my pasta is soft."

I agreed with her. She started putting pieces of lettuce into her bowl. I took two apples from a basket of fruit, and six packets of peanut butter, and then we walked to the end of a nearly full table and sat across from each other.

"Is that all you're having?" she asked. Her voice sounded slightly impressed.

"I'm not that hungry," I said.

"I guess six peanut butters is kind of a lot."

I nodded, but she kept her eyes on me. She didn't eat the tomatoes in her salad. She left the big quarter slices on the side of her bowl.

That night, the heat of September ended so abruptly that there was talk of snow. Clara walked ahead out of the dining hall, said, "Are you kidding me?"

We stood in the grass. I looked at the ground, which was brown and hard. In Temagami the leaves had already turned autumn colors. There were people from the city who planned vacations just to see the change. They would spend hours not hunting, or fishing, but sitting on the cabins' small wooden porches. Cameras in laps, they became very deliberate about breathing in, leaning their heads back. Above them, branches converged over each other, and the leaves made such a dense print that you felt like you were wearing it. I always felt the urge to laugh at them, but then, as time went on, felt sad instead that I wasn't similarly awed.

At first the snow was only slight, almost still rain. But then the gray of the sky fluttered white and it *was* snow that started to fall.

"Has this ever happened before?"

"I'm sure it has—"

We stood without coats, lifting our faces, holding our elbows. It was quiet for a few minutes, the moment gathering itself. I imagined our voices years later straining to recall this day in late September. Middle-aged and thinking back through the chill in our clothes. The memory more vivid and bearing than reality had been.

Clara left to speak to a boy she recognized from her philosophy class. I sat on a bench just beside the grass. My eyes were already starting to get restless. Like standing in front of a good view, you either have to build your house there or turn away.

"Isn't it cold?"

I looked over. A boy sat down, his shoulder against my shoulder.

"Yeah, it's a bit cold." I smiled at him.

He said he was Sam and I said I was Natalie, and then we asked the only questions we could ask. He was from Mississauga, and we were both in a class called Material Religion.

I looked at his chest. He wore a brown sweatshirt that matched his eyes and hair. He had rough cheeks, where acne had once been. "Can you believe it's snowing?" he asked.

"No, I can't."

He said, "It must be called something. Everyone out like this."

Faces turned up still, I thought, *If we look for too long, we'll join together and become a single cell. The kind that can't think or speak or behave.*

It seemed quiet even though people were speaking all around us. The cold air flattened the echo of our voices into an even tone. The ground was now white. Water leaking out of a pipe onto the sidewalk was slick, difficult to walk on. Sam leaned back against the bench, air in his cheeks. I looked at him, and I wondered why he'd sat down next to me. And then I looked across the way and I saw Clara leaning into one hip, the boy from philosophy smiling at her.

Sam smiled too when I looked over at him. And I decided to say, "You know, people are going to have sex tonight."

His eyes creased quickly, as though I'd said something worrying, and then he laughed a breath of cold, visible air. "What?"

"Yeah," I said. As though I knew. As though the line hadn't taken all of my confidence.

"Why?" Sam asked. "Because of the snow?"

It still fell slowly, floating.

"Is it like the apocalypse? Is it like, people have sex before the world ends?"

I said, "I'm not sure."

I imagined bodies heaping together, exactly the same as the snow. In the morning, a small plow burning a thin fume into the air would clear a path toward the dining hall even though it would've melted by the afternoon.

Sam shook his head at me, as though I were somehow unbelievable. And I wondered why certain people sit next to each other at certain times.

A few moments passed. He asked me what other classes I was taking. I started making a list. Intro to Psychology, a seminar in poetry—

"Ohh, you'll have Jones, then."

"For poetry? I think so—"

"Have you heard the rumor about her?"

I said I hadn't.

He said, "They say she slept with a student last year."

"Really?" I felt my head tilt. "Is that true?"

Sam laughed. "I don't know." But then he said, "She's still teaching, so there must not have been actual proof. These things only get serious if you're caught, or if you make a complaint." He gave a silly smile, which made me think of a spool of yarn, a sheep. "And if it was me, I wouldn't complain."

I opened my mouth but then closed it, not knowing what to say. I hadn't met Jones so I couldn't tell him whether or not I would complain.

Sam looked down at his knees. "Do you want to go inside?"

He pushed his hands inside his pockets, I noticed his jeans, dark blue. I couldn't picture his thighs. "I might stay out a bit longer," I said.

Sam nodded, as though he'd expected that. When he stood, I stopped looking at his pants. He said, see you?

I said see you.

And then he turned, brushing the snow from his hair.

My room was white except for my duvet cover, which was green. My desk was brown, and my chair. My shoes at my door were black. And all of these things together were me.

In bed, my stomach felt small, which made my whole body feel cold, and slightly sick. I wrapped myself in my bedsheets. I was hungry, but I was going to bed.

The lights were all out and the blinds were pulled down. My stomach made a sound. Like hands digging wet sand. I curled over onto my side so that I felt absolutely frail. And I wondered if I wasn't still a child who needed to be fed by other people. If I could handle going to class, and talking on benches, and milling through the dining hall, and putting enough on my plate, and not caring whether or not Clara thought it was cool to only eat apples and peanut butter.

I felt a slight nausea. I'd noticed that the room didn't get that dark. The white walls seemed to carry spare light from the window. I thought of hanging a towel across it, but I didn't have nails or tape. I shifted underneath the duvet. In Temagami, my parents would be sleeping. I imagined wood drifting through the dark on the lake. The bottom of a boat leaking through a hole in the water. How often did they think of me?

I thought of our kitchen and what my parents would have eaten for dinner. Wondered how long it would take for their routines to tighten around my absence. How had they delegated my tasks at the lodge? Did they wake up earlier and think of me, and hope that I would be back soon to sweep away leaves and untangle fishing rods and tell the old hunters hello? I felt a long, stretching sadness and wondered if it was a sign of true belonging. I thought of the wooden front desk where I'd stood and checked people in and out, the guilty boredom, was it really so bad? Wasn't there, in Temagami, a knowable way forward?

I thought it was probably just easier to be sad in the way that you were used to being sad. I decided that I had to be patient.

Less quiet, less myself. Closer to the person I intended to be. It would start the next day. I thought, *Tomorrow, find a subject that you love, and become more capable in it.* I felt these words soften my brain. I wondered if I'd heard them before, if it was a quote from someone famously wise, or just by an adult when I'd been younger.

I repeated the words, imagined they were a salve I was rubbing in. And this was how I fell asleep. Pretending that I'd never missed a class, imagining a grassy walk toward my next school building, a hill whose downward slope quickened my steps. The seat where I would find myself. Ears ringing with study, and close attention.

three

Jones taught poetry on Friday afternoons, dressed in black. I'd wanted to take a seminar called History's Biggest Losers, but it was full. Nature Poetry had one spot left.

Jones walked around the classroom while she spoke. Her fingers circled through the air as though she were explaining how wheels worked.

"It's always difficult to begin courses like this because there's so much possible material, and even as a full-year course, eight months isn't really enough time." A drink from her mug. "What's exciting is that everyone in this class will be bonded by the attention you give each other's poetry, and by the vulnerability it takes to share and receive feedback on each other's work."

The classroom was quieter than any other classroom. We rested our hands on the desks, some pressed flat, some open. A boy across from me had a serious leather notebook. He wore a jacket that fit his shoulders perfectly. It was black denim with a shearling, white collar. Several patches had been sewn on the front—a blue rocket that had *World Space Force* written on the side, white cursive writing that said *No Heroes*. I wondered if I should buy a more specific jacket. One that could quickly show the core elements of my character.

"Let's discuss etiquette. In this room, you must be thoughtful listeners. Critique is important, valuable, but I won't tolerate meanness, or blatant insensitivity."

Her eyes didn't move quickly, they moved with precise attention. She had short hair, cut below her ears. When she looked at me, I looked toward my desk, where I had a notebook open.

"Okay, briefly on category, because there's never any resolution. *Nature* is almost impossible to define. It's difficult to argue that any subject you choose is not part of the natural world, so we won't spend too much time on this. I won't limit you to greenery, or ask you to pretend that you live on some pastoral hill, but I will ask that you write, partly, about what is ecologically observable."

There was permission in the way she spoke. And I thought quickly of the rumor of her, whatever Sam had told me. Somehow, I couldn't imagine her taking any particular interest in one of us. Her voice was lofty, well-composed.

The girl beside me shifted in her seat. I looked over and saw her jaw tight, her hand writing.

Jones said, "There are many ways to think of poetry and to think of the work that poetry does. The poet wants to make the world expressible in some way. She wants language to be enough—for the words she chooses and the way she arranges them to support the life of her ideas in the world. This ambition leads us to consider the difference between what we wish to express and what we are able to express. What is the role of language in this difference? How might it be shaped, and used to minimize mistranslation? And how, ultimately, can we reconcile the fundamental limits of our abilities, of our tools, which prevent the poem from ever being perfect. That prevent us from fully being understood."

For the first time since arriving at school, I felt the promise of learning something that I'd never imagined. I felt the words that Jones spoke, affecting, pressing. Filled with an effervescent quality, a suggestion of new possibilities. There was a world where people cared about saying things a certain way, where they debated using one word over another and felt that the effect of this debate was consequential. It seemed impossible that this world was the same one that contained Temagami. It seemed impossible that it was the same one that contained me.

As Jones spoke on, I could see how she would be the kind of professor that students went out of their way to impress. I tried to write down important things she said, but the tone of her voice made each of her words feel so crucial that I ended up drawing faces in the margins of my page instead.

After class was over, Jones left quickly, coat over her shoulder. We started moving our things back inside our bags, no one really speaking. But then the girl beside me, Rachel, asked, "Have you read her work?"

I looked over. "No, I haven't."

"You haven't?"

Rachel pushed her glasses up onto her head. The skin underneath her eyes was pale, hinting blue. She had a small bump high on her nose and a tone of voice that made her sound suspicious.

"What did you think of the class?"

I said I liked it.

"Do you want to be a poet?" she asked.

I smiled, thinking she might be joking, but she was serious, and the seriousness of her face made me adjust mine.

"I don't know," I said.

Rachel kept her head on a tilt. "I want to be a poet."

We left the classroom. I thought, going forward, I shouldn't act as though anything were an impossibility. I should think that the world and all of its jobs were open to me.

"I've been reading all of Jones's work, to prepare. You know she published her first book when she was twenty-two?"

I raised my eyebrows.

Rachel said, "She's only thirty-eight now."

I nodded again. I wondered if nodding was as good as speaking.

"Which means she's very accomplished. Not very many people have that kind of record of teaching *and* publication at a young age." Rachel paused and then added, "Thirty-eight *is* young, especially in publishing."

"Right, sure."

She looked at me suspiciously. "What do you want to be?"

I laughed and said, "Oh, don't ask me that," but she had gotten serious again. The coherence of her desire and its pursuit made her face bright, made me feel like she was washing her hands while I was wringing mine. I felt jealous of her.

"Do you have a place in mind for the first poem?"

For our first assignment, Jones had told us to go somewhere we considered to be part of nature.

"I guess I'll just find a park," I said. "Somewhere nearby."

"It might be hard to concentrate downtown," she said.

"Do you have a place?"

"Yes," she said, "I have an idea."

I thought that if I asked her what her idea was, she would think I was trying to copy her, and I didn't want her to think I didn't have any of my own thoughts. She held her chin high. I watched her look up toward the street signs.

"Do you live on-campus?" I asked her.

"No," she said.

"Do you live with your parents?"

"I live alone."

"Really?"

She looked at me defensively. "I wanted to see what it would be like. The dorms can be loud, and I just want to concentrate—"

I rushed to say that she was right, they were loud, and how cool, anyway, that she lived in her own place. I told her that the city was so different from where I lived, had she heard of Temagami, it was so so so different.

She met my eyes. I stopped talking. Something about her made me want to chatter, made me want to say *so so so* forever. Maybe it was that the quiet between us felt hard and serious. She took self-assured pauses, seemed not to care if we walked side by side but didn't speak. It was my inability to meet her on this silent bridge that led to her eyes pressing against mine. Maybe doubting my intelligence, or depth of personality. I wondered if she didn't like me or if she looked at everyone this way, unable to stop herself from deep scrutiny. I thought she'd probably already decided that I was silly, and I imagined she didn't have a lot of time for silly people, people who weren't sure who they wanted to be, whose words could be forced out under the pressure of another person's eyes.

Rachel looked up at the street signs again and then said, "I've been walking the wrong way."

I turned around to observe the right way with her, but she hurried from my side and, without saying anything else, crossed the street before the flashing seconds ran out of time.

four

The early snow made the leaves brittle and they fell before their colors turned. Only a few trees in the park had any red or orange. The rest of them were already bare, the fallen leaves brown, dead.

Around the edge of the park there was a gravel path that runners circled like a track. It was almost raining; a haze, which seemed to want to materialize, made the air feel faintly pricking. I walked toward a square of benches and sat. I had to write Jones a poem. I tried to think about nature. I tried to feel if I was in it, had I picked the right place?

I leaned over my knees and looked at the ground. On my way over to the park I'd seen a bumblebee smeared into the sidewalk and now that was all I could think about. I moved my hand along the grass, and cold water sprang to my fingers. I wrote a few things down in my notebook. *Wet, green, mud.* And then, after looking around for a while, I wrote, *There was a bumblebee smeared into the pavement.* The words on the page looked much different from the bumblebee. Was that the disconnect Jones had meant, between words and their meaning? I looked up.

The benches around me were mainly empty. I felt the first drops of rain against my face. A man sitting across the way ate a muffin. Small birds hopped near his shoes. My chest started to feel cold, as though suddenly there was skin exposed. I looked down to make sure it was my imagination and when I looked up again, my eyes were drawn to a different place. As though caught by a seam in the air. Across from me, I saw a woman looking.

The woman wore a brown coat. It folded in between her crossed legs. She held the handle of her umbrella as though at any moment she might use it to shift gears.

She sat very upright. And I wondered if it was her uprightness that made the coat look so nice, expensive? Or if it was the coat itself that made her look so upright? I thought she looked the way you would expect a doorbell to sound. Bright with the anticipation of company.

I tried to avoid staring directly at the woman. I looked at the ground near her shoes, the branches above her head. When my eyes did fall on her, I made sure that they were also falling on something else. The trees to her right and left. I couldn't tell her expression, but the air around her seemed shyer, it seemed to softly petal from her.

The woman stood. As she got up, I looked back to my note-book. I stared at the ground again. A rock, a stick, a few leaves. I could only think of generic descriptions—veins on a leaf. What was another word for veins? What is a good word for a poem?

Because I could think of nothing, I took out a book that Jones had assigned. But then, instead of reading, I tried to think of all the reasons Jones would sleep with one of her students. I wondered if it was possible for someone to be irresistible-looking. Was that it? I couldn't imagine any one of us being so beautiful that it caused her to overlook the relative dumbness we would bring to conversations. And then I thought, maybe it was a poem. Maybe a student had written an irresistible poem.

The woman crossed the park. It wasn't until she was close that I could hear her shoes. Her boots had left a narrow path through the grass. Like the paths left by deer in the forest. Her heel marked her step, but then her toes were padded and flat. They didn't sink into the mud.

Now I could see her face properly, could see she was looking right at me. And I thought maybe I was in her place. I should move from where I was. I closed my book and I shuffled so that I might stand, but the woman held out her hand.

"Sorry," she said. "You don't have to leave."

I looked up at her. Dark hair that fell over one side of her face. She held her arms across her stomach as though the walk had made her cold, and then she said, "I'm Nora. Do you mind if I sit?"

When Nora spoke, it felt like a trick. It made me wish that the day was darker, or that a candle could be lit.

She sat down as though we'd been waiting to meet. I tried not to turn my head, but moved my eyes as far over as I could to look at her. The air seemed newly full. Nora turned her face toward me.

Neither of us spoke and after a moment I wondered if she'd mistaken me for someone else, but there was no way of asking her that, so I pretended that nothing was unusual to me, and I turned my book to a different page. I looked down at the poem in my lap. The journey, she writes, is full of branches and stones. The wind and bad advice—

"Mend my life!"

Nora leaned over my shoulder and said, "Mary Oliver?"

I opened my mouth and then closed the book self-consciously. Nora smiled. Catching her eyes felt like sitting in something wet, foolish.

I said yes. And then I said, "I'm taking a poetry class."

"Oh, so you write poems?"

I said, "Not usually." And then I asked, "We haven't met before, have we?"

"Not before now."

I blinked dumbly. I wondered what would make me sit down next to someone I didn't know and start a conversation. But then I thought other people did things like that all the time. On planes. Or buses. Or bars—especially in bars.

Nora propped her elbow on the back of our bench. Her eyes felt like buttons open on my shirt. "So, you're in school," she said.

I nodded at her.

"Should I guess your major?" she asked.

I tried not to smile too widely but could feel that I had. And I was almost overcome with embarrassment, but then she smiled back.

She looked down at my shoes, the collar of my shirt, quickly, my waist. What was I wearing? I felt my clothes hanging on to me. I wanted to tell Nora that they weren't really mine. But I didn't speak, and she was still surveying, gathering a guess.

I wanted her to name a subject that I'd never heard of before, and then for me to say no, and say something even more surprising. But instead, I said, "You won't be able to guess."

"No?"

"I haven't decided on a major yet."

I shifted on the bench. Nora kept looking at me. I was worried to look back in case her eyes stayed put, in case they didn't follow the usual give-and-take of eyes.

"You should guess what I do," Nora said.

She uncrossed her arms and her coat fell open over a blue sweater, the kind of color you'd wrap a baby in. I looked at her face and tried not to mind that just as I could see her, she could see me too. I wanted to keep my look sweeping, but then I found myself caught between her lips and nose. Puddling in that soft dip.

"You're thinking hard," Nora said. She smiled and the dip lessened. I got out.

"I don't know."

She watched me for a second. I thought of the rough tongue of a cat.

"Do you go to U of T?" she asked.

"Yeah." I paused. "I'm new."

She smiled as though this was quite obvious and then turned away to look out over the far ground of the park. As her attention strayed, I worried suddenly that she might be a teacher at the school. That she might have come over because I was a student, and this was a way of making people feel welcome.

"Are you a professor?"

Nora looked back at me. "Is that your guess, then?"

"Oh," I said. "No."

Nora laughed. "I'm not a professor."

I felt some relief.

"I'm sorry I interrupted you," she said, and gestured at my notebook.

"No," I said. "I didn't have anything to write about anyway."

"It's hard to write a poem."

"That's what I'm finding."

Her face turned again, and she looked over the grass. I tried to look around too, but everything seemed plain.

I said, "Do you talk to a lot of people in this park?"

"Are you trying to track a strange pattern of behavior?"

"Oh, no—"

"How old are you?" she asked.

I felt surprised. "Why?"

She looked kindly at me. "You don't have to say."

I wondered if she was flirting with me, and wished that I could tell her that I was twenty-five or thirty. A good, solid age.

"I'm eighteen," I said.

She nodded.

I tried not to look shy. "Is that what you expected?"

"Yes," she said. She closed her coat, brushed a strand of loose hair off her face. "Do you want to know how old I am?"

I looked at my lap. I did want to know. If she had asked me if I wanted to know what she'd eaten that morning, I would have wanted it.

"Only if you want to say," I said.

Nora looked at me. I wondered if it was a knowing look, and I tried to think of something I could say that might cause the thumb of her attention to shift. But then her hand flattened the back of her coat and she stood over me.

"I should leave you be," she said. "Good luck with your poem."

"You too," I said. Impossible to take back. She turned to leave, and I felt the feeling of a missed step, a sudden panic that I wouldn't see her again. "My name's Natalie," I told her.

She turned around. "Natalie—"

My name—it seemed to belong to some deeper part. Was this deeper part my truest self? I felt it buried in my chest, in my stomach. I felt it rattling as though there were a way for it to be freer than it was. I thought I should have told her my name earlier, given her more than one chance to tell me, Natalie.

"It was really nice to meet you," she said.

And I sat quiet as she left. Staring at her last glance.

five

That night there was a party in our dorm. The cold rain that had fallen all afternoon and evening finally stagnated but left a wistful fog that didn't part as the students coming across the grass walked through it. I could see only a vague movement of arms and legs. Loud cackles of laughter from a mouthless swarm.

I looked at myself in a mirror on the back of the door. Then I peeked down the hall. I saw a girl wearing jeans and a small corset-looking bodice. I shut my door and looked back at myself. I wondered if I should cut up one of my shirts, but I felt too unsure about where to cut. I decided to tuck my shirt into my jeans, and I rolled up both sleeves, which I thought made it slightly more corset-y. I put a beaded bracelet on my wrist. The beads were agate, but I'd lost the little paper that tells you what it means. I thought it was something to do with inner tension and grounding.

I had a drink in my hand, free-poured by a guy who said, sorry, we're almost out of orange juice. I'd only drank a few times before, and it had always been tentative. A short warmth, a slight tipping of vision. Now the warmth was expanding, and the conversation around me unraveled new ways to stumble. I sipped.

I saw Clara and a few other girls from my floor. Seeing them all together talking made me feel as though I were watching them through aquarium glass. I thought maybe I should have more friends, and maybe I should be having a better time. I moved toward them, and Clara said, "Hey, it's Natalie."

Clara's group moved through the party to the stairwell, and I followed. They were going back up to our rooms. There were people standing on the steps. I noticed how hot my cheeks were, felt the sudden pulse of my blood, sticky, like a melted popsicle. So quickly, drunkenness became an inescapable fact of my body. I lifted my head so slow. And my foot slipped on the next stair, and I had to put my hand down.

"Whoa, there."

A voice that might soothe an uncertain horse. I took the hand reaching down toward me and let myself be pulled up. Sam's face.

"Are you drunk?" He smiled at me, big teeth. Clara and her group had gone.

"No," I said. "Not drunk."

"I'm going down, are you going up?"

"Trying to," I said.

"Come down, with me," Sam said.

I shook my head at him, and he shook his head at me.

"Okay, okay. Like passing ships then." He nudged me gently as we passed each other. And I went upstairs, thinking he'd been funny.

On my floor there was a long table in the common room set with half-full cups. There was a deck of playing cards being flipped, a pen was stabbed through the side of a beer can and two mouths tried to fit overtop of it.

There were chairs pulled along the walls of the room, and I sat down beside a girl who kept putting her head in her hands. I asked her if she was all right and she swayed back and forth. I remembered a video we'd been shown in high school about alcohol poisoning, and I realized how difficult it was to know what to take seriously.

I asked, "Do you need anything?"

The girl shook her head, and then put it down again.

I walked around the party doing nothing. I walked through the halls, and then through a door that led to a stairwell. I would sit on a step until I heard voices and then I would stand quickly and jog the rest of the way up as though someone needed me. My face felt heavy, and my throat felt hard, an insoluble lump. I looked into the cup that I held. It was hard to imagine that I was the same person as earlier in the day, sitting in the park, speaking to Nora. I thought if Nora saw me as I was right now, she wouldn't come over and ask me how old I was. She would stay, sitting in the shape of her coat. Maybe the sun would have come out.

I wanted to go back to my room. I went down the next stairs and stepped sideways into the hall. There was a crowd gathered outside Clara's room. The door was closed. Someone said, "She wouldn't tell me anything, she's in there alone."

My room was a few doors down.

"I think she's crying," someone said, but I couldn't hear anyone crying. Sarah knocked on the door, no answer.

I couldn't get by the crowd, so I asked, "Did something happen?" And then the girls said, "None of us know." I tried to listen against the door. They said, "I think she's just really drunk." And I imagined again, an educational video, a group of girls huddled around a door while someone lies inside, not in the safety position. If she passed out on her back, would she start choking?

I tried the handle of her door. "Clara?"

The girls stood behind me. I looked back at them and they nodded. I pushed the door slowly so that Clara had time to tell me to go away. She was curled on her bed.

I said, "Hey."

She raised her eyes. When she cried, they looked more blue. "You can come in," she said. "But shut the door."

I pulled it closed behind me.

I moved toward Clara and her bed, and she made a slight effort to sit up. She was wearing a skirt. I noticed little blond hairs over her knee, but her shin was smooth, and so was the side of her thigh. I didn't know what to say. Clara wiped her face with the back of her hand, and then she asked, pointing to her eyes, "Is it everywhere?" She had wiped streaks of black all over her cheeks. I nodded at her. "I must look stupid," she said. "You don't have to stay in here."

There was a drawing against the wall opposite Clara's bed. A charcoal fire, painted yellow and red. "That's good," I said.

Clara held a tissue to her nose. "It's my fireplace."

I laughed a little and she cleared her throat and then walked to the mirror on her desk, where she sat down and wiped her face. She told me to sit, so I crossed my legs on her bed and leaned my back against the wall. There was still a heat in my throat, and I was still holding a drink in my hand.

Clara came back to the bed. "Was Annie in the hall?"

I couldn't remember. "I think she was around. Do you want me to get her for you?"

Clara said, "No, no." And then it seemed like she might cry, so I looked around the room and tried to pick something else that we could talk about.

"Can I have a sip?" she asked.

I passed her my cup. She drank.

"Do you like being away from home?" Clara asked.

It felt nice to be asked something, but I realized there wasn't a truthful answer that could be given quickly, so I said, "I think I do. I've always wanted to live in a big city."

She said, "I grew up here."

"Really?"

Clara tilted her head to the side. She held my cup against her face. "This is strong."

"I didn't mix it."

"Someone wants to get you drunk," she said, and offered it back to me. Clara looked down.

"Did something bad happen?" I asked.

She shook her head. "It's fine." She took a slightly shallow breath, but her eyes looked more solid now, and she seemed more like herself. I realized that I liked sitting by her. I liked it better than sitting alone, than going up and down the stairs, not knowing what to say.

And then there were several knocks on the door. And Clara's name was said loudly.

"I should go," I said.

"You don't have to."

But the knocks came again, and I didn't want to sit in a crowd.

"I'll see you around," I told her.

I opened the door and the group of girls walked in past me. I turned down the hallway to my room and saw Annie trying the handle of my door. She squinted at the key in her hand. I walked up to her.

"I think this is my room," I said. Even though I knew it was. I couldn't tell if she was drunk or if I was so drunk that everyone else seemed drunk. Or maybe I was starting to be less drunk and everyone else was starting to be more.

Annie said, "I'm sorry, I'm an idiot."

I told her she wasn't. She asked who my roommate was.

"I have a single."

She leaned against the wall.

"I didn't ask for a single," I told her. I didn't want her to think I was anti-social.

"Clara has a single." Her voice was marbled with alcohol.

I told her that I would have been happy to have a roommate, and said something about built-in friends. Then I started to worry that she might think I'd put something really strange on the roommate-matching form that had led the university to decide I shouldn't have a roommate even though I had wanted one.

"Did Clara say anything?" Annie asked. She wasn't thinking about me.

"She didn't say what was wrong," I said.

Annie looked toward the ground. "She's upset with me."

"Why?" I watched her face crease. "She asked where you were," I said, wanting to comfort her.

Annie looked toward Clara's door but didn't respond. "I have to find my room," she said, and held up her key before walking unsteadily down the hall. I imagined her sitting small and sad in the middle of her bed and decided not to go back to my own room. I walked by the common room again.

I took a beer from an open cooler, but then I left it on one of the tables. Playing cards were scattered across it, getting wet in drinks that had spilled. Now a ball was being passed around a circle and a group of people were yelling out different types of dogs. Rottweiler, lab, poodle, hesitate, hesitate, half a word, dachshund, big laughter.

I sat on a small couch that had been moved off to the side. Through a window, I saw that the fog was still over us. A solemn drift—I imagined that the common room was actually full of stretchers and that we were all soldiers waiting to be bandaged, to be told about the severity of our wounds. I imagined a new roll of gauze, and my blood accidentally wiped on someone else's hand, and them not worrying about that at all. I thought of Nora. I thought of her coat, which had folded between her legs so neatly. I thought of her walking away to where she lived, and I wondered, where, where did she live?

I wondered how long I would have to sit in the park before I met Nora there again. I tried to think of what I might say. I tried to think of all the things in the world that were interesting and how I might relate to these interesting things. Or, if I wasn't interesting, how could I at least be very fun?

I looked around. Sam spotted me from across the room and he grinned drunkenly. His legs wobbled as he came over, which made him seem taller. I said, "Sam, why don't you sit?" He sat down even while saying, no, I'm okay.

"I'll get you some water," I told him as I started to get up, but he held on to my trailing hand and I was pulled back down toward him.

"Natalie," he said. He motioned for me to come closer to him, and then he cupped his hand by his mouth as though he might whisper something to me. I leaned my ear toward him, felt his hand quick on my jaw, and his lips touched the side of mine.

I pulled away. "I'll go get you water," I said.

He reached for me again, but his hand fell through the air, and I heard the drunken sound of my name as I walked away.

I went to my room, and I lay flat on the bed. When I closed my eyes, yellow light spread itself through to black. I could feel the place where Sam's lips had touched me. I thought of his eyes spinning, dizzy, his body sitting down, doll-like.

I looked at the ceiling, light-headed. I wondered what Nora and I had looked like on the bench together. I wondered if in her presence I was hardly visible, a knot in the wooden bench that a passerby would notice only if they went very slowly. Only if they had a keen eye for detail.

I wondered what it would look like for Sam to meet Nora. I thought of him sitting on the bench, and her approaching. I thought of them shaking hands, not knowing each other, but being polite. Sam would say, *Isn't it cold?* His opening line.

Nora would nod her head and then her hair would fall across her face. It would spread across her cheek, in the way of her lips.

Sam would squint. Think about reaching out, tucking the loose strand behind her ear, out of her eyes. He would want to touch it so badly that he would put his hands in his pockets and pinch his leg. And then he would try to look past her altogether, try to look above her head, toward the sky.

Are you all right?

He would nod at her. He wouldn't cup his hands around his mouth and motion for her to come closer. He wouldn't lean toward her, wouldn't press his lips. He wouldn't touch her, except to shake her hand in the beginning. And I'd already thought of that—they'd let go quickly.

six

On the streetcar, I sat next to Rachel. The sun reflected a black glare off the tall buildings. Jones wasn't on the streetcar with us, though Rachel looked at the doors whenever they opened, in case she appeared.

I said, "Do you think Jones takes the streetcar?"

Rachel squinted into the sun. "Probably. It depends where she lives."

I asked Rachel if she'd been to High Park before. She said yes. "That's where I did the first assignment."

After that, we stopped speaking. I could tell Rachel didn't want to talk. She had a notebook in her hand, which she wouldn't stop looking at. She was crossing things out, staring long at the page only to change one word. She was too distracted to care about any effort I was making to say things to her. I thought this meant that her lack of interest in me wasn't necessarily personal.

It was just that nothing in the world was more interesting to her than the way her thoughts could be written down.

I leaned my head against the window, skipped my eyes along the sidewalk, which passed quickly. As we moved farther from downtown, there were fewer high-rises, more houses. A brown fence belonging to a stretch of backyards had collapsed. I thought, *Fix that, won't you,* and I wondered if I was really not a girl, but a gruff older man.

The streetcar slowed, doors opened, Rachel craned her neck.

I said, "I wrote the first assignment in Queen's Park."

I looked at the side of her face. Her tiredness reminded me of soft fruit. Plums and grapes. The streetcar's doors closed, and Rachel leaned back again. She turned to me.

"I imagine it was hard to concentrate there," she said. "It's quite a busy area."

Hard to concentrate, the rattling of the streetcar's wire reminded me of a set of blue crystal bowls that my parents kept in an old glass cabinet, which shook when you walked by it. Every time I passed it, my mother said, *Careful, that's your grand-mother's crystal.* And I wondered how I could help it. My body, a permanent quivering weight.

Almost as quickly as the streetcar sped up, it slowed again. The doors opened.

"Hey, there she is," I said. But Rachel had already seen her. She shot me a look, like a finger pressed against her lips. And then she turned back to the notebook in her lap and quickly began to scribble.

Jones glanced at me without recognition. I wondered, if she had told us all to meet at Queen's Park, if I would have seen

Nora again. And then I thought, *I shouldn't think of her, I should try harder at school.* I opened a book that I was supposed to read for Material Religion. There were statues pictured on the right-hand page, missing noses and arms. Underneath, it said, "Statues of young Tutankhamun and his consort"—I imagined myself his consort. Her statue was worse off than his. No feet, and missing more of her arm.

Rachel kept looking up at Jones, who stood a few rows from us, at the front of the car. She put her hand on the back of an empty seat, which kept her balance as we rode. I wondered what kind of thoughts she had. During the day, did she carry her mind like a net above her head and then in evening write poetry at a desk?

The streetcar spoke, *Next stop, High Park Boulevard.* I wondered if there was anything I could do to get that voice to break its automation and say something else. I thought Nora might be able to. If she sat close to the speaker, the recording might trip and the streetcar might find itself suddenly awake.

Rachel stood. "Are you coming?"

We stepped off the streetcar and onto the sidewalk. Jones walked slightly ahead. A dozen other students gathered by the gates at the entrance of the park. Once Jones felt we had properly convened she led us farther in. Students sidled beside her, keeping her pace, trying not to ask the same questions. Rachel stayed beside me, watching closely. We sat in a circle near a tree and bench.

In our circle, we pulled our poems out. It was the first time we would hear each other's poetry. Jones didn't ask who wanted to go first. She looked around once and said, "Okay, James, let's go with you."

My own nervousness distracted me. It was difficult to concentrate on the people who went before me. I heard:

The leaves crunch as I walk over them,
The sound is nothing.

Jones said, "You want the words to feel crucial. For every line."

James looked down. I noticed Rachel writing. I held my pen and tried to fake thoughtfulness, but then Jones said, "Natalie, do you have any thoughts on James's poem?"

I felt my body quicken. I wondered if it was important to consider James, or if I should only be considering the words that he wrote. I noticed James take a deep breath in. I tried to think of the leaves—he'd said they'd crunched as he walked over them? Jones's eyes. I could feel them, two cups, useful measures.

I said, "I liked the last line—the sound being nothing."

James made pleasant eye contact with me, and Jones inclined her head as though I'd done a good job, as though I'd realized something.

We went around the circle until we'd all read. When we'd finished, I only remembered the poem that Rachel had read. Her words had been different from the rest of ours. They had held fast. Been sturdy. I'd noticed quick recognition in Jones's face And she'd tilted her head as though to hear better. Was this a tell? Was this a rumor?

Halfway through the lesson, Jones offered us a break, where we wandered down different trails. And then, for the second hour of class, Jones spoke without interruption.

"Wilderness," she said.

We all listened, very still.

"See, you're all on edge, worried that I'm about to be boring."

Soft laughter, buttery, eager.

"Most contemporary nature poetry is about guilt, or mourning. Nature poetry used to be about terror. Terror about uncontrollable elements, about not having the right clothes and shelter. We may feel now that the wilderness is very far out there. Really, if you think of our collective attitude toward environmental issues—theoretically upset, and sometimes quite afraid, but ultimately complacent—it seems that we have stopped believing that we are still dependent on, and subject to, the natural world."

Rachel was closing her eyes. Not peacefully. She closed them with absolute attention. As though she were deepening the connection between herself and Jones by cutting away the rest of us. My neck felt hot with thoughts of dying. Jones paused for a minute. The trees swayed with wind, and it felt as though Jones had known, and waited for this.

"How does your sense of moral decency extend to the natu-ral world? Do you experience a desire to be out in nature? What factors contribute to or limit this desire?"

A guy put up his hand and told us about how he'd recently gone on a canoe trip through Algonquin Park. He spoke at such length that I was sure he must have a really good point at the end, but his story kept on wandering and eventually Jones interrupted him, saying, "And how do you consider all of that in conjunction with our course material?"

He trailed off. Rachel smiled. A few others spoke more successfully. They described the difficulty of understanding their relationship to nature, described the difficulty of drawing conclusions about any of their experiences. In my notebook, I tried to draw the tree that was nearby us. Next to it I wrote *the difficulty of drawing!* And then thought vaguely about what had caused me to choose the tree and if this was some kind of relevant desire.

"Okay," Jones said, "for this week, more poems rooted in the outdoors. Think about how the things you observe are reflective of your relationship with the natural world."

The hour had ended. This time Rachel did walk toward Jones. They stood beside each other by an overhanging tree. I watched Jones's eyes open slightly wider, perhaps a necessary adjustment to take in Rachel, whose words I couldn't hear, except for the brightness of their excitement.

I considered following a group back toward the streetcar, but then I decided that I should stay in the park and try to write. I stepped down a path by a small creek. The reeds had bent completely underneath the water so that the water's edge looked like a marsh. Dulling colors of red and yellow sank into the mud by my feet. I wondered if, somewhere here, there was a poem. But when I thought hard, there was nothing new, nothing of mine to say.

As I walked along the path, the ground became firm again and the pavement led back to the road. I felt my phone vibrating in my pocket. I took it out, and the screen was lit up—*home*. I decided to answer. My parents put me on speaker. They told me there was a storm in Temagami, and that the bad wind had untethered some of the boats from the dock. They'd been free-floating down the west side of the lake.

I said yeah and wow, but the lack of interest in my voice embarrassed even me. And I wondered if the boats would have been more interesting if I'd seen them myself.

"Have you made friends already?"

"Yes," I said.

They were silent. I wondered if they believed me. I'd never had that many friends in Temagami. My mother had told me that as a baby I didn't really like being held. That I wasn't good at being passed to strangers, and that I wasn't soothed when they rocked me at night. This had always bothered me. It struck me as unusually cold and discerning for a baby. I wanted my baby-self to be bright and bouncing.

"Yeah, there's Clara who lives in my dorm. And Rachel. I have a class with Rachel." I wanted them to be impressed by this bounty of friends. For them to believe that it hadn't been me but Temagami that had limited my friend-making abilities.

"Oh, there's also Sam. And Annie."

They made acknowledging noises, but none that sounded too impressed.

I fielded a few more questions. But my answers were short. My parents didn't push too much, and I thought maybe they felt the same way as me. The life that is most interesting is yours. They couldn't imagine the street where I stood, or the class that Jones had just taught. And I thought maybe, for ease of thinking, they just pictured me living in a Temagami that was farther away.

We hung up. I felt far from everything. I realized that I was sad about Rachel's poem, and about my own, which hadn't been as good as I'd wanted. Which hadn't captured Jones's attention.

I went down the road. There was a grocery store, door propped open. My shoes made a smacking sound against the floor, and a man with a cart eyed me disapprovingly. I wondered what I would buy at the store if I was older and wearing proper, silent footwear. I thought I would hold a phone against my ear as

I shopped. Talking, not to my parents, but to a very close friend whom I respected very much. I imagined this version of myself carrying a basket of lemons. So many lemons that it would appear as though I were trying to cure something. My friend on the phone would ask for my advice. I would give some, effortlessly, and I would hear that she was comforted and happy to be talking to me.

"Excuse me."

I was holding up a man in a rush. Getting out of the way, I knocked over several tins stacked beside me. Luckily, it was nothing that could be broken or bruised—how would I have dealt with that? I went down the next aisle quickly. There were rows of Halloween candy, which I skimmed, and then I stood in front of a box of mini-cupcakes. Chocolate with orange frosting. I wondered if I should buy them. I wondered if I should read the label, make sure I could pronounce the ingredients. Wasn't that supposed to be a good indication about the rightness and wrongness of certain foods? I thought of my mother holding a box and declaring something to be too much. I thought of Clara putting aside her tomatoes. Was there an ingredient I should be particularly fixated on? Sugar seemed obvious, and maybe fat?

I wondered if this was the kind of choice that would begin to orient my adult life. What kind of food to eat and how much. Maybe there were certain things I should start to discipline myself against. I decided to carry the cupcakes around with me until I could decide.

In the next aisle over, I thought nothing was as good. I picked up a jar of olives and then put them back and held the cupcakes more firmly.

"Just this way."

At first, I thought that the man was talking to me, but then he looked over his shoulder to see if someone was still behind him. His shoes also smacked the ground.

"Sun-dried tomatoes," he said, and then knelt. He ran his finger along a few jars until he found the right one and then he stood before the woman following had caught up. "Here you are," he said.

There was a pull through my stomach. At the end of the aisle was Nora, taking the jar passed to her by the grocery clerk.

"Never where I think they'll be."

The man's cheeks were red. "Is there anything else you need?"

"This is perfect." She held up the jar. "Thank you."

He nodded, then for a moment he still stood there, saying nothing, only smiling. Nora's face became briefly concerned, and then he seemed to notice his own awkwardness, realized that the need for him to stay had passed, so he apologized and turned away from her, almost jogging.

I watched Nora. She wore the same brown coat. Tied loosely, I thought it looked like a robe. She reached inside its pocket and pulled out a half-eaten packet of cookies. I looked away quickly, toward the olives again. She was only eating cookies, but I wanted to laugh like she'd told a joke. It felt like a dare when I looked back. She chewed slowly. Lips together. I wondered if her coat would look the same if I wore it. I wondered if she would ever take it off and offer it to me. First she'd have to like me better, and then I'd have to be extremely cold, or hurt. If I fell into a river, she might put it around me.

"Nora?"

I heard myself speak. I thought I'd only tried to breathe, it must have been that her name was resting whole in my throat, and that it had slipped. Nora turned, pressing her fingers to her mouth as she swallowed a bite of cookie.

"Natalie," she said.

I felt relieved to hear my name, but realized as she walked toward me that I didn't have anything else to say. I looked at the shelf as though it might give a clue, but she'd already stopped beside me. I tried to look away from the shelf slowly, as though I were leaving an important decision to speak to her.

Nora met my eyes. I smiled too quickly. She gave me a fugitive look and said, "I still have to buy these." She held up the folded cookie wrapper.

"Shortbread cookies?" I hoped it might seem like teasing.

She nodded her head guiltily, as though it were an embarrassing type of cookie to like. "They're my favorite."

She turned toward the shelf beside us. I looked at her nose and cheeks, her chin, her jaw. I wondered about moving closer to her. I wondered how much less beautiful I was than her. And I wondered if this was something Nora knew and thought about while we spoke. How I looked, compared to her.

"I can't decide—" Nora leaned over. "Do you know anything about olive oil?"

I watched her bend toward the shelf full of bottles. I looked hard at the labels, hoping for sudden knowledge, but none came and I said, "No, I don't know anything."

She laughed lightly. "I thought you were going to say that you did."

"I wish I did," I said.

"Why?"

Nora stopped looking at the olive oil and faced me. I found myself squinting at her, and I put my hand above my eyes as though I were standing outside. "So that I could help you decide," I said.

She looked curiously at me. And then she chose a bottle for herself, opaque, green. She smelled familiar, like a shampoo I'd used before.

I said, "Good choice."

She appraised me, the fake expert. "Yeah?"

"Yeah, definitely that one."

Nora held the bottle in her arms. "This isn't my usual store," she said. "What were the chances of catching you here?"

I wondered about the difference between catching and seeing. Because she was right, she had caught me.

"I don't ever come here," I said.

I wondered if it had been strange of me to acknowledge Nora in the store, but then I thought, she had been strange in the first place to sit with me in the park. The appearance of strangeness didn't show on either of our faces. I wondered if the feeling was mutually hidden. Her eyes tried to rest on mine. Every time she looked at me, I felt as though she were tucking something secret in my pocket. Something for me to look at later, when she wasn't around.

"What are you thinking?" she asked.

"Thinking? Nothing."

"You seem like you think a lot."

"No," I said. "I don't think so."

Nora asked, "How did your poem go?"

I wondered why she'd remembered that about me. I wondered if she'd thought of me after the park, as I'd thought of her.

"I'm not very good," I said.

"You're probably modest," Nora said. "Are you?"

"I don't think so."

We looked at each other. Eyes and eyes.

"Are you checking out?"

We walked together. Nora passed her things through first. She took out her wallet and she paid so quickly that it seemed invisible. She held her grocery bag in the crook of her elbow. I put my box of mini-cupcakes on the conveyor belt and watched them slowly move toward the cashier. I had to put my arm deep into my bag to get my wallet out.

We left the store together. To offset the embarrassment of the cupcakes, I tried to look around the street as though everything were interesting to me. As though my mind were working differently than Nora might expect it to. I wondered how I could cultivate the possibility that I was different from anyone she'd ever met before.

"Which way are you going?" Nora asked me.

I looked around, said something about bearings.

Nora said, "I'm this way." A different direction from the one I needed to go in.

I asked her, "Are you going home?"

Nora said yes, and then she said, "I like this time of year."

She looked around, so I did too. The air was cold and bitten. Across the street there was a man in a sweater so woolen that I thought of a hill and a hundred white sheep grazing. Nora was watching me when I looked back to her. I tried to look back strong, and not easily embarrassed.

"What are you going to have for dinner?" I asked her.

"I'm not sure yet."

"Yeah, there's time to decide."

She breathed out, faint laughter. "What are you going to have?"

I looked down at the cupcakes, but planned on saying something else.

"Am I keeping you from having one?"

"Oh, no," I said. And then, "Did you want one?"

Nora shook her head with a light smile.

"Well—" Nora said. The cusp of leaving. I felt the beginning of absence. The beginning of myself standing alone.

"Do you think I'll see you again?" I asked.

I pressed the box of cupcakes harder into my stomach. I felt like they might press through my skin and sit as though I'd eaten them.

Nora looked at me as though I were real. "Do you want to see me again?" she asked.

I nodded at her. Nora looked out toward the street, her mouth set to the side. I tried to read its setting—apprehension?

She shook her head. "I'll give you my number."

I passed her my phone. She typed a number in. I looked down at it.

"You can call me if you'd like. But don't feel bad if you change your mind."

"I won't," I said, meaning change my mind, but Nora had already begun to walk away.

———————

I went back to campus. I didn't want to take the streetcar alone, so I walked. On the way I ate two cupcakes, sweet and chocolate. My teeth chattered—sugar, or nerves. I watched the sun begin to drop. It was setting earlier and earlier in the day. I wondered if Nora was home yet, and this thought quickened the time. As I walked, I read Nora's phone number over, and in a panicked moment stopped to copy the number with a pen on the back of my hand. I thought the phone could be dropped or stolen. I walked faster, but when I got back to the dorm, my phone was intact and the pen on my hand was unfaded, and possibly it was even more deeply etched.

seven

I walked across the field at the front of campus, my shoes crunching down, turning the freezing grass wet. In front of me two people blew bubblegum-scented smoke back, and a soccer net that had been left out overnight was dragged into a shed. The goalposts left long creases in the grass. The light was a wintery yellow. It snapped overhead, made pale shadows to walk beside.

I looked toward the old building ahead. I thought about all the classrooms filled with wood desks so old that they had turned dark and red. The strong and sure voices of the professors who taught, a trance. I wondered if soon, someone would tell me what I should be. I imagined a teacher taking me aside, telling me that I had an unrealized aptitude. A calling so exacting they couldn't believe I hadn't realized it yet.

That morning I'd sat beside Clara and her friends in the dining hall. I'd had eggs, a bowl of oatmeal, and a cup of coffee. The sight of everything laid out seemed to suggest deep personal balance. I could imagine my father preparing this tray for himself. And I thought of him looking at me as I ate, commenting that I'd begun the day *right*.

As I walked, I felt a happiness that seemed to drift from me to the air, which was gently cool. Would it last as far as the edge of the grass? Until the field ended and the pavement of the road made for a firmer step? I felt my contentedness stretch. I imagined myself with the loose muscles of a young man. A face brimming with possibility and good luck. I imagined a tall hill and striding legs. A loose-fitting shirt that would show my tan, barrelled chest. I watched the sky continue overhead. And then I stepped off the grass and onto the pavement.

I followed other students down a carpeted hallway and then sat against the wall opposite the classroom door. There was about to be a test, so I opened my textbook on my lap and looked down at the chapter heading, "Destroying History's Treasures." There was a picture of a hammer smashing a face to pieces. I tried to think of the statue's name. Could that be a question on the test?

Two people sat near me in the hallway, in the middle of a conversation.

"He's mean sometimes," one said. "Very cold, very hard."

"That's like my mother."

"Really?"

"Really," they said. "She didn't ever care when we cried."

"Really? That's when my father stops."

I stared down at my textbook. I tried to remember being punished as a child, but I couldn't. I imagined beginning a conversation with *he's mean sometimes*, but no one assumed the position of meanness, and I thought instead of a path from my house down to the water. Stone steps with moss in between them and a wooden dock that spiders crawled. I saw night falling, a lawn chair that I was almost asleep in, and then the sound of my parents' laughter so awake and without me that for years I dreamed of discovering a secret joke that might cause the same sound.

The hallway filled with more people. I shut my textbook and tucked my knees into my chest. I wanted to call my parents and tell them something. I should say that I missed them, I should say that I missed Temagami. Although I wondered if those were the things that I really missed, or if I was longing for that soft spot—the age where your parents look at you and you look at them back, and you're just their child. And you don't yet feel the strain of being something else. Of being yourself.

I stared at the ground. I felt dazed by my desire, which scraped at all the life already behind me. And then I felt a hand brush my shoulder, and I looked up at Sam.

"I was saying your name." He smiled.

I stood up. "I didn't hear," I said. I wondered if I liked him less after seeing him drunk, and I wondered if he remembered leaning in, so quick I didn't think of it as a real kiss.

"Did you study?"

The door to the classroom opened. Sam propped his elbow against it and let me pass before him.

"Yeah, but I don't think I remember much."

"Are you nervous?"

It hadn't occurred to me to be nervous, but now that he mentioned it— "A bit," I said. "Are you?"

"I hate tests," he said.

The professor told us all to be quiet and Sam mouthed, *See you after?* I gave him an okay sign, which made him smirk. I felt my throat tighten slightly. Did he remember trying to kiss me? If he did remember, did I want him to say sorry?

I walked by Queen's Park on my way back to the dorm. I looked carefully at the benches, but there was no sight of Nora. I held my phone hard. Calling her seemed like *such* a decision to make. I hoped that we could just meet again, accidentally. I closed my eyes for a second in hope. As though this would give the world a second chance to consider my desire: Nora sitting not far. Her eyes catching mine—a coin falling to the bottom of a well, silver hitting flat against shallow water, the metallic sound of a wish made. But when my eyes opened, the park was cold and wet, and I was still alone in it.

In the common room, cobwebs were glued to each end of the hallway and a plastic skeleton sat on the couch. No one would say where it had come from. In the evening we burned our fingers on hot bags of popcorn and played horror movies on the small TV.

All the lights were turned off. The screen flashed, an ankle chained, a close-up shot of hands staked to wood. Someone said, "This is gore, not horror."

Clara put her face against someone's shoulder. Annie sat on the opposite side of the room, her hands tucked into the front pocket of her sweatshirt. They hadn't spoken since the night of the dorm party, and *their* group of friends had become Clara's group of friends. I wondered about Annie. Wondered if I should try to talk to her, but then Clara pulled my sleeve.

"Are you coming? We're meeting about costumes."

Credits rolled on the screen. I looked toward her blankly. I didn't know what she was talking about, but she leaned toward my ear and spoke quietly.

"Look, I'm an introvert too. But it won't be bad, we're just planning for the party." She let go of my sleeve. I said okay, and she pulled me by the wrist toward her room.

In Clara's room, the other girls were already sitting on her bed.

"I think we should go as animals. Foxes or deer."

"But that's not funny."

"Are we trying to be funny?"

"I saw a costume where this girl went as a shark, and her boyfriend went as a guy that had survived a shark attack."

"But that's a couple's costume."

"I'm not suggesting it, I was just sharing."

Someone else said, "We could go as different Disney villains? Like, Cruella De Vil?"

"Or, one of us could be Cruella and the rest of us could be her Dalmatians."

Clara made a faint groan to express her disapproval, then said, "Let's just go to the store and look around."

We walked in a group, taking up most of the sidewalk. The buildings around us were pale and gray, the Dollarama was just ahead. There were costumes in the window. Inside, a kid pulled his father's hand toward a bloodied mask. And the father said, "Really, this one?" The boy nodded.

"Those actually terrify me," Clara said, pointing to a display of shriveled masks.

"Should we get face paint?"

"Should we get ears?"

"Should we be cats?"

"Cats aren't funny."

"I don't care about being funny," Clara said. "I just want to have fun."

There was some nodding, but there was also the strain of us all being different people, wanting to dress as one. Clara led us through to a row of headbands with cat ears. There were cat tails and noses, a small leotard that a child might wear. Sarah held the leotard up to herself and said, "Maybe?"

A woman moved her young daughter away from us. Sarah had started doing a bit with the cat tail, purring at us, to show that it could be both cute and sexy. The young girl looked over and her mother pulled her arm, frowning at us over her shoulder. I wondered if what we were doing was wrong, or if it was just the sight of girls our age, newly unparented, which somehow made others feel like they were looking over the long drop of a cliff.

"What do you think?" Clara nudged me with her elbow. I stood in front of the rack of ears, looking but not touching. Clara took one off the wall and pushed it onto my head. "Okay, that's cute."

She put one of the headbands on herself, and turned to the rest of the group. They reached for their own cat ears. Someone shouted, "What's a group of cats called?"

Sarah paused to consult her phone, and then cried out, "It's a clowder."

And our costume was decided by the following fit of laughter.

We were going to get to the party late. After coming back from the store, we all got ready together in Clara's room. She passed around a bottle of gin, which was divvied into matching mugs we'd gotten during orientation. Clara rubbed the tip of her finger in the eyeshadow palette, the pink and purple shimmered. "So pigmented," she said.

I sat with my back against the wall. Clara's laptop was open on her desk. She pressed play on a makeup tutorial. Clara spoke over the girl in the video, said, "She's only fourteen, but look at her wings." She motioned to the girl's eyes. "They're perfect."

"Are you going to do that to me?" I asked.

She held my chin. I felt the wet tip of eyeliner flick over the corner of my eye. I was conscious of not dropping all my weight onto her hand. The back of my neck started to ache, and I wondered what the point was.

I shook my head at Clara when she uncapped her lipstick. She raised her eyebrows. "Ohh, you wanna get kissed?" She smiled to herself and then put the lipstick back. "Okay. None for me either."

We walked to the bar. It was close to school, but it was also night, which made everyone seem like they were teetering on an unseen edge. The block was mainly fast food, there were also a few head shops and a place where you could unlock your phone. Clara said the place we were going didn't usually ID, we just had to look like we belonged. She looked at me specifically, and I tried to muster a whole year's worth of confidence as I walked across the threshold.

The bar was dark, and the floor was slightly wet. There were purple lights in the ceiling, our noses looked like shadows when we turned to the side. I saved Clara a seat at our table with the other girls while she went up and got us both drinks. When she placed one in front of me, she said, "It's a whiskey sour."

I took a sip. It tasted bitter and then, as I swallowed, sickly sweet.

"I hope they play something good so we can dance," Clara said.

I thought if they played something good and everyone got up, I would walk quickly to the bathroom and sit there for a while.

Clara swallowed with difficulty. "Do you like this?" She pointed to the drink.

Noticing her own wince, I said, "Not really."

"Me neither." Her eyes wandered behind me. A few boys wearing jerseys walked in, and then another group of girls, also wearing animal ears, though I thought they were foxes. Behind them I saw Sam, who had already spotted us and was coming over.

Clara turned to me. "You like him, don't you?"

I hesitated, not sure how she meant it, and then Sam got to us before I had answered.

"What are you guys, cats?" Sam asked.

Clara said, "Of course we're cats. What are you?"

Sam shrugged. "Nothing," he said.

Clara raised her eyebrows at me.

"Hey," he said, to me. "You ran out after the test."

I felt suddenly bad. "Oh, sorry, I didn't know I should wait."

Sam laughed. There was already sweat on his temples. A louder song had started playing. Clara jumped up. "Come on, come on. Time to dance." I sat more heavily on the chair, but it didn't really matter, Clara grabbed my hand and Sam followed until we were in the middle of the bar. I could smell the salt drying on our skin, the taste of alcohol sharp in the air. My back touched someone else's. We were so close to the speakers that I couldn't really hear. The music was buzzy, it tingled the very base of my throat, I had to stop myself from covering my ears. I leaned back and forth, but my legs felt still. Was I dancing? I couldn't tell. My tongue felt like it was brining, I opened my mouth slightly to try to let the taste out.

Sam leaned closer to me. I looked up at the ceiling, the purple lights seemed like tired, sunken eyes. Sam shimmied forward so that I would shimmy back. And Clara laughed at all the shaking. I felt a quick dizziness that made me step to the side. A hand touched my waist, steering. But it stayed there even after I was rebalanced. I was wearing one of Clara's tops, it was tighter and shorter than I was used to, and it was beginning to ride up. Soon, I thought, the hand would touch my skin. And what after that? The hand started to grab more firmly. I could feel its heat against my hip, feel the fingers clenching experimentally.

Sam's face came into close focus and the dizziness stiffened. He looked at me eagerly, and tried to lean in, but I straightened my hand against his chest. I didn't want him to make a mistake again. I turned back toward the table. I felt for my coat on the backs of all our chairs and then I put it on. Clara pulled herself out of the dancing.

"What's wrong?" she asked.

"Nothing, I just have to go."

Sam walked up, and Clara turned to him. "What did you do?"

Sam looked at me. "Did I do something?"

I shook my head. "No, I just have to—"

I walked around them.

Outside, cars pulled up to the side of the street, a few people leaving. The cold air made me feel worse. My temples throbbed, and my ears were ringing. I wondered if Clara would yell at Sam, not knowing why I'd left. And then I wondered if Sam would be angry the next time we were together in class. I thought it must be a lot of work to keep leaning in. I should've probably said something to him. Something presuming, but responsible: *Oh, sorry, I'm not interested.* But what if he looked confused and said, *Interested in what?* Or worse, what if he looked hurt and indignant, and I had to give a good expression back. A conciliatory smile that would make us both feel like losers. I thought I should probably not say anything to anyone.

I zipped my coat, the cold was getting in. I walked for a while without looking up, and then I started to worry that Clara or Sam might try to find me, so every few minutes I would run ahead. I passed a subway stop, but couldn't relate it to where I was in the city. Hoping for a recognizable intersection, I ran for a few more minutes. And then I stopped because I thought somehow I had circled around—the purple lights in a window ahead were the same as the ones inside the bar.

I walked close to the purple lights, expecting to be somehow at the beginning again, but it wasn't the bar, it was a store. In the window there was a mannequin dressed in lace and a long whip balanced on a black stool. *Sexxxy* was written out three times in thin, slanted letters. I wasn't sure why the misspelling of the word made it seem like it had more to do with sex. But the added letters—the triple *x*—stuttered in my stomach. I thought of going in but wondered, if I did, if I would be forced to take off my clothes. I thought of myself being told to strip all the way down. Did I have what it took to be the star of a peep show? Who did I think I was? Definitely not sexxxy enough for that.

Should I go inside? I thought of Sam's hot hand. And then I thought of the time I'd looked through my mother's bedside drawer and found a tube of raspberry nipple balm, half-used. I took off my cat ears. I wondered if Nora ever went into sex stores. And then I imagined her sitting on the stool in the store window, her legs crossing as she looked at me.

What are you thinking?

Ummm, nothing.

Did you want me to put that on?

The mannequin beside Nora wore a black bustier. Tassels hung off the bottom. My face flushed. When I was fourteen, a girl named Elsie had sat on my bed and unbuttoned her shirt down past a lace black bra she'd ordered online. She'd asked me if I liked it, and I'd looked at the loose cups on her chest, the dark crevice between skin and material.

Do you want to act like the guy, and I'll act like the girl?

We sat next to each other at the fake movies, and I practiced taking her hand, and she practiced reacting nonchalantly. She told me to try to undo her bra. She was going to refuse politely, and then I was to try my best to convince her to keep going.

I don't know if I'm ready, she said. She put on a whining voice, the tone of play refusal.

I decided to deepen my own. *Don't you trust me?*

I do, she sighed. I reached toward her bra again, expecting her to swat me away. But she changed the game, and my hand pushed against the half-empty cups, and she pulled my face toward her, kissing it. At first our teeth clipped together, but then we figured out, lips. She held the back of my head, her hand was sweaty. Her tongue periodically swished into my mouth. My brain felt like it was swelling. Puffed up and pink, my whole body, a tissue expanding— And then Elsie leapt back. The bedroom door had opened. Time sped. Elsie was holding her shirt together and my mother was gasping my name so persistently that it felt as though I were running away and she was calling for me to come back.

I decided to go inside the store. It was a long, narrow space, and when the door opened, the woman at the cash register looked up from her phone. I walked behind the nearest rack. A row of black corsets spidered from their hangers. The woman at the counter went back to tapping her phone. I watched her through the straps of a leather harness, and then, when I was sure she wasn't really looking, walked along the far wall of the store.

Any moment I expected that I would be told to leave. My mother would take my arm and shout, *What are you doing? You aren't supposed to do that.* And I would no longer talk to Elsie, and she would no longer talk to me. The embarrassment being worse when it was ours, together. Better to divide it. It's half the embarrassment if you stay apart.

I took a box down from its shelf. Inside, there was a vibrator shaped like a tube of lipstick. I pretended to consider it and then I put it back, but no one was watching. At the very back of the store, where I could no longer see the woman at the counter, I put my hand around a bending blue dildo. Above it there were others, glass and metal, a tentacle ridged all the way down.

I wandered away, back toward the front. There was a basket by the counter filled with little tubes of lube and penis key chains. The woman at the counter looked up from her phone.

"Looking for anything in particular?"

"Not really," I said.

"Are you buying a gift?" she asked.

She put her phone down. There was something about her that seemed sarcastic. Not her voice, it was the way her mouth set after she spoke. A slight smirk, which suggested she didn't think she needed to take me seriously.

"You probably want something cheap. Is it for a party?"

She had a metal stud in the middle of her tongue, a silver ball that she clicked against her teeth when she was finished speaking. She turned the music down. I took a key chain from one of the baskets. It was squishy. You were meant to squeeze it so it would bulge. I dropped it.

"People find the bigger ones funnier," she said. The metal on her piercing clicked.

I looked at a display on the wall. She picked up her phone again and started tapping it. I wanted her to know that I wasn't walking around trying to make fun of anything. That I was a bit drunk, and I'd never been in a sex shop before. She raised her eyes as I kept looking at her and, feeling caught, I said, "I like that," motioning to where her piercing would be on my own tongue. She said thanks. I asked her if it had hurt. She said no.

She pointed at the basket of key chains. "Do you want a bigger one?"

I looked down at all the different colors. "Do *you* think it's funny?" I asked.

She leaned on her other arm. The leaning didn't soften her face; her mouth was still set, both her eyebrows slightly raised.

"I don't find it funny," she said.

I decided to say, "Neither do I."

Her mouth twitched. She had a different face when she smiled. "It hurt a little," she said, and she stuck out her tongue. "But not too bad."

I wanted her to come around the counter and walk around the store with me and take things off the shelves and touch them like they were no big deal. I wanted her to tell me about who she dated, tell me about a life in which she was someone, unafraid, and forward. But instead, she pulled out a bunch of pamphlets and put them on the counter between us. She spread them out so I could see. "You can take any of them if they're interesting to you."

There was a bright-pink one with the header *Queer BDSM Crew*, a beige one with a bubbled font that said *Learn about Sex and Allergies*. I felt myself beginning to flush, so I took one about eco-friendly sex toys. I opened it, hoping the information would stifle my embarrassment, but instead of reading it, I thought about the woman's piercing again. I wondered if it was heavy on her tongue. Wondered if it got in the way when she kissed—

"I have to go," I said. And, without waiting for her reaction, stuffed the eco pamphlet in my pocket and left.

I was the first one back to the dorm. I wondered how long Clara and the rest would stay out. Dancing by the big speakers, drinks shaking in a glass. I thought of Sam, and the makeup I was wearing felt heavy on my eyes. I took off my clothes. I thought of the woman in the shop, and I pressed my face down against my pillow. I thought of Nora.

I thought, *You could call.*

I couldn't call. I wondered if I could text her, but thought it might seem childish, unconfident. I wanted her to think I could handle myself.

What would be the harm in calling? She'd given me her number, and that must have meant something. That must've at least meant, I don't mind talking to you later.

I pressed down on her name, which then expanded to the top of my screen, and I felt like I'd been struck. Fear so hot—reeling and reeling, a fish getting away with endless line. I thought I would hang up even before the ringing began, even before there was any chance she might hear—

"Hello?"

I hesitated. "Is this Nora?" I knew it was Nora.

"Yes," she said.

"It's Natalie."

"Oh, Natalie." A recognition that made her voice soften. "You called."

"Is that okay?"

"It's okay," she said.

It was quiet. I felt the possibility of more loneliness than before.

"Are you all right?" she asked.

My throat hurt. Ahead of myself, there was the long tunnel of my whole life. I wanted her to tell me how I should spend all my time. I wanted to see her hands again. Hadn't they looked clean? Hadn't they made everything she said seem good and well-put?

"I don't know," I said.

I remembered that I'd been drinking. I remembered someone talking about kids who didn't drink in high school, how they always made up for it in university, and I wondered if that was me, if I was out of control.

"I guess I don't know very many people here," I said. "And everything is harder than I expected, but I really liked it, when I was talking to you."

I paused. Nora was quiet. I thought she should hang up. She should hang up hard, and she should tell me not to act like this again. You can't call people whenever you feel like it, what time was it?

"Natalie," Nora said. And the way my name sounded like a flame whispering out made me feel like I could cry. "You're new to the city."

"Yes," I said. My voice sounded like stinging eyes.

"And it's hard to be new anywhere." Nora paused. "Do you want to meet again?"

"Yes," I said.

And the warmth that spread against my chest felt so hot that I looked down to make sure it was just inside.

eight

The next morning Clara wanted to talk about Sam, but I was thinking about Nora, and not answering anything to her satisfaction.

"So it wasn't something he did?" Clara asked.

"No, nothing—"

"He *seems* like a good guy."

"I just think of him as a friend."

Clara nodded encouragingly, but I didn't say anything else, and eventually she turned to Sarah beside her, who, luckily, had made out with a guy called Ben. We could talk about that for the rest of lunch.

I left my afternoon class early, and I stood in my room trying to pick out clothes that would be good to go and meet Nora in. I knew I had nothing. I thought of asking Clara to borrow something of hers again, but I didn't want to explain where I was going. I had a black sweater. It had little buttons at the top that

I felt made it seem more dressy. I considered tucking the sweater into my jeans, and spent a while pulling the material into its most flattering form.

The streetcar moving west was almost empty. The light-blue day had darkened in on itself as though it had been punching its own leg into a deeper bruise. I looked up *things to ask people you don't know.*

1) How do you relax after a day of hard work?
2) What's your claim to fame?
3) When was the last time you climbed a tree just for fun?

As I read, the neighborhoods changed. When I looked up next, the street lamps were on, and the road was wider and quieter. Only two more stops.

29) If you didn't have to sleep, what would you do with the extra time?
30) If you could make a twenty-second phone call to your future self, what would you say and why?

In Nora's neighborhood the houses were all tall and brick. The leaves that fell from old trees had been raked away from the grass. At night, the branches looked tipped with silver.

The steps leading up to Nora's house were stone, unevenly cut so that you could imagine where they'd been before—a boulder on the side of a cliff, rocks set in a forest hill. Nora's door was made of glass. When I walked up to it, I could see the light on inside. A warmth that seemed to fog the windows. I thought, *You can't buy that kind of light.* It must be a quality of Nora and her life.

I knocked too quietly at first. I could tell as my hand left the door that she couldn't have heard. Heat pressed against my neck and cheeks. I lifted my fist again, but then saw Nora's face through the glass as she walked toward me.

She wore red. There was a thin gold chain around her neck, I tried to adjust my sweater again.

She answered the door smiling. A look so welcome that I wanted to immediately thank her and tell her how good a time I was having.

"Come on, come in."

She said that I looked cold, and I noticed myself shivering. She stood to the side, ushering me. I stepped onto a long cream carpet. There was a wooden table to the side where Nora kept her keys and a pair of sunglasses. The dish in the center of the table looked like the inside of a clam, swirling pearl and fragile gray. Nora told me she was boiling water for pasta. And then I followed her to the kitchen.

On the walls there were mirrors hanging like artwork. The ceilings were tall, and their tallness made me look up.

"I'm just about to put it in," Nora said. She lifted a lid off a pot of water boiling on the stove. There was basil and garlic cut thinly on a cutting board. Behind her sink there were little plants on a ledge, all slightly underwatered so that the soil looked loose and wanting.

"You have a nice house," I said, to speak.

She smiled and I felt the air pull. I thought of a violin player. And I thought of their violin. Dark-brown wood and the violinist tucking their chin. Bow against strings. The friction that might make that creaking noise or, worse, that screeching noise. Difficult to forget once it's been made.

Nora stirred pasta into the pot of water and then tapped the spoon against the edge so that it would drip off before she placed it on the counter.

"Can I help?" I asked her.

"That's kind to offer," Nora said.

I smiled, unsure if she meant yes. She moved toward the fridge, and I tried to lean against the counter rather than standing so upright. I looked around for something casual to talk about, but then Nora asked, "Did you have class today?"

"I did," I said. "But I left early."

"Ooh," Nora said. As though that were a little bit of fun. "How come?"

I watched her elbow shake as she grated Parmesan cheese onto a cutting board. "It was hard to concentrate."

"Is the class boring?" Nora asked.

"Oh, no," I said. "I was just—" I shook my head. "A bit out of it."

The pot behind Nora bubbled more loudly, some water spilling over the side. She turned around to stir it.

"Are you sure I can't help you?" I asked.

"No," she said. "Don't worry."

I wondered what else I should say. All my potential conversation starters bent together, limp and unsayable.

"I feel bad," I said.

Nora turned around. Eyes still narrowed from stirring, from the heat of steam rising up. But, looking at me, her face became dulcet, and she said, "No, no. Why don't you sit?"

Nora led me toward the next room through an open archway, where the light was dim and a wood table was already set.

The table was long. On the far wall of the room there was a cabinet with plates and glasses and serving bowls and trays. There was a small stand at the opposite end of the table with an old bottle filled with amber alcohol, and then another with a long neck and liquid as clear as water, a green pear at the bottom.

"I'll play some music," Nora told me.

I thought, *She shouldn't live here alone*, as though I needed to protect her from something ominous in her own house. I thought it must've been the sight of the pear at the bottom of the bottle. Or maybe it was the air of the dining room, which smelled of must. I looked over my shoulder for a man. I looked over my shoulder as though I might be hit heavily in the head, but there was no one.

"Don't worry, sit," Nora said. Did I seem so worried?

I pulled out a chair and I sat down.

"Do you drink?" Nora asked.

I told her yes, and she got two glasses from her cabinet and poured wine into them. She handed a glass to me, and I felt like I had when she'd first approached me in the park. As though she'd mistaken who I was. As though she were suddenly looking at someone she knew quite well, someone she was quite fond of.

Nora put her phone on the table and walked back toward the kitchen. "You can put on whatever music you'd like," she said.

But before she reached the kitchen, I said, "Nora?" And she turned around.

My stomach tightened as I watched her face, waiting for me to speak. I looked at her sweater, which was slightly loose on her shoulders. I wanted to know why she dressed the way she dressed. I wanted to know how much her jeans had cost, how many people she'd slept with, and where they'd met, and how it had all started.

"Nothing, sorry."

Nora kept looking at me.

I said, "I forgot."

I brushed my fingers through my hair. The ends had started to tangle. I thought about tying it up, but then thought no, I shouldn't, it looked nicer down.

"The pasta might overcook," she said, but gave me a warm glance before going back to the kitchen.

I wondered if I should have told someone I had come here. I picked up Nora's phone. I didn't know what to play. I typed *dinner* into the search bar, and scrolled through playlists. Dinner with Friends, Dinner & Wine, Soulful Dinner, Romantic Dinner Vibes. I picked Dinner & Wine because it seemed most precise, and if Nora checked it, she would see that I hadn't been presumptuous, I'd been very literal.

In the kitchen, a cupboard opened and closed. Nora dropped the lid of the pot on the stove. It sounded like she was hurrying.

"Almost there," she called.

I opened my mouth to call back, but then I felt too embarrassed to raise my voice, so instead I coughed into my hand. The playlist I'd chosen was full of slow, voice-forward songs. Not really ambient. I could hear the words too clearly, a man singing *your love holds me underwater, I'm in the deep sea under the waves—* in a husky strain.

I pressed the side of her phone and it lit up, but was locked. I worried that Nora would come in while the song was still going. I skipped to the next one, but it wasn't any better, so I turned the music down really low. And then Nora walked back into the room.

I tried to hold her phone more casually, as though I wasn't locked out and was scrolling through some more choices. Her phone didn't have a case on it. It felt slim, and newer than my own.

"You must not drop it often," I said.

She looked confused, so I waved the phone noticeably and then her face scrunched around her nose as though she'd thought of laughing. "I try not to," she said. She put a pepper grinder down.

I looked at the table. A violin player. I imagined his hands shaking, his legs shaking, his body turning into a tremble. Nora turned into the kitchen again. I imagined myself breathing until she came back.

She set a big bowl of pasta between us. We took turns dishing it into our own separate, smaller bowls. The noodles steamed.

I ate, burning my tongue and my throat as I swallowed.

"Really good," I said. "Thank you."

"Really hot," she said, and she covered her mouth with her hand while she chewed.

It was quiet for a minute. And then the next song was louder than the one before. We both looked over at her phone.

"I just put on a playlist," I said. "You might want to change it."

She glanced at her phone, maybe to see which playlist I'd chosen, what mood I'd wanted to strike. She didn't change it.

"Do you want pepper?" she asked.

"I'm okay," I said.

She twirled her fork through her bowl. "I got worried at the last minute, I didn't know what kind of food you liked."

"Oh, I like everything," I said.

Nora lifted her glass to her lips, I glanced down at my own glass and decided to sip it. "You like the red?" she asked.

I looked at her sweater, but she'd meant the wine. She bowed her head slightly. I nodded quickly and touched the glass. I took another sip. Another and another. The wine, and my burnt tongue, made my mouth taste of blood.

"Do you live alone here?" I asked her.

"Does it not seem that way?" She looked around as though she herself might not be sure.

"I just wondered."

She watched me eat another bite. And then she said, "Originally, I lived here with my wife. But—we're separated now."

"Oh," I said. I nodded as though I understood completely. Original floors, original beams, original tiling, original wife. And then I tried to think of something I could say that would be equally serious, but there was nothing "Were you together for a long time?"

Nora twirled her fork and twirled her fork and twirled her—"Yes," she said. "We met when we were eighteen."

"Really?"

"Yes," Nora said.

I thought of saying something consoling, but then I'd already started to imagine what her wife might be like. I tried to picture them sitting together and what they would talk about.

"Has it been long since you separated?" I asked.

"A few months."

"I'm sorry," I said.

"Oh, no," Nora said as she shook her head. "No need for you to be. *I'm* sorry, I'm being a bad conversationalist."

"No."

The speed of our apologies led to another pause. I stirred the pasta with my fork and then I tried to say more.

"So, what do you do?"

She smiled at me. "I'm a grant writer."

I didn't know what that really meant, and decided to say, "That's cool," because I thought that would be polite. When it led to more silence, more of Nora twirling her fork, I pushed my fingernails into my thigh and asked, "What does that mean?" She looked up at me. I said, "You know, in a daily sense."

She laughed a little at this, and I thought it might all go okay if I could keep it up, if I could keep asking for clarification, and she could keep laughing, and I could keep asking.

"Well, *in a daily sense*, I work with different organizations, mainly non-profit organizations, to get them funding for projects."

"Is it interesting?"

"It can be," she said. And then, more serious, "I think it's important."

I nodded as though I agreed with her.

Her eyes lightened. "What do you want to be?" she asked.

I chewed. I felt myself wanting to answer her a certain way. An answer that was actually a joke. That made it charming to be unsure. I thought of Rachel saying, *I want to be a poet.* The magnet of her desire pulling.

I didn't meet Nora's eyes. I followed the neck of her sweater, my throat constricted. "I want to say something really great."

"What would be really great?" she asked.

"I don't know," I said.

"So you'd like to do something impressive?"

"No," I said. "I'd just like to have a good answer."

Nora looked at me thoughtfully. I wondered if I'd said something thoughtful.

"I really like your house." I eyed the room around to show her that I'd really looked at it, but Nora frowned.

"Oh, I should have given you a tour."

"No, I didn't mean that you had to."

"I'll show you around." She wiped her mouth with her napkin and then she left it on the table. About to stand, she looked at me, still sitting, and hesitated. "Only if you want to," she said.

There was a second of silence. Her mouth opened and then closed. Her hands pressed either side of her hips as though she wasn't sure what else to do with them. "Okay," I said. "Show me around."

We left our plates on the table and I followed Nora back through the kitchen. She showed me her living room. A small green velvet couch, a black coffee table. There was a narrow fireplace on the back wall of the room with two logs placed side by side.

As Nora pointed me through each room, her house didn't appear as I expected it to. There was no real sense of cohesion, each room being dedicatedly different from the one before it. The kitchen had been modern and clean, the dining room expressly old, almost grim. And then the living room, which fractured into pieces: the plush couch, the smooth table. It was sleek and stuffy, depending on what you decided to look at.

I wondered if grant writers made a lot of money, or if Nora's wife made a lot of money.

"Here," she said.

She began to go up the stairs. I touched my way up the banister. I thought of the small red pocket knife my father had given me when I was nine, a protective mechanism.

Nora's foot creaked on the landing. "It's an old house," she said. I asked how long she'd lived there. "Seven years," she said.

I tried not to widen my eyes. I thought, *I was eleven then.*

"That's a long time," I said.

And she said, "I guess it is a long time."

I wondered if she'd loved the house better than her wife had, which was why she was there instead of her. But maybe that wasn't really how divorces went.

Nora moved to the end of the hall. "In here," she said. And she opened the door and stepped inside.

A bedroom. Against the wall, where you would expect, there was a bed. A white duvet, with a darker spiral pattern sewn onto the fabric. The walls were almost bare. There was a round mirror above Nora's bed, too tall to see yourself in. And a bookcase near the window. The only color in the room was of the books—their varied spines.

I stood in the doorway. I didn't know if I was supposed to follow her in or just poke my head through, but Nora had walked into the middle of the room.

I nodded at the room, trying to show a sense of appreciation for the space. I knew I should say something. I knew I should take a step forward.

"It's really nice," I said. "It seems cozy."

"Cozy," she said. As though the word didn't exist.

I looked at Nora's bed. On the low table beside it there was a glass of water and a lamp.

"Are you nervous?"

I looked at her, surprised. Conscious immediately of my mouth and eyes. "Nervous?"

Before, she'd said *don't worry*. But I thought this was different than that. *Worry* might've been the way I spent my day—a worried girl. *Are you nervous?* was in this moment. It was standing by the door. It was her bedroom.

"Should I be nervous?" I asked. I wanted to be joking, but I thought my voice didn't have enough assurance to be found funny. I went to cross my arms over my chest but stopped, so that they rose slightly and fell. I thought it might seem defensive, which might cause Nora to say we should go back downstairs.

"Don't be nervous," she said.

She met my eyes and I looked away quickly, started examining the door's hinges. I worried about smiling too forcefully. Maybe we could both just look at the hinges.

"I wonder if you've read any of these books." Nora waved at her bookshelf.

I felt I should move now, step forward. My pulse felt as though it were beating from deep inside my bones and I thought a few times over, *That doesn't feel like my heart. That doesn't feel like me.* I followed her into the room.

Nora pointed toward a book. "I'm sure you've read this one."

"I have read that one," I said.

"And this one," Nora said. She pointed out another.

"Yes," I said. "That one too." Her face was close to mine.

I could feel her looking at me. How long could we look at these books? I looked toward her bed.

"Do you want to sit?"

"On the bed?"

"If you want," she said.

I followed her to the edge of the duvet and then watched her crawl all the way back to the headboard, where she could lean against the pillows.

I sat at the foot of her bed. I touched one of the corner posts and scratched the wood with my finger. Nora pulled her legs toward her chest. I stared at her knees, and shins, and her hands resting on them. The very thought of her thinking to pull in her knees made me feel soft, overcome. And then the action, her arms, which had to reach and hold, the muscles in her hips, which had to shorten. I wished that I was also an action of her body. Something that one of her thoughts might control.

"Are you comfortable?"

"I'm okay," I said.

"Tell me something," she said.

"Like what?"

I looked toward her, but I couldn't hold her eyes, so I glanced at the mirror above her bed, which reflected the wall.

"Anything you want."

I wasn't sure if I should smile or frown. I chose neither, and then I wondered if I had an expressionless face.

"I'm sorry I called you so late the other day."

"I didn't mind."

I paused. I felt full of disbelief. Why would Nora want *me* here, sitting on her bed? I was sure she could ask anyone to dinner and they would come. So what did it mean that she had asked me? I didn't know what I had to offer her. If I were unusually pretty, I thought I would have known that by now. If I were particularly smart, or charming—

I hesitated, but then forced myself to speak. "Is this a date?"

Nora's legs stretched out and her foot almost touched my knee. I could hear the sound of music still playing downstairs. I wondered if it was romantic.

"It feels like a date," she said.

I felt embarrassed. "Do you go on a lot of dates?"

She shook her head. "No."

"Why not?"

Nora shrugged. "I've been married for a long time."

She looked down at the bed. I worried that she seemed sad. I said, "You know, you could ask a lot of people out and I'm sure they would say yes."

She laughed and said, "Oh, really?" I said yes. And Nora said, "We can go back downstairs if you want."

"What would we do downstairs?"

Nora pressed her lips together. "Probably keep eating pasta."

I nodded, looked away.

And then Nora said, "Or, you could sit beside me."

I looked at the open place next to her. The pillows stacked, the duvet still flat. "What would you like?" I asked her.

Nora shook her head. "It's up to you."

Her hair curled over her shoulder. On her neck I could see the soft path of a vein, and looking at it, I felt that I shouldn't be. As though it were too personal, this awareness of her body, this thought of her neck which made me feel the heat of my own blood. I wanted to know what she liked about me.

I crawled forward and sat next to her. I extended my legs as well. I knocked my feet together.

"Can I turn on the light?" I asked.

"Sure," Nora said. "There's a lamp beside you."

I leaned over and put my hand underneath the shade. After a moment I found the switch and turned it on.

She crossed her legs over one another.

"What were you doing the other night when I called you?"

"I was sitting here," Nora said.

"Do you like living alone?" I asked her, not sure if that was rude.

Nora tilted her head. "Not really. I find it lonely."

I tucked my hair behind an ear.

She said, "Your ears aren't pierced," and I touched my earlobe as though I'd lost an earring.

"No," I said. "I almost had them done a few years ago. But then I didn't."

"Were you afraid?"

"No," I said. "I just changed my mind."

"That happens."

"It was embarrassing," I said. "I was already in the chair."

"Had they drawn the dots on yet?"

I nodded, and Nora covered her mouth to laugh. I smiled at her. And then Nora reached toward me, and she tucked my hair behind my other ear, as though checking they were both the same. I met her eyes. And then, feeling how the moment might blink past, I leaned forward and kissed the side of her face. I did it quickly, without thinking, so I felt the panic afterward, as I moved away from her.

"I'm sorry," I said. I thought I should move back to the end of her bed, and keep still. But Nora put her hand lightly on my shoulder.

In high school there was a joke. A joke and a test. If your ring finger was longer than your index finger—or if your pinky finger was the same length as all four finger widths, or if you woke up with clenched fists—

There was everyone in class grabbing at each other's hands. I had *It isn't true* on my lips. But it doesn't matter how often you repeat that, if your thumb is shorter than the knuckle on your middle finger, and you feel the bristle of a certain someone walking past, and you feel the uncertain guilt of a lie, some allegiance to yourself being broken, then you've made a discovery.

As we kissed, I thought of bicycle wheels spinning, the promise of continued motion. I thought of a pond freezing over with ice, the weight of your legs beginning to slip. I was out of breath before I remembered to breathe, and I could hardly believe that I was myself, pressed against Nora's face. I should have been trying to remember things for when I wondered the next day if anything was real. But in the moment there was no thought of remembrance, no possibility of stop or go, there was only a spiral moving through a cork, the deepest parts of my body being pulled out.

Nora sat up and knelt in front of me. She lifted her sweater over her head, a fluster—imagine a bird flying toward you, incomprehensible wind and feather, that was Nora's body moving forward, the heat of her skin suddenly underneath my hands. She kissed my neck. When it tickled, I laughed and she smiled, and then I kissed her open mouth. I passed my hands over her back. They rested on her bra, unmoving. And then Nora moved her lips from my mouth. "It's a front clasp," she said. Almost a whisper, not instructive. She might've been teasing me, but I didn't know, so I said, "I've never done this before." I felt my nose prickle, the feeling so intense that I wondered if it would coil up into my brain. I put my hand against my face so that it might stop. Nora paused, and looked at me.

"I don't know what I'm doing," I said. "I don't know anything."

I felt her hip resting against mine. I wanted to look at her without her being able to look back at me. But I felt her eyes, drawing out my instability. I thought if she kept looking, I would cry.

"Front clasps scare everyone," Nora said. I wanted to smile at her, but it wasn't there.

"Do you know what I mean?" I asked her.

I could feel my fear rushing over my head. *Don't cry,* I thought, *don't speak anymore.* Nora nodded. She rubbed the side of my face with the back of her fingers. I realized, *yes,* I liked the feeling of her comforting me. I leaned into her hand, and she pulled my head against her chest and she held me there. I felt still. I heard the quiet ringing of her bedroom. She leaned her mouth to my ear. "I'll show you."

She let my head back up again and looked at me as closely as anyone ever had.

"Only if you want to," she said.

I said I wanted to. She kissed me again, and then she pinched the front of her bra and twisted it away. Without knowing why, I closed my eyes.

Nora hesitated. "Natalie," she said.

I breathed hard. "Sorry, I'm just shy."

Nora leaned forward. "Natalie," she said. "You can look at me."

"What if I'm bad at this?"

"I'll show you."

"Will you be disappointed?"

"Why would I be?"

"Because I'll be bad at it."

"You won't be."

"How do you know?"

I opened my eyes and looked up at her face.

"You'll show me?" I asked. She said yes, I said, "What will you show me?"

She kissed me again. My shirt started to ride up my stomach and I left it. Her hands moved down, and unbuttoned my pants. She waited to pull them off until I told her to, as though there might be more to their undoing. She held one of my hands for a while. My skin felt cool when she lifted her mouth, and the air felt like it touched me as presently as she did. She whispered in my ear. What words? I don't know. I felt constantly on the edge of a fall. I raised my eyes toward her face. At first I copied her and then I didn't, and then her thighs pressed closed on my cheeks and I thought, *This is how it begins.*

And now, there is only afterward and before. And afterward, Nora closed her hands around mine and she kissed her own fingers—she had meant them to be mine. I remember, her hands had seemed so sure and pressing that I thought that when they opened, there might be something else cupped inside. Instead of me, something precious and new. A bright and wavering yolk.

nine

In the morning, the porch pumpkins were wet, and the raked grass was full of frost. The air felt like a haze, as though it were still rousing itself out of sleep. On the streetcar, I touched the seat beside me with my hand and let it rest there as though holding a place.

In the entrance of the dorm, the air smelled like the elevator moving up and down. The common room was empty and so was the hall, but when I closed the door of my room behind me, there was very shortly the sound of someone knocking. I turned around and answered it.

Clara stood there smiling. It was early, but her face was already made up. She wore earrings shaped like little gold suns. "Natalie," she said. "Can I come in?"

She sat on my bed. I sat on the chair by my desk.

"You weren't around last night. Your parents don't live close by, do they?"

"A few hours away," I said.

I pushed my hair away from my face, straightened out my sweater. I'd forgotten about my parents, but now, thinking of Nora, I felt strongly that I'd disappointed them.

"But you *were* gone last night, weren't you?" I started to answer, but Clara continued excitedly. "Are you seeing someone? I've never even asked if you have a boyfriend—it seems like so many people still have boyfriends from high school."

"I don't have a boyfriend from high school," I said.

"But you *are* seeing someone?" Clara asked.

I was quiet, but some thrill passed through me.

"Oh my god." Clara leaned forward. "Were you really with someone?"

When I imagined myself saying Nora's name to Clara, the night before fell through my body, and I felt I could buckle. And I thought, if I were to try to speak, all of my inadequate explaining would loosen the reality into a spooling memory. And last night would be further from me than it ever had been, and worse, it would be articulated so poorly that I would have trouble seeing what had really happened. I would only remember the terrible way I'd tried to say it to Clara.

"I'm not really seeing anyone," I said.

"I get it," Clara said. "It's just casual. What's his name?"

I paused and then shook my head no, and Clara said, "Oh please, Natalie, no one here is as interesting as you. You have to tell me something."

She rubbed her knuckles against her thighs. Was I interesting to Nora? I wondered, if I told Clara about her, would Clara tell me what was interesting about me so that I could learn to accentuate it?

"I'll tell you a secret too," Clara said.

I paused. I wondered if Clara had also gone to a stranger's house last night. And maybe this stranger had also been older than her, and had been recently separated, and didn't go on many dates, but had asked her to come over—

"What's your secret?" I asked.

She gave a small breath out. "Well, on one of the very first days of orientation—" She stopped. Her voice had become quite small and sincere, and there was a real sense of her needing someone to talk to. She shifted on the bed. "Will you promise not to judge?"

"I won't," I said. "I'll just listen."

"Okay." She started again.

It happened on one of the first days of orientation. Maybe the second or third night. Clara and Annie had gone with a group they didn't know to a house party downtown. They'd both had a lot to drink, but for some reason, Clara said, she didn't feel anything. It was Annie that had been stumbling around, trying to grab onto Clara's hand, she couldn't stay upright. Clara didn't want to stay at the party. She'd tried to use the bathroom, but there had been three people crammed naked in the bathtub. All of their legs and arms piled over each other and the tub was only filled about a quarter of the way. "It looked terrible," she said. They left. Clara said she'd had to drag Annie out of the party. "She'd just been leaning against the wall, not saying anything. But I couldn't leave her there alone, she didn't know anybody." They got into a taxi. Clara said, "Annie kept falling asleep and I kept waking her up. When we got to the dorm, I laid her down on her side. And I let her stay in my room because that's what you're supposed to do. Keep your eye on somebody." In the morning, Annie had woken up first. "She was sitting up and she was looking at me. I had a headache and, surprisingly, Annie seemed fine." And then, Annie asked if they should talk about what had happened that night. "I said sure, what about last night? Thinking, if anything, that she would want to apologize." I nodded at Clara. "But then she made up a whole story."

"What story?"

"I'm just going to tell you exactly what she said."

"Okay."

"Well. She said something crazy."

"Okay."

"She said that I'd kissed her." Clara opened her eyes very wide to express the magnitude of her shock. To show that it still hadn't worn off. "I just couldn't believe it. I told her she'd been really drunk, and I'd just taken care of her the whole night."

A cold feeling rustled through me. I looked at the floor between Clara and me. And then I looked up to where her hand gripped her leg.

"What did she say?" I asked.

"She argued with me. I told her she'd been almost passed out and that didn't happen. But she wouldn't stop saying it—over and over again—as though she really believed it."

I tried to imagine. I thought of Annie sleeping. I thought of turning her onto one side. I thought of her mouth. Blurry with drinking, I wondered if the thought might appear quickly, *Touch her lips.*

I started to ask, "Are you—"

"Am I what?"

"Never mind."

"No, tell me," Clara said. Her eyes looked like faraway spots. I didn't speak, it felt hard to.

And then Clara said, "I'm not gay."

Our conversation felt suddenly blunt, hammering against my chest. I wanted to ask Clara if she thought Annie was gay and if that was why she was angry, or if it was all about the story she couldn't believe Annie had made up.

"Or I guess, I wouldn't be gay, I would be a lesbian, right?" Each word seemed heavy, but I shrugged and so did Clara and she said, "Well, I'm not." Clara craned her neck back as though wanting a clearer view of my face. "Do you believe me?"

I felt that I could see the small skeleton of our conversation. Bones so brittle, easy to break even while being gentle.

"I believe you," I said.

"Why would I lie?" Clara asked.

I shook my head. I thought of the bathtub, bodies misaligned. I wondered where she and Annie had kissed. In the car? In her dorm room? At all?

Clara said, "I keep having this feeling that she's about to tell everybody."

The unease in my stomach reminded me of sitting in front of Nora. And I wondered if everything I felt from now on would recall me to her.

We sat silently. And then Clara adjusted in her seat. "Is that why you didn't want to kiss Sam? Because you're seeing someone else?"

I shook my head. "I just thought he was a friend."

Clara's eyebrows pulled together. "So, who *were* you with last night? Is he in first year? Is he older?"

I looked at her without saying anything.

Her expression became more urgent, and then annoyed. "Come on, Natalie. Aren't we friends?"

I said we were.

"What's his name, then?"

Could I tell her at least that it was *her* name? But I knew *her* would turn into *Nora*. *Her* would turn into *you*. Would turn into, *So that makes you a lesbian, right?* I was starting to feel sick. I hoped that Clara would notice and say she should leave.

"Come on, Natalie." I thought of her story about Annie.

"Paul," I said. *Paul?*

She raised her eyebrows. "Paul?"

I started to picture Paul.

"He sounds older," Clara said.

Very very old, I thought. I started to imagine the apostle. I imagined Paul's beard. Always long, always raising his hand to shield against the light pouring down.

"How long have you been seeing him?"

I said not long.

She said, "Well, what's he like?"

I told her that he was a grant writer, and that he lived on his own.

"Is he funny?"

I paused, not sure. I said, "He has a nice laugh."

Clara tapped her feet with excitement. "Have you guys—you know?"

"Oh," I said. My stomach hurt and I wondered how often it was possible to feel this way. Like wood being split. The feeling must eventually be unhealthy for you. "Yeah," I said.

"Wow." She looked at me again as though I were cool. "This is major."

I smiled weakly at her. And then I rubbed my hands over my eyes.

"Are you tired?" she asked.

I told her I was, relieved that she might go.

"I'll leave," she said. "Maybe you'll sleep?"

"I have a class."

Clara smiled at me. "Then I'll find you later." And she got to her feet.

I lay on my back. I watched a video of a bodybuilder "Running for 24 Hours (Without Practice)." His shoulders looked so heavy. His legs, so thick, rubbed together so that, two hours in, he had to bandage in between them.

I thought I would only watch one more video before going to class. I watched a video called "12 *actually* good classic book recommendations," and I wondered if any of the books mentioned would make an impression on Nora if she saw me reading them. I imagined myself carrying a bag of these books with me the next time I met her and telling her, yes, I was reading them all. I was so keen, so ambitious—I imagined her looking at me with wonder. As though my desires and actions had a beautiful architecture.

I searched *day in the life of a grant writer.*

8:30 a.m.: Have a strong cup of coffee and finish off and send any projects that are in the chamber!

10:00 a.m.: Dive into a new proposal! I keep a master calendar to juggle all my clients. Starting a new project usually entails some deep research into the funding organization.

12:30 p.m.: Lunch break! I made my own hand-rolled sushi!

It was almost 12:30. I wondered if Nora was taking a break for lunch, and I considered texting her to ask. But didn't know how to sound casual without also sounding dumb. I looked up *how to date an older woman.*

Part 1: Exude confidence. Older women who date younger men aren't looking for a new son or someone to babysit; they want a man who knows who he is, no matter his age.

Part 2: Use your age to your advantage. Don't think of your age as something that's holding you back. After all, there's a reason she likes dating younger guys. Impress her with your energy and ability to try new things.

Part 3: Be assertive. Know what you want and don't be afraid to ask for it. While you shouldn't interrupt an older woman when she's talking, you should be comfortable holding up your end of the conversation. Use a clear, firm voice. Avoid topics that make you sound too young, like fights with your roommates, or asking your parents for money.

I tried to sense an abundance of energy, an ability to try new things stirring within me. Was that alluring to Nora? And then I thought about exuding confidence, which I was sure, to this point, I hadn't. How do you show your confidence to other people? I tried to think of subjects I felt confident about, but instead noticed my pulse. Quick and out of rhythm. The center of my back ached, and I looked up *disc herniation.* A picture of a woman holding her spine, a red glow emanating. I thought, *Yes, I have that.* I imagined my own X-rays, my black-and-white spine lit from behind, a doctor's finger pointing to the pain. *We've never seen one this bad,* he'd say. I hunched, crooked. *It's a miracle you're upright.* I sat up straight. *At your age, this usually happens after some trauma, some fall?* At my age, I thought, and I wondered if I shouldn't go to class. I wondered if I should call Nora and tell her I'd been injured and that I needed help getting to the hospital.

What happened? she would ask. And she would look at me, her concern like a mouthful of honey—I could dissolve. *What happened?*

Or maybe, and probably more likely, I would call and she wouldn't answer her phone at all. She would see my name appear and think of the great mistake she'd made. And perhaps she would feel a spring of pity, a jolt of dissatisfaction and regret. I wondered what I had to do to make myself think less. I went to class.

Jones was late. At first, everyone was quiet, expecting her to come in at any moment. But fifteen minutes past the start of class, some students began to ask if we should leave. Rachel and I sat beside each other again. Not because of any affinity, just because we had sat together on the first day, and neither of us wanted to risk skewing Jones's perceptions of who we were. Rachel was looking down at the desk, leaning her head against open hands. She wore a big silver ring on one of her thumbs. It had a signet I couldn't make out. I almost asked her about it but worried the question would grate on her, and decided to leave it be.

A few boys at the end of the table laughed at a phone they were passing around. Rachel put her hair up. I looked at my blank notebook and considered writing down a stream of consciousness, so that Rachel would think I was brimming with ideas. But before I could begin, she sat up straighter and said, "So, have you been enjoying the class?"

I thought she asked questions as though she were not also a student. I sat up straight as well. An unconscious copying that became conscious as I copied it.

"I am liking it," I said.

"What do you like about it?"

I paused. "Umm..."

It seemed that Rachel had instantly regretted starting a conversation. The filler of *umm* pulled the corners of her lips down, seeming to inspire so much boredom that she could, at any moment, be overcome.

"Jones is a good teacher," I said.

"She is."

"Yeah, I like her," I said. Boring.

Rachel said, "You know, she was nominated for an award recently."

"Really?"

"Do you know the premise of her new book?"

I told her I didn't. Rachel looked around. For a second, I worried that she wouldn't explain it, but then she carried on in a quieter voice.

"All of the poems are about nature in the domestic realm. Houseplants, bouquets of flowers."

I smiled at *domestic realm*, imagining some cavernous place with a sink full of dishes.

"Have you read any of her other books?" Rachel asked.

I said no. She put her hands inside her backpack and came out with a book. On the front was a potted plant set beside a tall outdoor tree.

"The cover's good, isn't it?" Rachel had turned to the author picture at the back. "And the pages feel good too, don't they?"

She passed me the book so that I could agree with her, and it was true, the pages did have a good feeling. I held the book open where she had, at the author picture at the back. I thought it didn't really look like Jones. And I thought it was strange that a picture like this could give such a false impression of a person. I wondered if it was because the way Jones looked relied so much on the way she moved, moment to moment. Her intake of breath before speaking, words so well-chosen that they seemed crisp and healthful. Maybe if Jones stood very still in front of us, she would resemble the picture more closely. But I couldn't tell. She'd never gone still before.

"What is it?" Rachel asked, and I realized I was taking a long time to look at the page.

"She looks different, doesn't she?"

"Younger?"

I shook my head and Rachel frowned, looking harder at the picture. A minute later, while she was still pressing her face close to the page, Jones walked in, and she had to stow the book away very quickly. Rachel gave me a darting look, as though I should've warned her. I shrugged to say sorry.

"Forgive me," Jones said, walking across the room. She was hurrying. Her hair looked wet. She dropped her bag off her shoulder. "I hate to waste your time."

Something about her rush made me feel like *she* should be trying to forgive all of us. We showed Jones soft faces, easy, breezy smiles. A boy sitting nearest to her said, don't even worry.

Jones seemed to relax a little. She said, "Let's go back a bit."

We nodded.

"Poetry is very often embarrassing. But that's all right. In this room it's okay to be embarrassed. It's not okay to be that in very many places, but it's okay in this room."

Jones looked toward the window, where it was not okay to be embarrassed. I felt a soft cradling of the room. A sense of camaraderie that we might all be making each other safe.

"As important as it may seem to become a good writer, it's also important to be a good reader. To be generative in your comments and your criticisms. Don't leave each other wondering about what a comment really means. Be specific, and well-meaning. Your writing might be personal, but your comments never should be. Our comments are only about making better work."

She looked away from the window, across us.

"Okay, let's talk about line breaks."

Rachel pressed her pen down into her notebook, writing and writing. I tried to read the words, but she was quick, and I was trying to be discreet.

"So we know that logic can break a line, and so can punctuation. And breath. So then, what about several line breaks in a row. Right? White space. Think about how you might justify your poetic choices. What does more or less space mean?"

I tried to consider. White space. Rachel's knuckles. Grazing Nora's teeth with my lips. How do you justify poetic choices? I thought of the pasta Nora had cooked, steam rising up toward our faces. The moment of her arms rising above her head, the few minutes that separate being known from being unknown. I could feel the pressure of her hands. My body—didn't I like being a stream? Didn't I like being dipped into, the breaking surface of myself that still rippled from the afterthought of her touch?

Beside me, Rachel had stopped writing, and had started packing away her things. Class was over. How had it happened so quickly? I put my books away too. Rachel got up and walked deliberately to the front of the room. Jones nodded at her, said, "Hello, Rachel." And then I couldn't hear anything else—I'd looked down at my phone and seen that Nora had tried to call.

ten

The day was dipping pink, and through the window the house was beginning to look dark. When Nora opened the door, her head was already tilted, and she said, "I've been thinking about you."

She kissed me in the hall. I felt the incredible relief of being wanted again and the rest of the day blurred unimportantly. Nora's face close to mine, I could feel the pressure of her body, the just-touching of her chest, her knee on my thigh.

Nora said, "I haven't felt like this in a long time."

Her hands slid along my sides. Her nose touched my cheek, her fingers undid my jeans, an unexpected rush. Her elbow lowered to her hip, and I thought quickly of how the night before had felt, the slower motion of our lips, her eyes watching more carefully, and then my thoughts disappeared and she pushed into me quickly. Sound rose into my mouth, as involuntary as a yawn or sneeze, and Nora kissed me. When I looked down,

I could see her bicep moving up and down, and I imagined that it was burning, and I thought, that sensation in her was also the sensation in me. The furious ache in her fingers, my mind skipping a beat.

I watched Nora in the kitchen. We ate from the same bowl, the pasta that was left over from yesterday. Where she leaned, with one arm on the counter, everything seemed matter-of-fact. Nora fixed her hair to fall over only one of her shoulders. I felt how my hair fell straight back. I wondered if its lack of styling was childish. I thought of the article I'd read about being assertive, about having a firm voice. But watching Nora, the only confidence that I felt was borrowed from looks she gave me. Was salvaged from the fire of my surprise—that she had asked me to her house again, that I sat in front of her now. I tried not to look at her too weakly. With too much need. Like a glass, already tipped over, already soaking the carpet and everything else.

"Tell me about where you grew up," Nora said. Her eyes had a chiseling edge. If I were a stone or a piece of wood, I would lean in.

"I grew up on a lake called Temagami."

"Is that a big lake?" she asked.

"Yes, it's big."

"What did you do there for fun?"

I wanted to answer quickly, as though having fun was at the forefront of my mind. As though life had been fun before it had been anything else. But as I thought of it, childhood seemed to become one long year that stretched away from me.

"I used to work at my parents' lodge," I told her.

I felt a strange uncertainty about how my life had passed so far. Had I just been sitting around? I'd gone to school. I'd separated a big pail of worms into smaller containers. I could remember the pleasant feeling of hiding from work, sitting on a sunny part of the shore. Sometimes my parents would drive me to get fries at the chip truck near the highway. At night, the TV played. Was that the same as everywhere else?

"Sometimes at night I would play cards with the guests, especially in the winter."

"And you liked it?"

"I guess I liked that part," I said. "What do *you* do for fun?"

Nora looked down as though I'd thrown to her the bulk of every problem she'd ever had. "That's a bad question, isn't it?" she said.

Nora stepped forward and touched my hand. Then she closed her fist around each of my fingers, as though bolstering each bone.

"You're smart," Nora said.

I frowned at her.

"You are," she said.

She gave me a solid, sure look. I wondered what she saw when she looked at me. What gave her the impression of smart?

"What are your parents like?" she asked.

"They're good," I said. I realized a certain unwillingness to say anything about them. My parents. What would they think of me here? Sitting with Nora, talking about them.

"Do they support you?"

I wasn't sure in what way she meant. "I guess so," I told her, and I remembered my mother dropping cutlery into my hand. Heavy fork, heavy knife, talking about a woman who had just moved to town. *I met her in the store, and told her about our book club.* And then she said, *She's very beautiful, isn't she?* My father had nodded, chewing. *What do you think, Natalie?* She watched my face carefully. I took as big of a bite as I could so that I wouldn't have to speak and I shrugged, noncommittally.

Nora looked toward me. I was interested in her interest. Her curiosity about me. Who was I, if she was curious about me? Not the person I'd expected myself to be.

"Can I ask you something?"

"Ask me something," Nora said.

"It's personal."

"Ask me."

"I was wondering about your wife."

Nora's face changed to be more concentrated. Her eyes, for a moment, searched mine. As though deciding if the reason I wanted to know was good. "Okay," she said. "What were you wondering?"

"Is *she* smart?" I asked.

Nora's forehead creased. "She's smart."

"Smarter than me?"

Nora said, "She's older than you."

"So, smarter?"

Nora shrugged her shoulders. I felt the sting of something sad.

"What do you like about me?" I asked.

Nora rested her chin on her hand. I wondered what divorce felt like. A tangle never coming free? And then I thought of the way Nora had looked at me when I'd first stepped into her house. And I thought of what she'd said, *I haven't felt like this in a long time,* and I thought I must be the result of some long-kept desires. Why had Nora gotten divorced? To set these private desires free? I felt my eyes begin to water.

Nora said, "Natalie, honey."

The soothing in her voice felt like the acknowledgment of some disparity. I further lowered my eyes. Maybe Nora and her wife had ended things badly. I might be a private revenge. Maybe soon, Nora and I would walk hand in hand down the street, and her wife would be sitting outside some restaurant, and Nora would push me forward and say, *Oh hello, have you met Natalie?* And later on, her wife would gather with a group of her friends, and one of them would say, *Does she think she can just trade you out for a newer model?* And the air would gather clearly, and I would see that Nora was never really interested in me. She was just trying to cast the broken bone of her life.

Nora said, "I didn't mean to hurt your feelings."

I told her she didn't, and she tried to rub a spot on the counter clean.

"Will you tell me more about Temagami?"

"Why?"

"I want to get to know you better," she said. She asked me what the lake looked like. She asked me about the lodge my parents owned. She asked me what I liked about fishing. She asked me more about playing cards. We moved upstairs. She asked me if I looked more like my mother or father. And I wondered if my answers to these questions were seeds that, inside Nora, might grow into more tenderness. What had she called me earlier? Honey?

I didn't know if I should stay over, but she never suggested that I leave, and then, at a pause in our conversation, her eyes slowly closed, and she fell asleep. Nora's breathing was uneven. Sometimes quickening, and sometimes falling slow, too quiet to hear. When I stopped hearing the sound of her breath or seeing the movement of her back, I worried that she'd suddenly died, and I had to press myself nearer to her. I pushed the front of my arm against hers, I felt her ankle with my toes, I waited until I felt some movement in return. And then I settled back and watched her still.

When it became clear I couldn't sleep, I shaded the light of my phone and looked up some of the books that I'd seen on her shelf. Ones that I hadn't read. There was one called *The Reification of Desire*. I found a PDF that had its introduction and acknowledgments. "One evening in 1996"—the author, Kevin Floyd, was upset to miss a conference where Judith Butler was speaking— "others who were there are likely to remember the snowstorm that hit western Massachusetts that evening." I imagined thick snow, cold car seats. "In the early to mid-nineties especially, a schism between Marxism and queer theory was impossible not to notice." I looked up a definition of Marxism and found that it scattered as I read. When I tried Floyd's sentence again, with anticipation of a new understanding, each word felt like its own torn piece of paper. I imagined them flying up in a wind.

I jumped down to the end of the book and read the acknowledgments. Nora stirred and I made sure the light was more hidden. "My gang of friends in and around Kent has sustained me in this work. Magicians all, they somehow managed, twelve months a year, to make northeast Ohio a consistently warm place." He thanked them for Halloween, he thanked them for Thanksgiving, he thanked them for poker and bonfires, and the "rare instance of pure foolishness people with our educational background really shouldn't be involved in." I wondered if I would ever have a gang of friends or anyone to thank.

I pulled Nora's sheets up to my chin. Her pillows were soft. I wondered again about Nora's wife. I thought about what she did when she couldn't sleep, because I was sure, somehow, that she had found herself in the same position as me. As Nora slept, I imagined a cold creek rolling through the grooves of her mind. A dream where her inner thoughts were rinsing themselves, basking in the streaming water. I thought it would be wonderful to go to sleep, full of complication, full of knots, and for those dense points to have drifted free by morning. I hoped that this happened for Nora as I lay beside her. I hoped that sleep would soften the hard way of life.

I read the acknowledgments of another book, *No Future*, by Lee Edelman. I read a part that said "my debt to Joseph is in a category of its own." And I read that part over and over again, imagining that I was the Joseph Lee Edelman had addressed. And I imagined the great debt that I was owed. A debt, as Lee writes, "of its own immense category." I imagined this category, perfect and whole. I wondered what it would be like to owe, and to be owed. To be married and to be not married. To lie beside a woman as she sleeps, and to find yourself not sleeping.

I put my phone away and I pushed my pillow onto the floor, and I let my head lie on the mattress. In the morning, I wanted Nora to wake up first and see me, head unsupported, body curled farther down than hers. I wanted her to wonder if I'd been uncomfortable during the night. I wanted her to wonder why the pillow had fallen. Had I been dreaming? Had I moved around in my sleep? I would keep my eyes closed as long as it took to make these questions real. For her mind to wrap around the thought of me, to hold it, think softly of it—I fell asleep imagining the possibility.

eleven

It became harder as the days got darker to go to night classes. Sam had stopped sitting next to me in Material Religion. When he saw me in the hall, he would give an acknowledging nod, but it felt as though some offer between us had been rescinded.

When I didn't go to class, I tried to read more diligently, but I still felt guilty about the waste. Professors were beginning to warn us, with Christmas break nearing, they were covering very important material. It was this material that we would need to learn for tests. But nothing to me felt as crucial as the trip I took most nights across the city, up Nora's steps. On the days we didn't meet, I was distracted by our not meeting. And so most lectures I heard were recorded fragments, extrapolations from slides online, videos from different professors at different schools speaking on the same subject.

On Friday I tried to go to every lesson. Jones was in the afternoon, and so I had something during morning classes to look forward to. I hoped through each hour that a professor might say something that I could remember and impress on Nora. I wanted to have something to say, a working knowledge of things.

I would try to collect the loose threads of the day before I slept. Readings would fumble over me like problems, *Clothing as Devotion in Contemporary Hinduism*, and *Men, Tattoos, and Religious Underpinnings*. I would try to remember a detail further, *as with scapulars, medals, and rosaries, tattoos can be efficacious conduits for protection and materialize love*—I would feel, sometimes, on the verge of solutions. I would feel as though I might think of a new kind of conversation, invent a word that Nora had always thought of but had never known how to say. And when Nora asked herself why she kept having me over, she would think of all these things we talked about.

Often, when Nora and I didn't meet, I would find myself sitting at the end of Clara's bed. Her hard, eager knocks would lead to her calling, "Natalie?" And I would open the door and she would say, "Come see me."

I noticed that over the weekend Clara had bought a lava lamp. I asked her about it and she grinned widely.

"You noticed," she said. "It's kind of an ironic lamp." She half laughed at herself. "Because—" A pause while she turned it on and it began to heat. "I don't really like how it looks."

"You don't like how it looks?"

Her eyes were bright. "I know," she said. "But I still wanted it." The lava was bright green and started to move up and down. Clara looked at it. "I hate it."

"You hate it?"

"I totally hate it."

We laughed at ourselves. Clara kept pointing to the lava lamp, which would make us start up again each time we were about to begin our work. We both had essays that we needed to write. Clara had asked me to come to her room, she said we could inspire each other. I started to type. *The Waste Land, by T.S. Eliot* . . .

"Your keyboard has an interesting intonation," Clara said.

I looked up at her. "Intonation?" I asked.

Clara nodded. She said, "Listen to mine." She tapped at her computer. There was a slight difference between the sounds.

I said, "Right." . . . *when Eliot writes, "Who is the third who walks always beside you?"* . . .

"How's Paul?" Clara hadn't started typing yet.

"Paul," I said, hesitating before remembering who Paul was to me. "He's good."

"You stay over at his a lot."

I shrugged, trying to direct more concentration into my essay. *"When I count, there are only you and I together, But when I look ahead up the white road, There is always another . . ."*

"How old is Paul?" Clara asked. "He must be older?"

"A bit older."

"I would date someone older," Clara said confidently.

I looked up at her. She stared at the poster above her bulletin board. An illustration of Paris's subway line.

"How much older?" I asked.

"I'm not sure where I would draw the line," Clara said. "Sarah's set her age limit to thirty."

I tried not to give anything away in my reaction. Thoughts of Nora pulled through my mind. I didn't want to acknowledge her accidentally, give her away by the darkening of my eyes.

"Paul isn't thirty, though?" Clara asked.

I said no, he wasn't.

Clara nodded. "Didn't think so."

"I do not know whether a man or a woman— But who is that on the other side of you?" This final section of The Waste Land moves away from the more typical poetic forms . . .

"You don't work out, do you?" Clara had put her laptop to the side. She looked at me with wide blue eyes. I wondered if she ever sat still long enough to study, wondered how she spent time in class without talking.

"Not really," I said.

"I don't really either," Clara said. "But lately, I've been feeling like I really should be. Have you ever been to the school gym?"

"No, I haven't."

"Neither have I, it's too intimidating." Clara picked up her laptop again and rested it on her legs. "I'm thinking of doing one of those workout challenges. I want to do the push-up challenge first. I follow this girl who does it every day."

I thought of the bodybuilder I watched sometimes. Thought of the metal bar he lined up with his wrists, elbows trembling, hips rising to push. His striated chest showed like rays of sun. I imagined Nora's voice, thick as the man's veins. Imagined her, commanding him, *Okay, lift.* I imagined her walking her fingers across his legs, *Okay, lift.*

"You could definitely join in."

I felt my face flush. I thought, *Don't think of Nora that way.*

Clara continued quickly, "It's just push-ups every day for thirty days, and you don't have to leave the dorm, we can do them right here." Clara pointed at her carpet.

"Right here?" I asked.

"On that carpet," Clara said. Pointing her finger again.

"Okay," I said.

Clara smiled at me, as though her life were better now, more full. "We should have a baseline. How many could you do right now?"

"Not very many," I said. "How many can you do?"

"Should I try it?"

I told her yes, she should try it.

She took off her sweater. She had a tank top on underneath, and she said, "I'm not wearing a bra," warningly. And then planted her arms.

"Knees up," I said.

"Okay, okay."

Clara breathed out hard and then raised herself into position. "Count for me," she said.

"One."

Clara lowered herself. Her back swayed toward the ground, but it stayed up.

"Two."

Her arms were already shaking. Her elbows clicked when they straightened. "Oh my god," she said.

"Three."

"It hurts my wrists."

"They'll get stronger," I said. "Come on, four."

Clara's face was red. She dipped into five and six and then her knees bent to the ground and she pressed herself against the floor. "My arms."

"That was really good," I said.

I waited until Clara sat up. It took a minute for her face to become less red. "Okay, you now," she said.

I brought my knees up, I lowered myself down. Clara said one and two and three, and every number was hard. I hovered above six, and then I tried to push myself out of seven, but I couldn't bring myself up, and I had to collapse.

"The same number," Clara said. And she shoved my shoulder excitedly. Our evenness was a delight to her. "You'll know exactly how I feel, and I'll know exactly how you feel."

I watched her bring her computer back to her lap and start typing with renewed purpose. I wondered what Clara would think of Nora's house. If she would like all the hanging mirrors, the empty, decorative bowls. Beside Clara's bulletin board, below the map of the Parisian subway system, there were photos of her family, and one of a huge white cat. I wondered who Clara would eventually be. And I couldn't help feeling that I knew more than she did about certain things. I was with Nora, wasn't I?

"Clara?" I said. She looked up. "Have you ever been to Paris?"

She frowned. Her eyes followed mine to the poster of the subway. "Of course I've been to Paris." And she smiled at me as though I were a bit of a fool. "Why else would I put that up?"

Snow swept by the window. We took off our coats, hung them slick on the backs of our chairs. Rachel brought a new book to each poetry class. Last week she had brought Adrienne Rich, *On Lies, Secrets, and Silence*. Spine broken, pages so thumbed I thought they might turn to dust in her hands. I had read the preview online later, in bed. "An honorable human relationship—that is, one in which two people have the right to use the word 'love'— is a process, delicate, violent, often terrifying to both persons

involved, a process of refining the truths they can tell each other."
I took this in. I thought of Nora. I thought of bringing my own
book to class. And then I decided to bring the same book that
Rachel had. I thought of a possible conversation. Rachel might
say, *Oh, I've read that.* And I might say something which gave new
insight. I found an article about the book that summarized:
"The pathology of lying, Rich argues, doesn't merely alienate
us from others—it engenders the greatest loneliness of all, by
cutting us off from ourselves." I thought I could tell this to
Rachel. And she might look receptively at me, and say something she'd learned back.

I took out the most worn copy of the book from the library.
When Rachel sat down beside me, I already had it open:

Women have always been divided against each other.
Women have always been in secret collusion.
Both of these axioms are true.

"Hey, Rachel," I said.
She said hi, but then we both sat quietly. I held the book
up a little higher off the desk so that she might see. I even
cleared my throat once when I turned a page. Eventually, she
looked over at me from the corner of her eye, and her gaze set
on the book.
Rachel frowned and said, "I was reading that last week."
I lowered the book. "Yeah, I thought it looked interesting."
Her eyes narrowed. "Are you copying me?"
I looked at her, surprised. Rachel looked unimpressed.
"No," I said. "I just thought it might be good to read."
She made a hmming noise.

I stared down at the next page, felt embarrassment breathing red over me. "There is a danger run by all powerless people: that we forget we are lying, or that lying becomes a weapon we carry over into relationships with people who do not have power over us."

Rachel said, "Well, what do you think of it?"

I looked up at her quickly. "It's interesting."

She looked amused. What had I read before? I needed to say something good, needed to show her that I might have insight.

I said too loudly, "It was interesting, in particular, when she mentioned the pathology."

"The pathology?"

"About lying." I felt out of breath. I thought, *Just stop now.* But continued, "You know, how we can be alienated and then, that endangers even greater loneliness."

"Endangers?"

"No, sorry, engenders."

Rachel nodded at me with an inflated smile. I felt sweat drip down my back. I wondered how stupid I had seemed. I wondered if Rachel thought I was deranged. But, as I looked at her, she seemed smug, as though realizing the dullness of my mind had helped her brighten her own.

Jones had come in; I hadn't noticed. I heard her speaking, but it came as though from another room. I felt tears in my eyes. I thought of Nora. I thought of myself, filled with timidity, kissing her cheek quickly. Closing my eyes as she got undressed. I thought, *I must embarrass her.* I thought, *Everyone is just suffering through variations of my inability.*

"Natalie."

A hand touched my shoulder and I flinched. Jones's arm drew away from me. I saw everyone else had their heads bent down, writing.

"Oh, sorry," I said. And I opened my notebook.

"Could I see you in the hall for a minute, Natalie?" she asked.

I looked toward her face, floating above me. I stood. Rachel stared at us.

Jones and I stood outside the door. I wondered if I was in trouble, and tried to imagine the worst thing I might've done. Had I accidentally spoken out loud? I wondered if I had been asleep, and had only felt as though I'd been awake, and I wondered if I'd cried out, said Nora's name.

"I'm sorry," I told Jones before she could speak. "I didn't hear the instructions."

She met my eyes. Gently, and not searchingly, A railing that might help the steepness of steps. "Do you need a minute, Natalie?"

What did I look like? I stared down at my feet. I wondered if I looked distraught. Wondered if there was something about me that gave her some suspicion that beneath what she could see, there were thoughts, dangerous and prone to wreck.

"It's okay if you need to take a minute."

I nodded at her, breathed in deeply. I wanted to say something to her, because I wanted her to say even more to me. I wanted to be comforted.

"I'm sorry," I told her. "I didn't mean to disrupt—"

"You didn't," she said. "No need to apologize."

She looked back toward the door. I worried that she would leave me in the hall and go back inside. So I opened my mouth, asked, "Am I doing well?"

She frowned and looked back at me. "Are you doing well?"

I felt embarrassed, but also, I had made her stay for longer.

"In my class?" Jones asked. "Is that what you're upset about?"

"No," I said. "Sorry. It was something else. I was just talking to Rachel—"

But I stopped. I didn't want to explain that I was upset by my own insecurity. I would rather her think that I was braving something difficult—a real, personal hardship.

Jones shook her head as I paused and then she said, "Don't let anyone else dictate how you feel about your writing."

"Rachel's quite good," I said. I watched her, felt more greed for her attention. I wanted her to agree, or disagree, or tell me that I was good also. Or, better, a fantasy where she lied and told me I was better than Rachel and on my way to surpassing even the best poets she had read. But Jones inclined her head and looked at me more sternly. Recognition of the fantasy?

"Good poetry isn't mystical. It's just the process of us all trying to find something true."

Her sentence rolled over me with a sense of discipline. I nodded at her, wanting her to let her guard down again. And I wondered if I might be trained by her lessons, feel myself change and sharpen. It would be like watching a warrior learn to fight, the pleasure of seeing someone become good and brave and capable.

"I'll see you back inside, Natalie."

I told her thank you, and watched her walk into the classroom.

I looked at everyone writing through the small window in the door. I felt that I would rather not go back in. I would rather leave and not feel everyone's eyes turning my way. Plus,

I wondered if Rachel would find it mysterious that Jones and I had gone out into the hall, and that I hadn't come back. Maybe she would think that Jones had given me an important and personal task—

I turned my head toward the end of the hall, and I began to walk down it. I thought, *I'm just taking a minute,* but I kept walking. Outside, and then eventually on the streetcar, I kept thinking, *I just need a minute.* But the minute was long, and I found I was walking the road toward Nora's house.

Nora was outside. The snow had piled along the gate in her garden; her driveway was long and narrow, and it was also blocked by snow. She didn't expect to see me, and when she turned her head, she leaned with both of her hands on her shovel and said, "Did they end classes early?"

I walked up to her.

Nora watched my face and then she took her gloves off. "What's wrong, Natalie?"

I said, "Nothing," but I felt that my blinks were wet and unconvincing.

She asked if I was crying, and I said that I wasn't. She put a hand under my chin. "No, really."

She staked her shovel in the snow and we went into her house. When I stepped through her door, the snow melted quickly off my boots and left slush on the floor. She said, "Never mind," when I looked back at it.

I peeled potatoes into her sink. She watched me out of the corner of her eye. Once I was finished, Nora put them in a pot. The starch rubbed off on my fingers. The water boiled quickly. The burner was set to high, and fire licked wishfully up the sides. Nora turned it down.

"What's happened, Natalie?" she asked. "Something with class?"

I wondered if I could spend my entire life coming to Nora's house, watching water boil, sticking potatoes through with a knife. I looked at Nora. I thought of Rachel, why had I said *endangers* and not *engenders*? Such a slim margin between saying something meaningful and exposing the fallibility of your mind. I opened my mouth, felt the way my tongue might tie.

"Natalie?"

She touched my hand. I wondered if I should mention Rachel, or Jones. I wondered if she'd read Adrienne Rich.

I said, "It's poetry."

Nora frowned. "What about poetry?"

"I read the same book as Rachel. But she read it better than me."

"How did she read it better than you?"

"I don't know," I said.

I looked at Nora, looking at me. Saw her face, tense with concern, and wondered again what she liked about me. How often could I ask her that? I wondered if I would ever find any true purpose, be able to say as confidently as Rachel, *I want to be a poet.* I thought dumbly of the notion, *true purpose.* The silliness of thinking that one day I might find myself at the heart of some prophecy. A path clear and in front of me.

Nora said, "Natalie?"

"I shouldn't talk to you about this." I thought of that article, I thought of the rules, avoid topics that make you sound too young, like—

"Why not?"

"It's stupid, it's not interesting."

"I'm interested," she said. I tried to tell if she was lying. Tried to see if she was annoyed, or bored. But her eyes were expectant.

"How did you decide you wanted to be a grant writer?" I asked.

Nora paused. "It was a process. It wasn't a job I always pictured, but there are a lot of good things about it, and for me, that makes it all right."

I told Nora, "I don't know what I like."

"You've just started school, there's so much time to figure it out."

"Everyone else already knows."

"No," Nora said. "That's just how it seems. It's very difficult to try and figure out what to do with your time."

I wanted to say something, but my mouth felt so dry. I wondered whether I was becoming less attractive to her. I thought the next thing I said should be delightful.

The snow continued outside the window.

"We could go somewhere," I said.

"Now?"

"We could do something."

"What do you want to do?"

I thought of becoming a different person, unbuttoning my sweater in a way that was smooth and alluring, standing in front of her undressed, my body more plush than it was, a lace bra rather than the solid white I was wearing.

"Should I drain the potatoes?" I asked.

Steam rose out of the sink. She leaned away. I wondered if I'd drawn too much attention to myself.

Nora eventually spoke. "So, you don't like poetry much?"

I looked at her, surprised. Was that the impression I'd been giving?

"It's my favorite class."

"Right, but there's Rachel, who you don't like?"

I considered playing this up. I imagined Nora walking me to class, asking Rachel for a private word. But I said, "I actually don't not like her. And she didn't really do anything wrong. She just doesn't like me." Nora frowned. "I think she just really cares about the class. And she feels it's all a competition."

"For best poem?" Nora asked.

I said, "She wants Jones's attention."

"And does she have it?"

"I don't know." I considered whether or not Jones gave Rachel any extra attention, but thought she didn't really seem to in class.

Nora reached into the sink and plucked out a potato. She put it, hot, onto a cutting board. She cut it in half. "Would you ever read me one of your poems?" She put a pat of butter onto both halves and then threw salt over them.

"My poems are really bad."

Nora laughed disbelievingly. She handed me a fork. "You're hard on yourself." Then she said, "I like that you came here."

I felt guilty for not being fun. "I'm sorry for—"

Nora shook her head instructively. "I like that you came."

"You do?"

She looked down at my fork full of potato, and she smiled as I tried to scrape up the melted butter, the dispersion of salt.

The next morning, I emailed Jones. I'd left my bag in her class. She had office hours in the afternoon, and she replied that I could come and collect my things then. Clara and I walked from the dining hall to Jones's building. Clara was meeting a guy there, outside.

"We're going to have coffee," Clara told me. "He suggested it." I told her that was nice, and she said, "*Is* it nice?"

I asked, "Why isn't it nice?"

"It's very cautious," she said. "It's the middle of the day. It's bright out."

"Maybe the coffee will be really good."

"Natalie," Clara said, and her shoulders rose as though she were about to sigh. "I'm looking for more than a good coffee."

I left Clara outside the building twisting her hands in front of her stomach. I walked up the stairs to the third floor, where Jones had her office. I'd never been there before. There was a bulletin board outside her door, which was empty, and then a nameplate that said *Kate Jones*. I walked toward the door, which was closed. It had no glass pane to see through. I wondered how I would tell if the office was empty, wondered if I should knock or sit down on the bench in the hallway and wait until she called me in. I sat down.

I looked at my phone. I watched a video. A man sits in his seat holding a vacuum on his lap. First the man examines the vacuum for almost ten seconds without speaking, then he looks directly at the camera. He says, "This is a very expensive vacuum." And then he begins to take the pieces apart. He picks up a wet cloth and he rubs the inside of the vacuum's pipes, not saying much while he does it. Afterward, he holds the cloth up to the lens. The rag is almost black. "Look at that," he says, as though he can hardly believe it. "And I clean my vacuum every other day."

The door of Jones's office opened slightly, only enough for a thin wedge of light to appear. The sound of soft crying was let out from the office. I could hear small intakes of breath, and the sound of attempted suppression.

"There are just a few boundaries—"

"I didn't realize I was breaking any rules," said a tear-muddled voice.

"You're a talented student, and I want to help you with your writing, but—"

"That's all I want." The voice broke again.

"I need to be able to give other students as much attention. We're talking about a reasonable limit—"

The student sniffed a few more times and then their breathing evened out. When the student spoke again, their voice was stronger and I thought I recognized that it was Rachel.

"I understand," she said.

I wondered if this was how rumors circulated? Slips of sound heard through the small gap in a door.

"Is everything okay now?"

There was a pause before Jones said, "Everything's fine. I'm glad we had this conversation."

It seemed abrupt how soon after Jones had spoken that her office door opened the rest of the way. Rachel stepped out. When her eyes fell on me, she made a startled sound, and then said, "Oh," as though I were the last person she wanted to see.

"Sorry," I said. "I was just waiting."

She looked like she'd been trying to stand still in a bad wind. She wiped her hands on her thighs. I stood up but didn't say anything.

She said, "You can usually just go in."

"Oh, okay."

I walked forward, but I didn't try the handle. I knocked lightly on the door. I glanced back at Rachel, and she looked coldly at me. And then Jones called, "Yes, come in."

In Jones's office there was only one window. The blinds were half-closed so that the light slatted over the desk and floor.

Jones closed her laptop. I took off my jacket and sat down. There were books stacked all over a shelf beside her desk. Loose papers on her left and right, two mugs of coffee, neither finished.

When I looked over at Jones, she was already looking at me.

"Oh, sorry," I said. And it occurred to me that if I was only there to pick up my things, I shouldn't have bothered to take off my jacket and sit down.

Jones said, "You never came back to class."

"No, I didn't—"

"I hope everything's all right," she said. Not a question, a gesture.

"Yes," I said. "Everything's fine."

We looked at each other. The light from the window wanted to lead my eyes away. I tried to think of something to say. Should I just leave?

Jones rested her hand underneath her mouth, a curl of fingers near her lips. What if I said something insightful? What if I said something that made Jones like my company?

"Your bag's just over there," Jones said, pointing to the ground near her bookshelf.

I wondered if she'd slung it on her shoulder to carry it up the stairs. Wondered if she'd thought it was heavy, or light.

I considered whether she would have been curious enough to look inside, but thought, probably not. I leaned forward in my seat.

"Are poems hard to grade?" I asked her.

Her lips pursed with consideration. I wondered what she would say if I took a book from her shelf and started going through it. Would she look taken aback? Would she say stop? Or would that boldness seem like ambition?

"Yes. They are hard to grade," she said.

"Why are they hard?" I asked.

Jones made a *hmmmmm* sound. Her eyes concentrated on the ceiling for a moment. "In poetry there are tricky relationships. Relationships between writers and readers, between writers and their poems." She paused, and I watched her hands stop. "The poet does their best to write their meaning, and after that there is a world of inference. There isn't a proper rubric that I can lay out for students."

"How do you know if a poem is written badly?"

Jones smiled, said, "Well, if you think of a poem as inviting a reader to interrogate, and a reader chooses not to interrogate, then the poet needs to consider whether or not their invitation was truly compelling.

"And did you notice, I said the poet does their best to write *their* meaning—the opposite might be the hallmark of a bad poem."

I asked, "What is the opposite?"

"Trying to write *the* meaning."

I made a noise like Jones, *hmmm.*

"Imagine writing a poem, saying love is this, and love is that, just for example. You think a reader will care more because you've been unspecific. Because you've told them very broadly, and philosophically, what love is, but it doesn't work." She pressed her lips together briefly. "It's much better to say, 'the woman I love lives in Vancouver, and it's terrible to love her because she never meets me on the bridge where she promises she's going to meet me'— than saying, 'love is harsh, and love mistreats me.' It's better to write from yourself, to write what's true, specifically, about your own mind."

I nodded at Jones, wondering how much knowledge I would have to accumulate before being able to also draw these kinds of conclusions. She looked down at her desk. I waited to speak. I wanted to be quiet for so long that when I left her office, she would think back to the silence I'd left, and be impressed by how much dead weight I had bared.

But only a few seconds passed before I asked, "Does it feel generous to be a teacher?"

She sat back and rested her hand against her face. "No," she said after considering. "It doesn't feel generous."

The steadiness of her voice made me believe her answer. But I thought if I was a good poet, with my own office, and my own students, I would feel very generous for letting them hear what I had to say.

"How do you know if your writing is good or not?"

She rubbed one of her eyes and then she shook her head. "Don't worry about being good. Worry about saying things precisely. Worry about saying things in a way that makes them more than what they are. Yes?"

"Yes," I said.

"Good." And she folded her arms with finality.

I fit my arms back through the sleeves of my jacket. "Thank you."

"Don't forget your bag," she said.

I leaned over for it. Jones turned her attention toward her computer and started typing. I opened the door and walked out, letting it close behind me. Rachel was standing so close to the office that I held a hand against my chest in surprise.

"You're supposed to leave the door open," she said.

"Oh," I said. "I didn't know that."

"I forgot something inside." She motioned toward the office. She had to shuffle by me and knock on it again. I moved out of her way, and Jones said, "Come in." Rachel went in and shut the door.

I waited there for a minute without moving. I tried to listen, but there wasn't a sound. Would the door open back up to allow that wedge of light? I waited, but nothing happened. And then I felt my phone in my pocket. I'd missed a call from Clara.

I stepped outside the building. Squinting, I felt dazed by the difference in light. I thought of Rachel and Jones back in the office together and wondered what else they could be talking about. I called Nora. While the phone rang, I watched my breath fill the air. The pavement was white with salt.

"Hello?"

"Hey," I said. "It's Natalie."

A small laugh before she spoke. "I know your voice, Natalie."

She said this as though she knew much more as well. And for a second I felt embarrassed rather than flattered. I thought, if Nora decided to never speak to me again, it wouldn't change anything that had happened between us. I was no longer completely and privately myself. I imagined her eyes gathering and saving an image of my body. Her mind held a sense of who I was. A feeling of me that she might always be able to recall.

"I know your voice, too," I told her.

Her voice was still light, without any of my thoughts. "Of course you do," she said. She asked what I was up to.

"I was just getting my bag," I said. "I forgot it in class."

"Oh? It's good no one took it."

"Oh, well, Jones took it for me. I had to get it from her office," I said.

There was a sudden, hard silence.

"Nora?"

"Why don't you come here tonight?"

"Oh, I'm supposed to—" I was supposed to study with Clara. But, I thought, I could probably tell her I couldn't and instead—

"If you're busy, it's fine."

Something tightened in my chest. I felt the barbed intonation of *fine*.

"I can come," I said.

"You shouldn't come if you're busy, Natalie. If you've made plans."

"It's because I'm about to have exams—"

"Don't worry, I understand."

Unfamiliar abruptness. I paused.

"Will I see you tomorrow?" I asked her. I thought I could still offer to cancel with Clara and go to her tonight.

"Only if you want to."

"Of course I want to," I said.

There was quiet. And then Nora said, "Are you sure you didn't leave your bag on purpose?"

"My bag?"

"Maybe you wanted an excuse to go see your professor."

I blinked, bewildered. "No," I said. But then I thought of sitting across from Jones. My bag in the corner of the room. I didn't have to stay, and I wondered if I had been wrong to. If Nora could sense some secret and inappropriate desire, one that I didn't even know myself. "I'm sorry, I—"

"No, I'm sorry," she said. Her voice sharpened, but now it seemed inwardly reprimanding. "I didn't mean to say that to you. About your professor."

I said it was okay. And I wondered, oddly, if she was jealous. If something about our conversations had given her the impression that I was after Jones in some way. "I left my bag because I was in a rush to see you," I said.

"It was silly of me to say anything." And then she said, "I didn't even ask you why you called."

"Oh," I said. "It was just to say hi."

"Hello," she said, voice returning to itself, as though nothing had happened a minute before.

When we hung up, I saw that Clara had texted, *meet me by Northrop Frye's statue.* I walked to find her. She was sitting on the bench beside the statue.

"Short coffee?" I asked.

"Terrible coffee," she said.

We moved to a bench outside the library nearby. It was cold, but the snow had been brushed away.

"I think he may have been a narcissist," Clara said. "He talked the whole time about a paper he was writing—he quoted himself several times."

She told me more things she didn't like about the guy she met: the smell of his hair, too much like coconut, the way he had zipped his sweater below the halfway mark.

There were ladders leaning against the nearby trees, and men on them, stringing lights through.

"What are you doing for Christmas?" Clara asked. "Are you going home?"

"I think so."

"You *think* so?" Clara raised her eyebrows.

"No," I said. "I will."

"Don't you want to go home?"

"I do," I said. But I could hear the sound of Nora's voice, *You shouldn't come if you've made plans.* And I wondered if she would be angry at me for going away. I wondered what her house would look like during the holidays. I thought, I could leave late. Tell my parents I had exams into the middle of the month.

"I'm excited to go away," Clara said. "I need the reset, school's starting to feel oppressive."

I nodded at her. She said she was too cold to sit still, so we got up and started to walk.

"I guess you're thinking about Paul?" Clara said. And she looked at me with a new understanding. "You guys must be exclusive?"

Were we exclusive? Fear hissed through me. Did Nora see other people besides me?

"Have you had that conversation?" she pressed.

"Indirectly."

"From my experience, you should have it directly."

I wondered what experience that was.

She said, "But I'm really excited for Christmas." And then a pause. "Do you celebrate Christmas?"

"Clara, I have to go."

She frowned. "Where?"

"I'll be back tonight to study."

I hurried away from her down the path. I heard her call, "See you later!" behind me, but I was running, and she already sounded far.

I climbed up the steps to Nora's house. I was sweating through my clothes, my jacket trapping all the heat in. Her street had felt longer and leaner than before, like a rabbit mid-run. I blinked sweat away from my eyes, ran the back of my hand across my face quickly. At the door, I felt my fist turn into a knock. As I waited, I thought that Clara must've been right. Nora was out with someone else, there were too many conversations we'd never had. I opened my jacket, hoping the cold air would dry some of my sweat. I looked out onto her street. Could she have gone for a walk? All along the row of houses, the driveways and sidewalks had been shoveled clear and the melting snow made a neat stream down to a grate; I could hear it trickling. It reminded me of Temagami, and I found myself longing to stare out onto that lake. I tried to follow the sight of the water all the way down the street, but in the middle of its path there was someone standing. The person turned away quickly and began studying the house beside them. I wondered if they'd been look-ing at me. I thought there was something familiar about them. A coat I'd seen before?

"Natalie?" The door had opened.

I turned around. "Nora," I said. She wore high-waisted pants. A black belt with a gold buckle, which felt eye-level with me. Was I shrinking? A brown sweater tucked in, her sleeves rolled to her elbows. I wanted to collapse with relief. She looked soft, and sweet, our phone call earlier seemed imaginary.

"What's happened? Don't you have to study?"

Everything in me wanted to go back in time, wanted to say right away, *Of course I'll come over.* I opened my mouth to give a good and charming answer, but I felt my next thought quiver, and I felt compelled once again to look over my shoulder.

Down the street, the person was still nearby, now looking more directly. I squinted, trying to see better. But the sun was high, and there was a whole street of houses, and trees, that the person might actually be looking toward.

"What are you staring at?" Nora walked through her doorway onto the step beside me. She looked out over the street. The person who had been standing near started walking the opposite way.

"Nothing," I said. "I thought that was someone I recognized."

Nora reached a hand toward me, but I stepped back.

"I'm all sweaty," I said.

Nora asked, "How did you get here?"

"I ran."

Her mouth twitched into a smile. I thought, *Exclusivity,* she said, "Come on." And I didn't resist as she reached out again, and led me inside.

Nora watched me talk on the phone with Clara. She looked at me with a pleased smile, and I felt like a mechanism, integral to her satisfaction.

"I can't make it tonight."

"Why not?"

Nora picked up my hand and looked at each of my fingers, and then she touched my palm to her lips.

"Are you with Paul?"

"Yes, I am."

"Are you going to have *the* conversation?"

I wore one of Nora's robes. I had tied it closed like you would a shoelace, in a big bow. It smelled like her, and when she wasn't looking, I brought the material up to my nose. Nora tugged on the end of my bow.

"Yeah."

I tried to pull it away from her.

"Well, I'm not mad at you. But you have to remember I am the most supportive friend."

"I'll remember," I said.

Nora let go of the tie, and pulled my ankles toward her. I tried not to laugh into the phone.

"Say it—I'm your most supportive friend."

Nora's mouth was cold, and she pressed her tongue against me. I tried to hold her head between my legs, to make it harder for her.

"You're my most supportive friend."

I turned the phone away from my face, but Nora laughed, and I began to as well, and then I felt the tips of her fingers below her mouth, and I inhaled. I worried that Clara might have heard, but then she said, "I'll see you tomorrow?"

The thought of Nora's fingers was also the feeling of them. I imagined how her hands, so everyday, so visible and apparent to everyone she met, could also be so intimate to me.

"Tomorrow," I said, and then I hung up the phone.

Nora—I wondered if the rhythm of back and forth was intrinsic to the earth. A wave pulling and pushing the sand and rocks. Legs running tirelessly—one after the other, the clicking spokes of time. Nora's fingers curled, were her hands different from mine? She felt immense to me. I looked up at the ceiling rather than down at her face. But I felt her attention, how it moved from my legs to my stomach, to my mouth, to my eyes. And I felt as though I might coil around her, become a trap without release. How could this feeling stay so contained? Spikes pressing into the get-away of a rabbit's leg. Steps quicken, Nora quickens too. And if my breathing was loud, I didn't care. And if Nora was watching, I didn't care. Your body claws and claws, and then eventually, there is that feeling. A rope burning against the side of a ship, fraying and fraying. Desire for the end, desire to get there. I felt solidly that my body was against something. Against the bed, against the ground, against a center that resisted me, even as my hips moved back and forth.

My clothes were washed and dried in her machines. I wore Nora's robe still, in the kitchen. She asked if I wanted to order pizza. I nodded, excited. I loved being in her house and having her ask me if I wanted to order pizza. I imagined the smell of the hot cardboard box, cheese stringing off a slice. It felt like the enaction of some childhood fantasy—to eat an ordinary pizza standing by Nora's granite countertop, in her robe, which felt thicker and warmer than my coat.

"Sure, let's order pizza."

I listened to her voice over the phone. Clear, not nervous at all. The way she spoke made me feel like the pizza people were charming and, potentially, the whole world was charming, I'd just not realized it before.

She held my hand, said into the phone, "Don't worry, we aren't in a rush," and then laughed brightly at the response.

Once we ate, Nora told me that I should study, just as I'd planned. I said, "I don't have to," and she told me that I should. She cleared off the table in the dining room and she watched me lay out my work. She sat opposite me with her own stack of papers, and she met my curious eyes. "You forget that I work too?" I nodded at her, surprised that she'd observed me so well.

I turned to a new page. I made flash cards for Material Religion, definitions that might be tested. Once in a while Nora closed her eyes, rubbed them, and said, "Okay, read me something."

"Okay," I said. "Oracle bones."

I read,

The desire to know the future has been a pervasive human quality throughout history and the people of the Shang Dynasty were not outliers along these lines.

"Is that a direct quote? It's phrased awkwardly."

During the Shang Dynasty fortune telling was considered an integral resource in decision making, and these "psychics" were consulted by farmers and kings alike.

Nora said, "Nice air quotes."

I said, "They were written in! Okay, listen."

The person would ask the fortune teller a question like,
"Should I bring my oxen to market next month?" A hole
would be drilled into the object and then a hot poker would
be applied, or the shell/bone placed near fire until it cracked.
If the crack went one way, it would mean the person should
go to market with the animals, and if it went another way,
they should wait.

"What do you think? Should I bring my oxen to the market?"
Nora mimed placing her hand on the back of an ox.

I said, "Ma'am, that's not an ox, that's a horse."

Nora raised her eyebrows at me. "Well, I had no idea."

I said, "I'll consult the oracle bones."

"And?"

"They take a while to heat," I said.

"Oh, I'm sorry," she said, and she looked at her pretend horse,
stroked her hand along its neck.

The sunset burned quickly, light ceasing as though it were trying
to race into the recesses of blue. The dryer had stopped, the
buzzer had gone off. Nora asked if I wanted to go upstairs. She
said, "Bring your books if you want to." Nora brought me my
clean clothes. She said, "You don't have to put them on."

The room was dark. I felt the usual bite of her teasing, her
eyes, confident with desire, rolling me in a certain direction. But
then, suddenly, maybe because of the shadows crossing the room
from the window, or because it was hard to see Nora's face exactly
without the side lamp on, I imagined the sight of birds circling
above trees. A sign that, somewhere below, something is injured,

or has died. I felt as though these birds were above me. I looked away from Nora, took my clothes from her.

I said, "I'll put them on for now."

She watched me as I got down from her bed and closed the door of the bathroom. I looked at the clean walls and the clean faucet. I saw my face. Unexpecting, I noticed the hardness of my cheeks, shadows beneath my eyes. I had been softer a moment ago. Was this the way we aged? Unwittingly—harsh, an accidental look in a mirror.

I hung up Nora's robe, pulled my own clothes over my head. I noticed the shampoo and conditioner Nora had lined up on the side of her tub. Noticed her soap and white towels folded tightly in an open cupboard. Something on top. I paused, moved closer. Lying on the stack of white towels was a brush so full of hair that it almost concealed the brush. I touched it. The hair was so tangled that I thought it might move. It was not exactly the color of Nora's hair. I wondered if the brush was being kept as a relic. Because it belonged to her wife, and that kind of thing was difficult to throw away, or to give back. Was it sentimental? Was it, *I want to keep your hair? I want to save your place?* I wondered if I should go ahead and clean the bristles. I pulled lightly on a strand, sensed I would have to really try to rip the hair free. And then there was the problem of how it would look—like a small animal once it was thrown out.

"Natalie?"

The clean bathroom felt infinitely less clean, and I felt I might turn my head and see a huddle of insects. I thought I might slip on something leaking, notice that the house we were in was actually decimated. Nora's room would not be her room, and I would be standing back outside, packed into the sweat of my jacket.

"Natalie?"

I came out. Nora stood by the door.

"Are you all right? You didn't answer."

"I'm sorry," I said. "I didn't hear."

She told me to sit with her on the bed. We sat with our backs against the pillows.

I said, "Nora?" She said yes. "I'm going away for Christmas. Back to Temagami."

I braced for discontent, but she said, "Of course. That'll be nice for your parents."

I wondered what she would be doing while I was away. And I felt the same desperation as earlier not to leave, to stay by her side.

"What will you do over the holidays?" I asked.

"Ohh, maybe I'll have a big party," she said.

I looked at her. "Will you really?"

Her voice dipped. "Oh, yes," she said. "A huge one."

I realized that I wouldn't like that. "Will you?" I asked again, and I heard how my concern coated each word.

Nora smiled. "No, I won't."

She looked at me. And her looking made me feel full of body, made me feel as though I were wearing a coat with pockets that were always spilling.

"Maybe I'll visit my parents too," Nora said. I looked at her. Her eyes were cool, collecting. I thought it was weird that she had parents. That she had thoughts that weren't to do with me. That she would leave this house and go to another, and be a person who had a mother and father.

I tried to imagine Nora walking to her car in the snow. Waiting for the frost on her windshield to melt, her tires getting slick on the road. Who was Nora's traveling self? Did her eyes get red when she didn't sleep? Did she catch her reflection when she checked her mirrors, think for a moment about how she looked?

"Nora?" I asked.

"Natalie?" She gave a side-smile.

"Are we—*exclusive*?"

She raised her eyebrows. My stomach felt punched. I thought how stupid the question was, hated that Clara had mentioned it to me, wished I'd never spoken, or thought of it. I covered my face in my hands.

"Never mind," I said. "Don't answer."

"Don't answer?"

I uncovered my face, looked at hers. "Okay, answer."

She lowered her chin. And then she said, "Natalie, there are things you don't know about me."

I wondered why I didn't think harder before I spoke, and I thought that from now on, before I did, I should imagine first what I might say if I was a proper adult. A good adult, who had tempered the jump of nerves from their body, the trigger-pull of questions.

"There are things *you* don't know about *me*," I said.

"That's true," Nora said, but she didn't seem worried.

"Why don't you tell me the things that I don't know?"

"Tell you everything?" Nora asked, and one side of her mouth turned up, as though I might be funny.

"Why not?" I asked.

Her smile faded and for a moment gave way to a look I didn't know. And I felt, eerily, that there might be someone lurking behind me. That Nora's eyes, when they were disturbed, preoccupied, saw more than I could ever see.

Nora began to say, "I like you more than—" and then she paused, realizing the possible hurtfulness of her words.

"You thought you would?"

Her eyes flashed up at me. I felt the sway of possible insecurity, the fear of inadequacy, but I tried not to think these things deeply. I tried to make my face still and accepting. Maybe knowing Nora better meant absorbing some hurt, meant understanding hard things. And maybe if I did, I would find myself lasting in her company.

Nora said, "I'm not seeing anyone else."

"You're not?"

She shook her head. Did that mean exclusivity? The word felt gold, shiny, a medal you could put your teeth down on. I looked at her. The dark center of her eyes looked wet and wavering; I felt I could be lost, vacuously absorbed. Nora sniffed and looked sad. I knew to hide my happiness. I changed the subject.

"You know, I was thinking I might cut my hair."

I watched the long look of Nora's eyes center on my face. "Were you?" she asked. "How short?"

The wetness in her eyes disappeared as she looked at me, and I felt a responsibility to make the moment better.

"Very short," I said.

"Really?"

I knelt on the bed and looked at the mirror above the headboard. I pulled my hair back, and held a constricting ponytail behind my head.

"You have small ears," Nora told me. "Come here." I sat back down, facing her. She pushed my hair back herself, then shook her head.

"What?" I asked. "Is it terrible?"

"No," she said. And she let go. "Do you want to see something?"

I said I did. Nora leaned over to her bedside table and riffled inside a drawer. She handed me a photo. The film had a soft and flattening light. She was in the middle of it. Her hair had been buzzed short, and her face looked bright and clear, as though she'd just been swimming.

"That's you," I said. I looked up at her.

"That's me," she said.

"Can I take a picture of it?"

"If you want to."

I laid the picture against her sheets and took a photo.

"Who took it?"

"I can't remember," she said. I thought the person who took the photo probably loved her.

"How old were you?"

"Seventeen."

"You look the same," I said.

She laughed doubtfully.

"So, I should do it, then? I should cut my hair?"

"If you want to."

I pulled my hair back again. "I don't think I'd look as good as you."

She gave me a surveying look rather than offering any assurance. And I wondered if I seemed childish, or if it seemed like I was looking for compliments. I wanted her to think that I was there solely for her happiness.

I decided to speak more. Isn't sadness harder to feel when things are moving quickly? "Where do your parents live?"

"Kitchener," she said.

"Do you see them much?"

And Nora said, "I see them when I can." She started rubbing her thumb against my temple. I could hear the faint sounds of the wood floor underneath us.

"Were your parents there when you got married?"

Nora's thumb moved less rhythmically. "Yes," she said.

"Did they walk you down the aisle?"

"No. We just stood up, together."

"What did you wear?"

"Oh, you know, this and that."

"You don't remember?"

"I remember," Nora said. Her hands returned to her lap.

"Do you still see your wife?" I asked her.

Nora looked around the room, disconcertingly. As though the air might manifest before us both. Become the one we spoke about. Wasn't this part of what Nora had to tell me? Wasn't this part of exclusivity?

"I see her, but not often."

She watched my face. I didn't let it fall. I wondered what I felt. Could it be jealousy? Nora was with me, and I was here with her, and it didn't really matter that she had been married, this was still the reality. I was here, and her wife lived somewhere else. Nora turned her head. Eyes up the wall, to the light hanging from the ceiling.

"If you're gone for Christmas, then I won't see you for a while," she said. Voice like an eavestrough dripping after rain. I saw wet umbrellas, a wicker chair that wouldn't dry for days. Where would Nora be on Christmas Day? Would she find herself on the phone, reminiscing with her wife over years of shared memories?

"I'm not leaving yet."

Her knee touched mine. "What's Temagami like in the winter?" she asked.

"It's very cold."

"We used to go a little ways north when I was younger. On vacation."

"To a cottage?"

"My dad liked to go hunting."

"I've been hunting."

"You have?"

I nodded.

She lay onto her side. "I'll see you again, before you leave?"

I lay down as well. I curled my leg over hers, like a husband would. "You'll see me," I said.

Nora's eyes began to close. I blinked against the dark, which had started to tug mine as well. I felt more tired than I had in a long time.

"I have something to tell you."

I opened my eyes. Nora's were still closed. Had she spoken?

"Nora?"

"Mmm."

"Did you say something?"

I watched her lips move. "Me?"

"What do you have to tell me?"

As I watched Nora, I imagined that I was a child sitting on the corner of her bed. I imagined that Nora had looked underneath it and said, *Someone's down there,* and I'd said, *What?* and she'd said, *Someone's down there, had you never thought of that?*

"What did your professor say, when she gave you back your bag?"

Her eyes were closed. Was she awake, or asleep?

"We had a conversation," I said.

Nora nodded against her pillow. "What did you say?"

"I asked her about how to write a good poem."

Nora smiled. But otherwise, it was as though she were sleeping.

"She said to be specific. And she said not to worry about being good."

Nora's eyes were still closed. Her mouth kept its soft upturn.

"She said it didn't feel generous to be a teacher, but I don't know if I believe her."

Nora whispered, "You're smart, Natalie."

I responded diligently, "I'm not."

Nora's lips settled to neutral. They opened very slightly with her breathing. Sleep?

"Nora," I said. "What did you have to tell me?"

But there was only silence.

"Nora?"

But she was asleep.

twelve

I took pictures at the bus station. I took one of my bag against the tiled floor. One of my ticket lying flat on my leg. My mouth obscured by a coffee cup that I deliberately held in the way. When I saw the bus coming, I took a picture of it on its way. And while I sat in my seat, several hours from meeting my father, I tried to decide which of all these photos would be best to send to Nora.

In North Bay, the bus stopped, and I walked around the parking lot looking for my dad's car. When I found him, he got out and hugged me. I pressed my hands against his back. I felt his nose against my hair, the soft whistle of his breaths against my head. When his arms loosened, he held me out in front of him, as though making sure I'd come back in the same condition I'd been left.

He said, "Look at you. You're a big-city girl now."

I mumbled no, no, and then asked him how his drive had been.

Not far from the station, we stopped at a drive-through and he ordered a large black coffee and a box of timbits. He asked me if I wanted a hot chocolate, and I said I was okay.

The roads were good, my father said, though it had snowed quite a lot the few days before. Even so, he turned on the radio, which updated us on the road conditions as we drove upon them.

"Would you pass me a honey glazed?"

The box of doughnuts was in my lap. I picked through them. Hard icing flaked onto his jacket collar.

As we drove, I remembered that one Christmas my parents and I had driven into Toronto to go shopping. In the mall there'd been geese attached to the ceiling, their wings open as though they were mid-flight. There were kiosks down the middle of the walkway and a man had waved us over, holding up a figurine of a wax hand. My father asked me if I wanted one.

I'd spent quite a long time trying to pick between my left and right hand. And then another long while deciding on the color. The biggest decision was the gesture. My dad said, *Why don't you give a thumbs-up?* I'd asked my mother what I should do, and she said, *Anything you'd like.*

The man held my arm and guided it into the wax tub, and then I sat while the mold formed. I hadn't firmly decided on a gesture, so my hand was cupped, thumb almost raised. When enough time had passed, the man pulled my arm out, and while I wiped off my hand, he finished off the figure. My parents paid. I held the soft statue. On the car ride home, I pressed the hand against the window, hoping someone would see and be perplexed by the strange purple fingers dragging oil across the window. And then I pressed the fingers against my face. The statue smelled like a page that had just been photocopied. I noticed that the position of the hand was just right for choking, so I pressed it against my throat until it felt restrictive.

My mother said, *Don't do that.*

I said, *It's choking me.*

She said, *Natalie, don't.*

"Any jam ones in there?"

I picked out a doughnut and passed it to my dad. My phone buzzed against my leg. Clara wrote, *are you gone??*

I wrote back, *Sorry, I was late for the bus.*

no goodbye?

The bus!

I checked that my message to Nora had sent. I'd chosen a picture of the bus arriving because it had seemed more artistic than the rest. Although now I wondered if it being most artistic had been a good enough reason to send it above one of the others, which would have been a clearer evocation of me. What could she even say to a picture of a bus arriving at a station?

"Are you yoked to that thing?" my father asked.

I looked ahead, at the windshield. "Has the lodge been busy?"

He told me that it was. "We hired Liam." I told him that was good, and my father said, "You would've been young—do you remember when we went Christmas shopping in Toronto?"

I told him I was just remembering it, that I had my wax hand made. I told him I wasn't sure where that was, I told him it must've been thrown away.

He gave me a disabusing look.

"What?"

"We wouldn't throw away your hand," he said.

"You still have it?" I was surprised.

"We must have it."

"Mom might've thrown it away, she didn't like it."

He frowned at me. "She wouldn't throw away your hand, Natty."

I shrugged at him, as though I didn't mind either way.

Eventually, we drove completely forested roads. High snowbanks narrowed the way. The snow hadn't melted in Temagami since the very beginning of the month. In the woods, it would be waist-high and hard.

My father pointed ahead of us. "Almost there," he said.

I smiled at him. "You know, I've been here before."

We drove up the driveway to the lodge. The wood siding was forest green, though it never did blend with the trees. Our house was behind it, rounded logs laid horizontally.

The car stopped and I got out. I wondered if Nora had gone to Kitchener today. Maybe she was also standing in a driveway with her bag—

"Natalie, come say hi to everyone." I'd started down the path to our house, but my father came, took my bag, and walked us toward the lodge. "Your mom will still be working."

Inside, a few guests had just returned from hunting, some from fishing on the ice. I could hear the sound of men laughing in the dining room. Liam stood at the front desk, taking off a thick orange jacket.

"Look who I've got," my father said.

Liam looked around, his eyes met my father's and then mine. He said, "Hey," in a spacey voice that made me wonder if he was high.

"We'll have to find your mother," my dad said.

"She went out to cabin 6," Liam interjected. "To bring new sheets."

"Why don't you go and see her?" My father looked at me. "She'll love it if you go and see her."

I went to the house alone while my parents finished chores at the lodge. Inside, it smelled of pine, and thickening broth. In the kitchen, I unplugged the slow cooker like my mother had told me to. I lifted the lid. There were beans and onions drifting across a big shoulder of meat. I stirred it a few times and then put the lid back on.

The inside of our house wasn't so different from the inside of the lodge. There was blond wood, floor and ceiling. Brown couches, one made of leather and the other of polyester. A framed map of Lake Temagami hung above a fire that looked in need of more wood. There was a square kitchen table with sticky place-mats. They were plastic, and had different kinds of ducks on them.

I walked along the hall. I tried to find things that had changed in the house since the last time I'd been there. But it didn't look any different than it had before. My parents hadn't changed their minds about anything since I'd been gone. Hadn't decided, after my leaving, to put up a different picture, to buy new art.

My room, as I went in, seemed less my own. The duvet on my bed was pulled flat, made for a long time without being touched.

I pressed down my hand and the fabric wrinkled, and I felt a sense of reassurance that I could affect it. I looked inside my closet at all the clothes I hadn't brought with me to school. I tried to remember what I used to think about when I chose what to wear. What did I used to think about before I'd met Nora?

I checked my phone again, but there was no reply to my bus picture. I considered taking a photo of my room and sending it, but I thought the appearance of so many wooden walls, of such a small and single bed, would make it seem that my life was tiny, and toylike. Would make her think of a rocking horse, a doll.

I wondered if I should try to call her. That would be more immediate. Her voice saying hello. I pressed her name on the screen and closed my eyes. I let the call ring out. It rang and rang, without an interrupting tone. I wondered if it would ring forever if I didn't stop it—but then the door downstairs opened, and I had to hang up.

I sat at the end of the table, and my mother and father sat across from each other. For the first few spoons of stew, they talked absently about who would be checking out and in the next day, and then my mother turned her head toward me.

"How's your school?"

She said *your* school, in a way that stressed how its belonging to me, and my belonging to it, had interfered with my belonging to them. It didn't sound like a mournful acknowledgment, nor did it sound like disdain. It sounded matter-of-fact—*my* school was not *their* school.

"It's really good."

"Tell me more about your friends," she said.

I told them Clara was funny, and quite popular. I told them she'd grown up in Toronto, that she studied chemistry and physics, subjects that were hard.

"You were always so good in high school," my father said. "Didn't matter what subject, you always got good grades."

My phone vibrated underneath my leg. I looked. *Natalie, did you call earlier? I'm in Kitchener, the house has bad service. I'll try and call you tonight?*

"Who's that?"

I felt like I was sipping wine at the table. My mother would turn and see the tall glass in front of me, teeth red. I imagined her lips parting, *Who said you could have that?*

"Clara," I said.

The relief of Nora writing to me made me eat more hungrily. I raised my spoon again and again. The stewed meat fell apart. I decided to explain more about my classes. Told them about Mary Oliver, and the Shang Dynasty. They smiled receptively, but I felt that their thoughts might have wandered. It didn't really matter, though; Nora had written, and I felt I was doing my part.

I did the dishes while my parents sat. My father lay on the couch, watching TV, and my mother worked on a puzzle that looked to be made almost entirely of indistinguishable pieces of the sea. After an hour I went upstairs and waited alone for Nora's call.

I sat in bed with the covers pulled up to my chest. I texted Clara, *How's your break going?* Hoping she would say that she felt strangely out of place, so that my experience would sliver universally. But she didn't answer, and then Nora wrote, *Tried to call but it wouldn't go through, I don't know if it's my service or yours.*

Immediately, I tried to call her back, but the dial tone lagged and then dropped. I got out of bed and opened the window. Long tree branches pointed toward me. The cold rushed in. I lifted my head, and phone out, against it. I tried again.

"Natalie? You got it to work."

"I'm hanging out of the window."

Nora laughed as though I was kidding.

"What are you doing?" I asked.

"I was watching a show with my mother. What are you doing?"

I wondered if I could ask her to come and get me. Wondered if she would, if I told her it was an emergency. And when she arrived, what would she say to my parents? What would she say if my mother burst in while we were kissing? Would we jump apart? Or would Nora be the one to look disapproving? As though my mother had been impolite—an intrusion on our privacy.

"Are you finding it hard, Natalie?"

I wondered what *it* was. Was *it* being in Temagami? Being away from her? Was *it* looking at my parents and feeling unknown to them? Did Nora mean all of this at once?

"Is that her? Will you say hello for me? And we'll miss her this—"

The phone went quiet for a second and then Nora's voice came back. "Natalie?"

"Who was that?"

I tried to shield the phone away from the wind. My hands were stiff. *Is that her?* The phone voice had sounded hopeful, and I knew immediately that it hadn't been for me.

"My mother," Nora said. "She was a bit confused."

I hesitated, but then asked, "Did she think I was your wife?"

"My ex-wife," Nora said, voice strained. As though this were a refrain she'd spent the day repeating.

There was a pause. I wondered if Nora was having a worse time than me, but then my shoulders shook with the deepening cold and it was difficult to move my lips.

"Are *you* finding it hard?" I asked her.

Nora let out a tone of laughter. It sounded slightly sarcastic, not the truest reflection of her feelings. I wondered if it was because the word *hard* had seemed like an understatement.

"Do you miss me?" she asked.

"Of course I do," I said. "It's all I do."

I worried that this sounded pathetic, but Nora sounded amused. "It can't be all you do," she said.

"Then it's every other thing I do."

"You miss me half of the time."

I agreed it was half and Nora laughed more truly. My nose was running. I realized I was smiling because my teeth started to hurt with the cold. I asked Nora if she'd gotten my picture of the bus, and this made her laugh some more and say, "You're too much, Natalie."

I felt as accomplished as I ever had. Wind blew snow from the roof and a white drift sprayed across the lake, and I forgot that a few minutes ago, before our call, life had been difficult, and I had been trapped.

thirteen

On Christmas Eve, I woke up sick. My mother said, "It's much colder here, in Temagami."

In the middle of the night, I had turned and turned, and when I'd woken up, my voice had been scraped thin. I pushed aside my blankets, which were damp, and I changed my shirt, which was wet. When I went downstairs, my mother looked at me and said, "You didn't sleep well." So definitive that I thought she might have spent the whole night beside me, watching the rise and fall of my breath.

I sat at the kitchen table. My mother handed me two pills. Underneath the table, I texted Nora that I was sick. I watched my mother at the sink doing dishes. "Is the medicine helping?" she asked.

"No," I said. And then I watched the back of her head, hair wispy and brown, her arms shaking as she scrubbed a bowl, and I said, "But thank you, for giving it to me."

She flicked water off her hands. "You should eat."

Poor you. I hope you're being taken care of. Nora.

"Natalie?"

"Yes," I said.

I miss you, Nora wrote. She missed me.

"Are you hungry?"

I miss you, I replied.

"Natalie?"

"Yes," I said.

"You *are* hungry?"

"Yes," I said. And then followed up, "Thank you."

I felt Nora's focus on me. Distant eyes looking this way, would the sky be altered as her attention turned toward—

"Do you remember Mrs. Adams? I think she taught you English."

"Mhmm."

"She was asking about you, asking how you were doing."

"That's nice of her."

I have something to tell you, Nora wrote.

"I told her you were doing fine."

I reread, *I have something to tell you.*

What do you have to tell me? I asked.

"Are you doing fine?"

I wished she had asked me a few seconds ago, when Nora had missed me. Now, my voice sounded half-hearted. "I'm fine," I said.

I looked at my phone. I waited, staring at no reply. Every breath I took felt pale. A bead of sweat ran along my forearm. My father walked in. He said, "Natalie," and asked how I was feeling. I said okay.

He poured orange juice into his glass. Then he filled my mother's as well. We were all sitting down.

Nora? I wrote, before my father said, "No phones at the table."

We ate quietly. I watched my mother and father exchange looks a few times, and I knew that these looks had to do with me, but all I could feel was the strain of not looking down toward the answer that might be there. The answer that Nora might have written.

"Is anything wrong, Natalie?" my father asked.

"What do you mean?"

"Is everything at school—manageable?"

I looked at them both. My mother held hard onto her fork. I nodded, but my whole body felt like a shrug, and I wanted to look down just once and see if Nora had answered.

"You hear horror stories," my mother said. "Kids getting very overwhelmed. Kids being alone in their dorms studying under so much pressure."

"I'm not overwhelmed," I said.

"You seem a little worn down—"

"I'm sick—"

"Natalie, why do you keep looking at your phone?"

I looked up quickly. The worry on my parents' faces made me feel like, if I wasn't careful, they would try to take it from me. I put it underneath my leg.

"Sorry."

We sat for a few more silent moments and then my dad stood from his seat and said, "I need to brine the turkey." My mother turned her attention to her last few bites.

I ate a piece of bacon slowly, and then said, "I think I should rest for a little while."

She said, "Good thinking." Eyes yielding to mine.

My window in my room looked onto the lake. It was so close to the trees that sometimes branches would brush against the glass and make a bad sound. In the very corner of the room, a new cobweb had been made, white strands that looked like fraying patches of air. I took out my phone: still nothing from Nora. My throat hardened. I felt like I should pack all my things and run with them through the snow all the way back to Toronto, where Nora might be, making an answer. I paced around the room and then sat on my bed and then lay down.

I scrolled through my phone. My nerves began to bunch. There were steady photos of living rooms with Christmas trees, mugs of coffee swirling with milk foam, ads for daily planners which, with their embossed gold lettering and straight lines, seemed so firm in their promises of stability that I almost started tapping through them. I closed the screen, tapped the next little icon. It offered me a choice between *For you* and *Trending.* I pressed *Trending.*

"*I've never felt better!* Ella Gossling responds to hate over her new relationship." I tapped through. A picture of Ella holding the arm of an older man I didn't recognize.

I read the comments below.

> *Didn't they first meet when she was 17?*
> *They are two adults! There's many relationships in the history of the
>   world where people have large age gaps.*

And then,

If the person you're dating is much older and more accomplished than you, they have purposefully sought this dynamic and will probably never want it to change.

I stared for a while at these words. Then I scrolled around to find more supportive comments:

Women crave men that are more powerful than they are. These are facts.
You are not your age! You are your energy!

I looked up *people that date people older than them.* I scrolled through a slideshow called "Celebs with Big Age Gaps." As the photos flicked by, I tried to consider what Nora and I would look like in one of these pictures together. I tried to imagine what her friends would think of me. Had she ever told anyone about us? And if she had, had it been in a confessional tone? Had it been a, *Listen to what I did—*

There was an article by a professor in psychology and relationship science who said "the success of relationships is dependent on whether or not each partner shares the same values, beliefs and goals. It depends on trust and intimacy, and the ability to resolve issues in constructive ways. This has nothing to do with age!"

I checked my messages again. Read the last few over.

I have something to tell you.	*10:15 AM*
What do you have to tell me?	*10:15 AM*
Nora?	*10:17 AM*

Would Nora tell me that she had been considering things, and that she had decided, helped by this bit of space, that I *was* too young for her? Really, I thought, it would probably be that I wasn't pretty enough, at least not pretty enough to make up for not being smart enough. And for being as young as I was, she had expected more youthful exuberance. I probably didn't smile as often as she would like, or suggest that we do something wild. I went back to my phone and typed *what are spontaneous things to do?*

Do a speech or a soliloquy unexpectedly in front of a lot of people. Ride a camel in a desert, or a horse, or an elephant.

I wondered if I should message Nora that I also had something to tell her. But then I thought of the faltering moment when she would say, *What?* And I would have to say, actually, no, I had made that up.

My nose had been running so much that I'd used up an entire box of tissues. I peeled an orange and ate it very slowly. Eventually I heard the sounds of cooking downstairs. I felt cold, and I couldn't stop myself from looking at Nora's old messages, so I decided to run a bath.

I lay in the water. I spread a clay mask along my forehead and then splashed it off before it could set. The water turned murky gray. Sometimes, when Nora spoke, she rested her hands on her face. A few fingers would cover her mouth. The end of her nail would rest between her teeth.

I pressed my finger and thumb together. I imagined that my hand was really Nora's hand. And when it reached down into the water, below my stomach, against my thigh, I pretended that

I didn't lead myself, sometimes touching the wrong place before the right place just to show that I was uninvolved.

The fantasy began with Nora touching me, but then, as it went on, my hand became my hand, and my body became Nora's, and I became very knowledgeable. I opened my face the way Nora opened her face. I let a sound escape, not embarrassed—I was her. The heat of the water was also the burning of my arm, was also all the tension that structured everything—the tone of a word, the weight of eyes, the body, acting as it does. I withdrew. My stomach floated to the surface, and I lifted myself to sitting, hot and dizzy. I pulled the drain out of the bath. The sound felt like it came from my own throat, and I felt an urge to cry, which made me curl forward. Did I love her?

I said Nora's name out loud, weakly, as though I were being watched by a large audience that needed to know what I was thinking. I felt tired of myself.

I waited until the bathwater was almost drained, and then I stood up. Once I stood, I realized that I'd forgotten the towel hanging in my room. I dripped onto the floor. I considered putting my worn clothes back on, but they looked so crumpled and sick that I didn't want to return to them. I opened the door a little. "Hello?"

I could hear sizzling downstairs. I called out again, one last check before running across the hall, but then my mother turned the corner and said, "Natalie?"

"Oh," I said. I made sure my body was covered entirely by the door.

"Are you all right?"

"I forgot my towel."

"I can get it," she said.

"And my clothes," I said. She turned away.

I felt nervous for her to go into my room. I thought she might find something strange there even though there was nothing to find. Maybe she would go into my room and suddenly know about me in the bath.

My mother walked back, the towel and a pile of clothes in her arms. My underwear had been moved in between my shirt and pants. I knew they'd been on top before. I pulled the clothes through the very small space in the door, watched my mother's hand pull away, and then pushed it closed.

"Your father's making dinner," my mother said.

"I'll be right down."

She spent a second standing there. I could see her shadow.

"I'll be right down," I said again, but she didn't answer.

I dried myself off. I looked at the door. I said, "I'm going to be right down."

I could see the shadow still, but again no one answered, and then I thought maybe the shadow had always been there. It couldn't be my mother; she must have already left.

fourteen

The last message I'd sent Nora had been on Christmas Day. When she didn't answer, I spent most of the day in bed. In the evening, there was turkey and ham. The turkey made my throat feel worse, and the ham was wet. The next day my mother thought I seemed better. I sat with her behind the desk of the lodge, carrying a book that I said I had to read for school. Over the next few days, I hid my phone behind *To the Lighthouse*, not reading more than a few sentences before checking to see if there were any ellipses forming in Nora's chat.

On New Year's Eve morning, when Nora wrote to me, the relief felt almost crushing. I wanted to fall to my knees, tell everyone, *She still likes me,* but instead I sat alone in bed and I held the phone close to my face. She had written *Happy New Years, honey!* and I spent a long time looking at the words. I wondered if I was crazy. I wondered if Nora had never written, *I have something to tell you,* wondered if that text was just a hardened bit of imagination.

A line I'd misheard as we'd fallen asleep, a dream that I'd taken too seriously.

I wrote, *I was worried about you.* And then I deleted that to consider my fun side. *Yay, New Year's Eve!* Or, *Ya! New Year!* But couldn't send either of those. I considered some emojis. The party hat and the party horn.

And then Nora wrote me again. *I haven't been well, I'm sorry. I meant to answer earlier.*

I looked again at all my messages, unanswered.

What do you have to tell me?	*3:00 PM*
Are you okay?	*3:33 PM*
Can I call you?	*8:54 PM*

I wanted to tell her that it hadn't been me who had sent those texts. It had been a child playing with my phone. I had leaned against the counter and, through my pocket, I must have pressed all those buttons. I thought I could never be cool, after sending all those messages, one after the other. I would have to live forever on the red cheek of embarrassment.

Nora said, *I even went to the doctor.*

I wrote, *You've been sick?* And it occurred to me that she might have been *really* sick. I thought, *Burial, beginning of eulogy, end of time.* I thought, *Nora's wife,* and I wondered who I would turn out to be if Nora died.

Are you okay?

I'm okay, she wrote. And then said, *I do have something to tell you, but in person.*

Is it something bad?

She said, *Not bad.* And then, *I'm sorry if I worried you.*

Time eased slightly, did I love her?

I'd like to call you later.

I wrote, *Call me whenever you'd like.*

She responded quickly, a face blowing a kiss. I sent her a telephone and a face that was happy but not the happiest. And then she sent me back a telephone and a face that was the happiest. Did I love her? I felt every stretch of my body, longing. Wanting to be, as these faces and words, at her fingertips.

By lunch, most people visiting the lodge had left. I went around to each of the cabins and pulled the sheets off the beds and then I helped my mother clean the plates in the dining room.

"You're in a better mood," she said.

"I feel less sick," I told her.

She wiped eggs from the plates into a garbage and then handed them to me. I passed them through the soapy water in the sink and loaded them into a dishwasher. She talked for a while about a show that she wanted me to watch.

She asked me if I was watching anything, and I told her I wasn't really. And then there were a few minutes where the only sound was of the water running and the plates touching.

"I wanted to ask you something."

I turned my head to her. Her hair looked a lot like mine. She told me often, when I was young, that I looked more like my father. My nose and my eyes. I wondered if my body was like her body. I watched her arms cross over her chest, her feet shuffling nervously.

"Can you take your hands out of there?"

I took my hands out of the sink and held them dripping at my sides.

"Are you—" Her voice teetered. Trepidation clutched my stomach. I imagined her saying, *Are you always angry at me? Are we always fighting?* But maybe those were the questions I had for her. I wondered if it had started as soon as I'd been born. If she'd looked at me and thought, *I'm not sure we're going to get along.*

"Is there anyone special at school?"

"Someone special?" I wondered if she'd heard me say Nora's name in the bath.

"You know. Are you seeing anyone?"

I leaned against the sink. "Why did I have to take my hands out?"

She said, "I thought it would be better."

I tried to feel bored, to look bored. "No one special," I said.

I put my hands back into the water, but my mother had stopped passing the dishes, so I was just soaking them. There were bits of food by the drain. I moved my fingers away.

"What about Clara?" she asked.

"Yeah?"

"Yes?"

"Wait, what about Clara?"

My mother paused. "I thought there might be something—"

"Oh," I said. "Oh no, Clara's a friend."

She pursed her lips together. I tried to laugh the same way you might shrug, or wave someone off with your hand. I considered telling her about Paul, but didn't know why I would when I could tell her nothing at all.

She passed me another dish. And then she said, "So, you haven't been watching anything at all?"

My eyes stung suddenly, and I tried to signal to my body, to my brain, that I was fine. You're supposed to smile at yourself when you're sad. You're supposed to meditate and exercise. I tried to breathe deeply, but the bottom of my lungs seemed so close, and I started coughing because I thought it would be better than crying. I held the edge of the sink, my mother came over to my shoulder. I coughed and coughed. She patted my back, and I felt my face, so hot, and my eyes, wet, but from coughing, not from crying.

"Are you okay?"

I tried to breathe enough to tell her that I was just coughing, but my mouth was so spitty that I gagged. She went and got me a glass of water. I drank some. I felt it at an impasse at the back of my throat, but I tilted my head, and it went down.

"I was just coughing," I said. My mother watched me, and I said more loudly, "Choking on nothing."

My mother cleaned one of the last plates. She wiped a napkin full of ketchup into the garbage. "It's all this talking when you're still sick."

I said it might be. And then we cleared the last few things silently.

The New Year's Eve party each year alternated among the houses of the neighbors who lived along our road. Because the road was long and began to round the lake, we counted "our road" as the four houses that lived side by side on that particular six-kilometer stretch. Beyond that final house, it was decided, we were no longer neighbors. We were something else.

I carried food from the kitchen to the dining room. Cubes of cheddar cheese, crackers in a bowl, seeds and salt flaked to the bottom. When the timer went off, my mother passed me an oven mitt and I pulled out two trays of phyllo appetizers. I piled them onto a tray, and my mother said, "Nicely," and I tried to adjust some of them. Before she walked the tray to the dining table, I put one of the pastries in my mouth. It was hot, but with my mother turned toward me, I couldn't spit it out. I nodded at her. Her eyes on my mouth. Hot steam, and the butter in the phyllo melting out. When I swallowed, my tongue tasted like tin, and I imagined my throat, a desert ridge, red and unwilling.

My mother looked pretty, and my father wore a sweater. When my parents' friends arrived, I stood in the kitchen pretending to be busy. My father walked in to get plates. I met his eyes and he rested his hand on my shoulder. Sometimes when my father touched me, I imagined that I was his son and that he was congratulating me. Or, I imagined that we were in a stable, and that I was his horse. His hands appraising, kneeling on the ground, he would hold each of my legs. And then, when he stood, he would look directly into my horse eyes, and he would remark how human I seemed, sometimes.

"Will you have a drink?" he asked me. There was alcohol on the counter.

I hesitated, but then said, "Yeah, I'll have one."

"I don't think I've ever made you a drink," my father said. "A *drink* drink."

I told him he was right and then I looked away as he poured. I remembered once, my father sitting in a lawn chair, his seat almost touching the grass, holding a beer. There was a dog around, I can't remember whose. And the dog walked up to my father and my father lowered the glass and the dog licked the beer quickly. My father laughed at the dog's pink tongue, laughed at the slapping sound, and then pulled the glass away. I was young enough that it wasn't strange for me to be on my hands and knees. I crawled toward my father like the dog, and I pretended to bark, and I pretended to be thirsty. And my father's laugh didn't stop, he tipped his glass toward my nose, and I tasted the foam, the vague bread, cold and then warm. I felt a little strange, crawling away like the dog, my dad speaking no human words to me. And I wondered if I had been funny, or if I had been bad. And then, sitting by myself behind my father's chair, I wondered if I was drunk. Wondered if I would stand up and embarrass myself.

My mother called my name and my father told me he would bring my glass out. I left the kitchen and stood beside her in the living room.

"Jake and Emily are here," she said. When I didn't move, she gestured toward the dining room. "Go on and talk to them," she said.

They stood over on the far side of the dining table. We were used to these kinds of gatherings together. The problem was that, although our parents were close, and although we were neighbors by some stretch, we didn't ever hang out at school—we weren't friends.

Jake took a handful of crackers that he ate while speaking. His sister, Emily, crossed her arms. Liam arrived and stood by us, distractedly.

My father walked up, and he passed me a glass. I was grateful that he didn't stay and watch me drink from it. I smelled the rim. It looked like milk, but it had a dark bottom rising up through the white.

"Why didn't I get one?" Jake asked.

"You can try mine," I told him. After I sipped it, I passed him the glass. And after he sipped, he offered it to the others, who tried it also.

"I was going to go over to Callum's tonight, but he just wrecked his snowmobile," Jake told me. He was two years younger than Emily and me. He told me about how many bones Callum had broken. He said that his foot had been turned the other way. That he'd had to go to Sudbury for surgery.

Liam asked, "Was he on the lower trail? I heard trees are down there."

While they spoke, I was free to think about other things. Emily looked toward the table of food, but she didn't move. I wondered if Nora was eating at this moment. I wondered when she would call, and then I wondered what I could say that would make her wonder if she loved me.

Emily tapped her foot while Jake spoke. When he paused, I said, "And what are you doing now?" to Emily.

"I'm working for Cassidy Tombanks," she said. Cassidy was a local real estate agent; she had signs of her face along the highway.

I asked her if she liked it and she said it was fine. I'd hoped that she would say more.

I tried to tell by her face what her passion was. "Do you still run?"

She shook her head. "Not really. That was more a high school thing. What about you? You're in Toronto?"

I nodded.

"How's that?" she asked.

"Oh, it's fine," I said. And I wondered if it gave her equal disappointment that I didn't elaborate or tell her something interesting.

"Is that your phone ringing?" she asked.

Through my pocket, the screen was bright. "Oh," I said. I turned away from her, held the phone up, close to my body. Nora.

I hurried from the dining table to the bathroom and shut the door. "Hello?"

"Natalie," she said. Her voice cracked over me. "What are you doing over there? All the way in Temagami."

I caught my face in the mirror, saw that I was smiling. I turned away from it. "My parents are having a party."

"And you're the life of it," Nora said.

"Hardly," I said, whispering.

I tried to imagine Nora and me at a party together. Not here. In Toronto. I imagined her bringing me to a friend's house. I wondered if the thought would make her nervous, if it ever entered her mind. Did she think of asking me to go somewhere with her?

"I've been thinking about you," Nora said.

"Really?" I asked. And then I said, "Do you ever think about— Do you think I'll ever meet any of your friends?"

Nora laughed quietly. "Natalie, have you considered that I don't have many friends?"

I thought. "Not really," I said.

The phone was quiet. I wondered if it was still my turn to talk. Then Nora said, "I sometimes worry that you see me differently than I am."

"What do you mean?" I asked.

Nora's next breath in sounded sharp. She said, "Natalie, ask me something."

I felt the desolate possibility of being wrong. "What should I ask you?"

"You can ask me anything that you want to know."

But her voice betrayed that there was something, really, that she wanted to say. Would it be hard to guess the right question?

"Nora—"

Her name. I held it in my mouth. I felt how it might taste, a fork across the table, the crisp, watering fat of meat. And I realized as soon as I started speaking that I wasn't going to be smart, or calculating. I wasn't going to ask the right question. I couldn't be keen or interrogative at the same time that my mouth was so loose with wanting.

"Nora, do you love me?"

My hands were suddenly cold. And I was sure for a moment that time had been interrupted. The phone became so silent that I looked down at it. The screen was black and then white. And then it looked normal, but the call had dropped.

I stared down at it. Had she heard me? What if she had been about to say yes, but now, as she had time to think about it, she had changed her mind before I could call again? I tried to call her back, but the phone wouldn't ring. I thought I should go outside, for better service.

I opened the bathroom door and stepped quickly into the hall. My mother was standing nearby. "There you are, Natalie," she said. "The kids are all by the TV, it'll be the countdown soon." I began to gesture that I had to go, but my mother said, "Emily said you were taking a call?"

"Oh," I said. "Yeah, Clara."

My mother smiled, said, "How nice."

It was, I explained, but in the middle of talking, the call had—

My mother said not to worry, and she took my phone, ignoring me, and said, "I'll plug it in for you."

"It's not dead," I said.

"It might need to be plugged in," she said. "That can help the connection."

"But—"

She frowned at me, and I thought, *Settle down.*

She said, "Just wait a few minutes. You can call after the countdown. Why don't you go and sit." She ignored my hesitation, walked me through the hall to the couch where everyone else sat. And then she left, saying, "I'll be right back."

I eyed the kitchen door. Wondered if Nora would try to call. And if she called, what if my mother decided to answer? Seeing it wasn't Clara, seeing I was lying. What if she said, *Hello?* And Nora said, *Natalie?* And my mother said, *No, this is her mother.* But before the course of these thoughts could bring me to stand, my mother had moved back into the room, and chosen a chair.

Emily said, "We should watch the New York countdown instead."

But my father said, "We live in Canada," and so Niagara Falls stayed on.

I sat. I didn't realize I was rocking back and forth until Liam, who was sitting beside me, laughed and said, "You good?"

My mouth felt very dry. It wasn't long until midnight, and I thought, *Just get to midnight,* as though the breaking of this time would bring resolve.

———

At 11:45 a bell rang by the front door. Everyone frowned at each other. The bell meant a guest at the main lodge.

My mother stood. "I'll check," she said.

I listened to her putting her boots on. I thought her leaving would be an opportunity to go to my phone.

I looked around the kitchen. I looked by the toaster, and coffee maker. But there was no phone plugged in. I started opening the drawers. I searched the cupboard above me. I thought Nora must've tried to call back by now, and I'd missed it. I stared at every object around, the toaster again, the stove, not my phone, not my phone. I heard the front door open.

I walked through the hall toward it. I tried to take calm and deliberate steps, think of the voice I would use to ask my mother where she'd put my— Someone from the living room called out that there were only three minutes left. My mother met my eyes.

"There's a woman here," she said.

My father walked toward us. "A woman?"

"She asked for a room."

I thought of Nora. Had she come here? No. I'd just spoken to her on the phone.

"She was upset," my mother said. And then she paused. "She may be in trouble."

I put on my shoes, and I followed my parents. We walked on a path through the snow. The lights on in the lodge shone out. My father asked, "Was she young?"

My mother said, "Not *young*."

I asked, "Was she pretty?" Not thinking clearly.

"Pretty?" my mother asked. She frowned to herself, and then she didn't answer.

Inside the lodge, the lamp behind the desk was on. My mother looked at us and said, "She was standing right here."

"Maybe she went to a room?"

"They're locked."

"Maybe she's using the bathroom?"

My father stayed by the desk, and my mother and I walked down the hallway to the bathroom door. My mother pushed lightly against it, called, hello. No answer. My mother stepped in, and I followed her. The tap hadn't been turned completely off; it hissed a narrow stream of water.

"Was she crying?" I asked my mother.

She shook her head and said, "Never mind, let's go."

We walked back to my father.

He said, "Anything?" My mother said no. He said, "Did she give her name?"

She shook her head. She drummed her fingers against the wood. "She just asked if we had any rooms left."

We stepped back outside. I looked around at the snow. The white, frozen light. My eyes fell on an interrupting shadow, and then I saw several boot prints that veered off the path. I pointed at them, and my parents' eyes followed. The woman's steps were close together. We walked where she'd walked, across an unshoveled bank, then up to the side of our house. We paused by the window. The narrowness of her shoes had made small marks. Her soles were smooth, not made for winter. They disappeared where she'd stood watching us.

My father shook his head. "Probably checking to see if someone was home."

"But our lights are on, and she would have heard everyone at the party," I said. "Should we try and walk up the road?"

I reminded myself that the woman who had come could not have been Nora. But still, I felt a strong desire to find her, to be certain about who she was.

"I think she's gone now, Natalie," my mother said.

My father said, "I'm sure she's okay."

I nodded at them, realizing that they were trying to reassure me about feelings I didn't have. I let my mother steer my shoulders toward the main path, but I kept glancing back.

"You'll trip, Natalie."

I looked forward, stepped across the old path of my own shoes.

Inside our house, a new year had begun, and we had to meet late hugs. I wanted to ask my mother about my phone, but I had to pass first through everyone's arms. And then the guests started to leave, so I sat out of the way and waited.

Once the door closed a final time, I went to the kitchen full of dishes. My mother noticed me and said, "We'll leave these for tomorrow," as though anticipating that I had come in to try to clean them. I looked again at the toaster, and the coffee maker.

"Mom—"

She turned and looked at me. I noticed her eyes—brown, like just-found clay. I wondered if I'd been picturing them wrong my whole life. She held an arm across her chest, and I saw how this made the buttons on her blouse loosen. I thought of her choosing that shirt and putting it on. She looked at me. Her face creased with concern. I wondered if there was anything I could say that would make her understand me. But instead, I said, "I can't find my phone. You said you were going to plug it in."

"Oh," she said. "I must have gotten distracted."

She took my phone from her pocket and handed it to me. Now, dead. I turned. She put her hand on my arm before I could leave.

"Are you still thinking of that woman?"

At first, I felt afraid she meant Nora, but then I remembered the privacy of my thoughts, and I said yes. She hugged her arms tight against my back. I wondered if she could feel my shoulder blades, my ribs. I wondered if feeling these things made her love me more, if they made her want to talk more often, to be closer.

"We can't take on everything," she said. Her breath ruffled my hair. "Things just happen. We have to do our best to forget them. Okay? Just forget it now."

My mother turned off all the lights on the way up the stairs, and I watched as she closed the door to her bedroom. I sat on my bed. I plugged in my phone and waited. Battery, battery. And then, it came to, and I read Nora's message.

Tried to call back, going to bed now. See you soon.

I pressed myself face down against my pillow. I grabbed my hair in my hands, and felt it pull, begin to hurt. I let go, I sat up. I thought of being in control. I tried to imagine that my body was a linen closet and that, inside, everything could be folded very neatly.

Had Nora heard me ask if she loved me?

I felt how easy it would be to cry. The sharp edge of so many thoughts, the cut of one opening into another.

I thought, *Be in control.* I imagined standing in Nora's room. Her moving forward, wordlessly. Her kneeling down in front of me. I imagined wearing a black belt that she would reach up to undo. A difficult buckle. Her fingers losing their deftness and then, her face looking up at mine below.

Front clasps scare—

I got up. I closed the blinds as tightly as I could. And without meaning to, thought of faces appearing in the window, staring in. A woman's face. A man's face. And then, from the bleary darkness, something faceless, but equally capable of looking.

fifteen

When my bus reached the city, it jolted forward and back, moving incrementally with traffic. I walked from the bus station to campus. On the way, I followed a man from my bus into a deli. He had an extremely angular haircut, and a leather backpack. He ordered a small black coffee and a bagel with smoked trout and cream cheese. I ordered the same thing after him, but he'd sat down to eat and I hadn't, so as I walked, the coffee kept spilling on my hand, and I couldn't unwrap the bagel while carrying my bag.

Clara found me outside the dorms. She'd seen me from a distance, and started running. "Natalie! It's been forever, I swear that's how long it's been." She walked beside me as I pulled my bag up the stairs. It bumped against every step. "Have you been doing your push-ups? I've been doing my push-ups. I'm seriously strong."

We ate lunch together. Clara told me every gift she had received on Christmas Day, and then turned to her bowl, holding a piece of bow-tie pasta in front of her throat before popping it into her mouth.

We walked in the same direction to class. Clara's good mood made me feel more at ease. It felt ideal to be walking through the park, wearing winter jackets, the haul of books in our bags not yet so heavy. Along one edge of the park, snow was packed down so tightly that it had become hard and slippery ice. A few people sat there tying up skates. They held on to each other's wrists, and I imagined the satisfying reliance of grabbing someone else for balance. I pictured my own arm aloft, being steadied. The jolt of almost falling turning into bright, blustery laughter.

Clara told me about a new class she was taking this term and I half listened while we walked. Then, almost there, Clara turned to me and asked, "Did Paul get you anything good for Christmas?"

I said, "I haven't seen him yet."

"I bet he got you something."

Clara's class took her up several flights of stairs. I walked farther through the halls on the main floor, and through the second classroom door. Jones was already there. I was the first one to sit down, which was unusual. Jones drew up her eyes, said hello.

I said the same. "Did you have a good holiday?"

"Just fine," she said. She looked down into her bag, and I watched her collect a pile of books and place them on the table. She seemed tired. As the room filled with students, Rachel sitting as usual beside me, I thought Jones grew more and more weary, aware that a whole lesson would have to come before it could pass. She gave us a small, labored smile and said, "Why don't I read you a poem?"

I thought Nora's street looked different as I walked toward her door. The tall trees loomed without their leaves, and even though they, and the snow, had been there before, they'd never looked so inimical.

Before I knocked on Nora's door, I drew myself up, full height. I felt some need to prepare. Should I bring up our last call? Ask what she'd heard before it had cut out?

I knocked lightly, as I always did. The lights inside wavered, as though run through by wind. And I saw the figure of Nora approach. I shuffled side to side. I felt my throat constrict, no air getting by. I wanted to press my face against the glass in the door so that she would appear sooner. But then I thought, better to try to gain a sweet and enticing composure. What if Nora opened the door and I stood there softly blinking, no rush. She would be forced to say how good I looked, and maybe she would be the one who grew nervous and unsure. Nora's face began to take on more quality as she moved closer. I wiped my hands on my pants to make sure they were dry, and Nora opened the door.

The hall smelled like baking fruit. The air tasted like sugar, brown, almost honey, almost leaking out. Before I had a chance to look at her properly, Nora's lips brushed against mine, and my pulse felt like a fist banging carelessly against an animal's glass. She held one of her hands against my back and I thought that every worry I'd had in Temagami could be over now that I was with her. Nora's hand touched my cheek, and I opened my eyes to see her looking at me.

"I'm baking. Are you in the mood?"

She took my hand, my shoes barely off. In the kitchen, I could feel the heat of the oven. Nora opened it, and I saw a pan of oats crumbling sweetly into a stew of cinnamon and pear. I tried to look at the pan for as long as she held open the door. But my eyes began to burn, so I had to look at her instead. "It smells so good," I said.

Nora looked away, at the floor. I wondered if she would tell me that she had heard what I'd asked her on the phone and that it had been too soon, made her uncomfortable, but she said, "You must be mad at me, Natalie."

I looked at her, surprised.

She said, "For how I treated you—"

"No—"

"I should have been better while you were away."

"No—" I said again, but I could hear how softly I spoke. And I remembered the inward spiral of no replies.

"I wasn't sure how to tell you what I have to tell you." Nora's eyebrows furrowed.

I tried not to seem impatient. Nora's eyes were tired, and her cheeks were shadowed. I wondered if she was still sick. Maybe this was what she would explain, some illness. She took one of my hands in a serious way and I felt my stomach hollowing. That was it, wasn't it? A disease. My shoulders felt heavy. I thought I should let her know that I would take care of her if she needed me to. I would sit by her, read her things, hope that she got well.

"You can tell me," I said, and I tried to look at her with confidence, but it seemed whatever look I had given filled Nora with private concern.

"We're good together, aren't we, Natalie?"

I felt weak. I nodded at her.

"When we first met, I wasn't sure what we would be. But I like you being here with me. And I missed you while you were gone."

I felt my voice shake back. "I missed you."

Nora held my hand harder. "Don't sound afraid," she said. "I told you it wasn't something bad."

I had forgotten that she'd said this. "What is it, then?"

Nora breathed in deeply. "Natalie, before my wife and I separated, we were trying to have a baby."

At first, my ears felt like they couldn't exactly hear. Partly because the words were so unexpected. Not an illness? I remembered a video I'd watched once of a woman being pranked by her husband. He lines up cups of milk but makes the last one orange juice. And the surprise of the orange juice, after the body's already prepared itself for milk, makes her gag and gag.

"We tried for two years, and then she decided she didn't want to try anymore. She decided it was too hard, not meant to be."

I didn't move. I felt the sweat between our fingers. I stared at our hands. Nora waited for me to react, so I asked, "But you felt differently?"

Nora said, "I wanted to keep trying."

I tried to imagine this desire. "Was that why you separated?"

"It was one of the reasons." She closed her eyes bracingly. Was I supposed to speak again, ask more? "I'm pregnant, Natalie."

I felt a strange dumbness fog through my mind. I opened my mouth, found how my tongue was dry, I felt enveloped. I imagined this was how it would feel to be eaten whole. A fish inside a fish, my thoughts subsumed by Nora's words into their own death.

"I've been going to a fertility clinic," Nora said. She looked at me with solid eyes. "I didn't want to tell you before I was sure it was really happening. I've had problems before—"

I breathed in deeply. Tried to keep standing, and looking, and talking. I tilted my head, and I hoped that this tilting would reveal something more to me.

"—we picked a donor a long time ago."

We. I felt myself fall out of Nora's life. I wondered if next, Nora's wife would knock at the door, and Nora would have me answer it and she would say, *Here, now, you can see that this makes more sense.* And she would still insist that I eat from the dish full of oats, and they would both watch me. The cinnamon and sugar, the limp fruit, each swallow making me feel more sickly.

"Are you breaking up with me?"

"I don't want to be unfair to you. I want you to know that I don't expect anything—"

Who was I if she didn't expect anything from me? I found suddenly that I wished for some undeniable role. I wished she would look at me and tell me that she needed me. That she would say, *You know, before the single-celled organism, there were no living things.*

I would nod at her. Feel the beginning of an origin story, reality laid to waste, a new sense of becoming taking shape. What if she explained that sometimes, body inside of body, fingers curled toward each other's stomachs, atoms break open into god particles. That when two people love each other very much, the body explodes.

I would say, *So, biologically—*

And Nora would say, *I don't expect anything,* but it wouldn't matter because everything would suddenly belong to me.

Nora shook her head. "I have fun with you, Natalie."

I flinched away. I felt strange and like a toy. Felt, uselessly, how Nora might explain our relationship in a later conversation.

"Are you breaking up with me?" I asked again.

Nora shook her head as though I wasn't listening. "I'm not."

I tried to turn away from her, but she touched my shoulder. I looked up at her face, and she said, "I'm giving you the chance to break it off with me."

I thought dumbly of Clara saying, *I bet he got you something.* My lips trembled. "Do you love me?"

Nora's mouth opened, but inside it was the same deadness of the phone. When she spoke, she said, "Natalie——" And the sound of my name made me feel brokenhearted.

I tried again to turn, but she held my shoulders her way. "Before I met you, I had this terrible feeling of loss. Nothing felt important, nothing felt worthwhile." I watched her eyes. "When I saw you sitting in the park, and I came up to you, that was the first thing I'd wanted to do in a very long time."

She held her eyes closed for a moment. When she opened them, they were red and wet. And I found that I wanted her to cry, I wanted her to be feeling what I was feeling.

"I didn't know how this would go—you're eighteen. I didn't know——"

I pulled away from her hands. She reached out again, and I tried to move, but she grabbed onto me. Her eyes—in that moment, I didn't wonder what the world would look like if Nora had a baby, I wondered what would happen if she didn't love me. I wondered if I might collapse and stay forever where I stood, a ruin that Nora walked by, that she tried to clear away only after some time.

My voice was weak. "What am I supposed to do?"

Nora's chest moved up as she breathed. "I can't tell you."

"Why not?"

Her next breath staggered as she spoke. "Because I care for you."

"You care for me?"

I wiped my eyes. I said I should go, I shouldn't stay. Nora watched me. How much could a person shake before someone asked them if they were okay?

"It was hard when you went away to Temagami."

"Because you were alone here?" I asked.

Nora looked hurt for a moment, but then she said, "Because I was without you."

I waited to feel the everlasting comfort of being loved, but the kitchen only grew more quiet.

"I can't stay," I said.

"You can't?"

I shook my head.

"Can we talk more?" Nora asked.

"About what?"

She said, "I'm not trying to hurt you."

I told her I really had to go. Nora took her hands off me. And for a second, I looked at the window in the kitchen and I saw how the snow hedged up against it, cold and still.

"I love you," I said.

Nora's mouth trembled. I felt no courage.

"I love you," I said again. My eyes stung.

Nora reached out and I thought, *Don't let her touch you*, but I found myself in her arms. I felt her kiss my hair. Her nose pressed against my ear. She said, "Oh, Natalie," as though I were a sad and hopeless thing. A fish hooked through the guts. Not caught to be released. *Oh, Natalie.* As though she really hadn't meant to—

As though she were not mine, even though I was so plainly hers.

sixteen

I went back to the dorms, taking the street through the dark almost-woods. The feeling in my chest got worse as I walked, like a blister. The trees looked even thinner in the winter. The light from street lamps and high windows fell onto the snow. I walked off the path and pushed myself down the rough bark of a tree and sat. The snow seeped through my pants.

I had a missed call from Nora. When I left, she said that she would call to see if I was all right. I asked her if we were broken up, and she said no.

In high school there had been a bowl of condoms brought into one of our gym classes. A woman had pulled all the girls aside and ripped the plastic open and fit the condom over her hand. She pulled it to her elbow: *Don't let any boy tell you that it won't fit.* The girls laughed nervously. I thought of Nora's hand holding mine. I thought of the sweat between her fingers, the not letting go.

Nora called again. I looked up at the branches above me, cold and dying. I imagined falling asleep out in the cold. Imagined that if I stayed very still, eyes closed, body turning blue, I would be collected in the night. Like a soldier badly hurt, maybe I would be brought to someone's home. The city would be gone, the trees overgrown and full. I would lie in a world where the city was yet to be built, a thin bed, a fire cracking near my face, making it red, alive again. When I opened my eyes, I would notice my wound. Because, of course, there was a wound. It had been washed, there had been bandages alternating for days, fingers dipping into my blood, pulling my skin closed. The wound would burn and itch, but it would make sense. It would be the source of all this pain.

I opened my eyes again. I thought of the pearly bowl that Nora kept on the table in her front hall. I thought of her dining room, and her lips as she passed me a glass of wine. Her voice made it seem as though everything she had was something to admire.

How would it all go on?

I thought of us lying in the thick covers of her bed. I thought of her kitchen counter, one half of a butternut squash steaming, cream simmering, the smell of onions turning brown in a pan. Where would a baby go while we were talking?

I wondered if Nora would drag a crib into her bedroom. I wondered if all the squash would be mashed, no longer for me, no longer for our evening.

The ground rustled behind me. I turned my head but saw nothing. I wondered if I would be eaten by something. And wondered, if I was, if the nausea of this moment would carry on. So deep within me that it could not be chewed apart.

Nora wrote, *Natalie, let me know that you're all right.*

I stood up. Why had I told her I loved her? The cold air felt like a finger down my throat, and as I started to move, I thought that I might throw up.

My eyes watered down at the snow, my legs were barely underneath me. Who controlled my body when so badly I wanted to lie back down?

A skewed trail of footprints led to the dorms. I thought, *Lie down,* but my body wouldn't. And soon I was carried up by the elevator, I was walked down the hall, I was let into my room. My body began to thaw, and I felt the renewed heat trying to ease my mind. But it had been dragged there disparately. And I felt that, really, I was still laid out in the snow, waiting for Nora to love me back.

Clara knocked on my door the next afternoon. When I didn't answer, she opened it—I thought it had been locked.

"Natalie?"

All the lights were off. I wasn't going to answer her, but she kept repeating my name, so I pretended to just be waking up.

I told her I was sick. "Poor you," she said. "Stomach? Throat? Head?"

"All of it," I said.

"A flu?"

I nodded. Clara said she'd check on me later. She said to answer her texts, and then left. I fell asleep again. When I woke up, the dark felt stiff. If I listened closely, I could hear my bones creaking through it. I typed *what is that creaking noise?* into my phone, and the light from my screen hurt my eyes. I found "Nine

Sounds Your House Should Never Make." Number nine, *you suspect hissing that could be a gas leak.* I listened, but there wasn't hissing. *You hear water running—but nobody is using it.* I closed my eyes. No water running. Nora had called again, but I'd been asleep. I wanted her to call me now, but thought she never would. She'd probably told herself it was enough to try three times.

I read a checklist, "32 Signs He Loves You Without Saying It." I looked up *pregnant lesbian having sex.* I watched a pregnant woman lying on her back, trying to peer over her stomach at the hand between her legs.

I looked up *sperm donors* and clicked through different profiles. Instead of pictures, they had sketches that showed the shapes of their faces and bodies. I wondered which one Nora had chosen, and I wondered whether, if any of them had been me, I would have been the one.

Clara came back to my room. She asked what I'd been eating, and I said nothing. She said, "I'll make you soup." She brought her kettle to my room and hit a packet of instant chicken noodle against her leg. "It might not be good," she warned. It was okay. Clara watched me eat. When I was done, she said, "You should wash your hair. That always helps when you're sick." She walked over to where I sat and rubbed a hand against my back. "Do you think you're contagious?" I told her no.

Clara said if I showered she would download a movie for us to watch when I got out. "Deal?" I asked what movie, and she smiled and said, "A classic movie."

I walked to the bathroom. I felt like my whole body was shaking, but Clara hadn't noticed, so I thought I must not be shaking much. I got undressed. I had goosebumps that wouldn't go away. I got into the shower as quickly as I could, while the water was still warming.

I let the water run over my face. I thought, *See, taking care of yourself.* I made the water hotter. *Why don't you meditate?*

I tried to think of nothing, but couldn't. When I shut my eyes, my ears rang, and I felt like the curtain might be pulled back and I might feel someone's hard touch. I imagined a child wandering in, starting to talk about nothing. I imagined Nora's arm, her hand pulling me toward her, her clothes getting wet. *I don't care,* she said.

I opened my eyes. I stared at the goosebumps on my leg, and I imagined a goose. Me, a goose. I breathed out. A goose washing its hair with very dexterous feet. A goose drying itself off with a towel. A goose going to its room.

Clara and I watched *E.T.* She said, "You've seen it before, right?" I said that I had, and she put a box of tissues between us. She cried at the end of the movie and, inexplicably, at some points in the middle. Her eyes were puffy. I didn't cry, so I said, "It's sad, it's so sad," over and over again. After the movie ended, Clara stayed beside me, our heads propped up by pillows. She watched a series of videos, beginning with a makeup tutorial. I can't remember when, but I closed my eyes. And the next morning, I woke up alone.

The next day, I skipped my classes and Clara asked, "Are you sure this doesn't have to do with Paul?" She had suggested a walk, but when I got to the front step of our dorm, I stood there saying, "I can't."

"Natalie," she said. Trying a stricter tone of voice. "Why don't you tell me what's wrong?"

I thought of the terrible mess I'd made. Why had I said *Paul* to her? Why hadn't I said *Nora*? Because that would be worse. Clara saying, *She didn't say she loved you? You said you loved her, but she didn't say she loved you?*

"I have to go to the drugstore," I said.

"I have some cold medicine in my room."

"No, I need to buy a—test."

Clara's eyes widened with alarm. I didn't know why I'd said that.

"Oh, Natalie," she said. "Do you think—"

"I don't know."

She said, "Of course, let's just go." And we walked.

Clara threaded her arm through mine and then she said, without breaking stride, "I'd like to meet this Paul guy." She kicked a small stone out of our way. "Does he know what's going on?"

I shook my head and she made an *uchh* sound.

"We have to be so careful, don't we?"

Clara looked closely at the box. I leaned on the sink. She passed the pregnancy test to me, and then she read the instructions out loud so that I wouldn't misunderstand them.

"It's actually more complicated than I thought," she said.

I watched her, and I didn't think about how Paul was actually all a lie, or about how the test would be negative. And I didn't think about how a moment like this would later have repercussions. There was no telling the truth now, no *Eventually, I will say Nora.* I wondered who Clara was really friends with, because it wasn't me, was it? It was some girl who dated Paul, and who now needed a pregnancy test. Clara closed the bathroom door, and a moment later I opened it and we waited together.

Her eyes pressed, but she said, "There's no point in talking about it, not even hypothetically." I didn't say anything. "Because in a few seconds you'll have an answer and then, if it's negative, we'll have gone through it all for nothing." I watched her chew her lip, staring at the timer she'd set.

I said, "You know, I told Paul I loved him."

"You did?" She searched my face quickly. "Did he say it back?"

I looked down at my legs.

Clara said, "Oh, Natalie," in a tone reminiscent of Nora's, and I felt that I might cry. Clara said, "You know, there are people that are our age that are already mothers."

I looked at her face. She looked young, and I wondered if I did too.

"And it might seem crazy, but some of them seem happy. They're always posting cute pictures..." She trailed off, looking at the timer. And then she nodded toward the test near me.

"What would you do?" I asked her, ignoring the prodding look.

"If I were you?" I nodded and she crossed her arms. And then she closed her eyes, as though really envisioning. Clara sighed. "That *is* hard. I'm just not sure how it would feel in reality. And you know, I've never been in love."

I felt my face redden. The implications of *in love* embarrassing me. I felt like a dog drooling around on everyone's hand: *she can't help it, she's just spitty—*

Clara said my name and I looked up. "The test's ready."

"Will you look at it for me?"

I watched Clara lean over and pick up the test. She squinted at first, as though she might see something scary, and then her eyes relaxed as she saw clearly.

"Negative," she said. She threw her arms around me, squealing, laughing as she held me. "Negative Natalie, negative Natalie . . ."

I called Nora when I got back to the dorm. The phone rang a few times, and then she answered, breath heavy.

"Natalie—I've been worried about you. You never called me back to say you were all right."

"I'm sorry, I forgot."

"I called, but you didn't answer."

"I'm sorry, I didn't see," I lied.

"Have you been busy?"

"With school?"

Nora said, "I don't know, I'm asking."

"Yeah, with school," I said.

I closed my eyes. "32 Signs He Loves You"—*He checks in about your day. He tells you he's thinking about you.*

"I hate how things went, the other night," she said.

I didn't know what to say. She could change everything about how they'd went, she could say—

"I have a doctor's appointment on Friday, for another scan. I was going to ask if you wanted to come with me." *He includes you in his decisions. He'll do things to make you happy.* "I know we had a hard night."

A hard night, I thought. I wondered if that was all it had been. The hardness of each day after had made me envision a whole hard life, but Nora had spoken as though the hardness had all but dissolved. As though one day you could walk home in the dark, your chest feeling as though it had just been stitched, and then the next walk back the other way, feeling healed, almost okay.

"I think I embarrassed myself," I said.

"No, you didn't."

"I said too much."

Nora let out a short laugh. "I told you I was pregnant, Natalie."

I pressed my forehead onto my knees. *He can't stop smiling at you. When you're at his place, he doesn't want you to leave.* I wondered if everything between Nora and me was ridiculous. I imagined trying to explain our relationship to someone else.

I would say, *Yeah, so, I see this woman, Nora.*

THE LISTENER: *Go on.*

Well, she's quite a bit older than me.

THE LISTENER: *Quite a bit?*

I'm eighteen, though, so there's no real problem with it.

THE LISTENER: *There's a story there.*

What do you mean?

THE LISTENER: *You're eighteen, and she's quite a bit older? There's a story there.*

Not necessarily. I might be really mature for my age. I might be very attractive.

THE LISTENER: *Are you those things?*

I don't know.

The listener leaves a reserved silence.

Nora asked, "What are you thinking, Natalie?"

"Umm." I paused, felt the listener trying to crane in. "I was thinking that we're an odd couple."

Nora let out a hard laugh. "Do you feel odd when you're with me?" she asked.

"Sometimes I do."

"Really?"

I said, "I think it's odd that you like me."

"You can't think it's that odd by now."

"It's odd that there's so much more to you than there is to me," I told her.

Nora asked what I meant.

I said, "Like how you want to have a baby. And how you've been married. I hadn't started thinking at all about wanting a baby. Compared to you, I think about almost nothing."

Nora said, "I don't think that's true." She told me it was all about context. She'd lived for longer, so she'd had more time to want things.

"Do you feel odd when you're with me?" I asked her.

"I feel present when I'm with you. Sometimes I feel guilty, but most of the time your company makes me forgetful of everything else."

"Why do you feel guilty?"

Nora said, "Because there's an inherent disparity."

"Because you don't love me?" I asked.

Nora paused. The listener held their face. I hadn't meant this to sound so sudden and I hadn't meant it to sound as sad and stubborn as it did. Nora answered, with her voice subdued, "Because of our age difference."

"Oh," I said. And then more silence fell. Nora asked if I was okay, and I said I was. And then Nora asked if I thought about the future. And I said that I did, but that I didn't know anything. Nora said that was all right, and then I said, "Can I ask you a question?"

Nora said to ask.

"What will happen once you have the baby?"

Nora paused for a moment. I tried to remember more signs of love—*She tells you she's pregnant. She tells you she's having a scan, and she was going to ask if you could go with her.*

"I imagine that things will change," she said.

"What kind of things?"

"It's a baby, Natalie." Nora's voice was almost scolding. "Things will be different."

I had hoped she would convince me that not much would change. I worried about the small things. About her house becoming more practical. About it becoming proofed against a child's hands and mouth, less desirable to me. And then I also worried that if Nora was distracted by a baby, she would hardly have time to imagine if she loved me. And when, if she did imagine, would she find a moment to tell me?

Nora asked if I was still there.

I said, "I'm still here," but I was thinking about the sound of a baby crying in the night. When Nora woke up from the sound, would I offer to take care of it, tell her to go back to sleep? And when her baby looked up at me from on its back, would my love for Nora spread to it? Would I be so good and generous that Nora would shake her head and say, *Can you even imagine that in the beginning I didn't expect anything?* And I would smile at her, proud that I had become something.

I asked Nora, "What would the baby call me?"

"You can just be Natalie," she said.

I felt some relief that I would be able to keep myself. "Everything isn't ruined, is it?"

I felt the line tense. I wished she would say no even if she didn't mean it. But she said, "I hope it isn't."

"You said we were good together."

THE LISTENER: *Actually, she asked if you were good together.*

"We are," Nora said. "We have fun, we laugh."

"We do."

And then she said, "I'm not lonely when I'm with you."

"I'm not lonely when I'm with you," I said. Hoping, as I said it, that this was still true.

seventeen

In February, the wind made the whole city feel like bone. Nora and I sat on the couch. On the coffee table there was a menu from Sal's Sandwiches and Soups that Nora had taken out of the mailbox and left there. Beside it, there was a voting registration form and a book called *Pregnancy: The Essential Lesbian Guide.*

"Okay, Natalie, I'm ready," she said.

I had to be careful not to look for too long at the pregnancy book or Nora would ask if I had any questions. All of my questions were bad, and couldn't be asked. On my phone there were so many open tabs.

Q: I don't like my wife as much during pregnancy. I am missing—

I tried to scroll down, but first had to make an account to read the whole question and answer.

Q: I don't like my wife as much during pregnancy. I am missing sex and she doesn't seem like the woman I married ... What should I do?

A: Tanya Anne, 41, personal trainer:
If you're going to be a father you should be mature enough to handle your pregnant wife who's carrying YOUR child and put up with any "weird" behavior. Rub her aching feet, do ANYTHING to help her feel—

I scrolled.

A: Mark Rutt, studied at Baker Highschool (1962):
I think men are supposed to just suffer their way through pregnancy and smile away the urges. A test of character. Because pregnancy changes a woman's hormones she cannot control her feelings. Tell her, "I know you don't feel like yourself but you still make me horny. You're more beautiful pregnant than ever. Please try to make some time for me."

Nora's hands rested on her stomach. Her clothes had begun catching, her belly button growing wider.

Before arriving at Nora's, I had looked up, *What does it feel like to be four months pregnant?*

Welcome to the second trimester! Four months is usually reason to celebrate: You're feeling better, people know you're pregnant and are asking you a million exciting questions, and you probably have a bit of a baby bump!

As I'd walked to her house, I'd tried to think of some exciting questions. I asked Nora if she thought the baby would be a boy or a girl, and she said she wasn't sure. I asked her if she would find out, and she said she wanted it to be a surprise. I asked her if she knew what job her donor had, and she said he was a social worker, and that he'd donated a kidney to his sister, and that he enjoyed cycling in his spare time, which couldn't be that spare as he had three children and a wife.

"He donated a kidney?" I asked. I wondered if those kinds of details were verified before they were allowed to be written. It seemed very easy to lie, and probable that someone might. "Do you know what he looks like?"

On her phone, Nora showed me his picture. The first thing I thought was that I didn't look very much like him. He had broad, round shoulders and a full-lipped smile. His eyes were stable, possibly kind. His chin was pointed sharply, which gave him a natural seriousness, a spirit of expertise.

Nora observed me looking at the photo. She touched my arm, and I realized I'd been staring for too long.

"Sorry," I said. She watched me thoughtfully. "Very handsome guy," I said. And I tried to brighten with this compliment, to also become a very handsome guy. But, looking between her and the photograph, I had never felt so solemnly myself.

Q: My pregnant girlfriend doesn't want to have sex with me anymore. How do I deal with this?

Nora had stopped kissing me at the door. A change. Usually, at the door was where she kissed me hard, a moment that dropped off into hands poking buttons through their slips. But now, as she answered my knocking and I came in, she would reach absently for my coat, sometimes not looking at my eyes until we were sat down, talking.

I saw that she watched me more thoughtfully, with a new intellectual interest. She wanted me to tell her more. She asked me questions, and then pawed at the answers as though beneath them there might be something more deliberate and well-thought.

I felt a thinness of character, of being. I wished that I would regain whatever luster had caused her, before, to want to just grab me when I walked in. I wanted the soft questions that she asked me after we had sex. Her thumb moving up and down on my hand, light touches that seemed to affirm feelings of tenderness.

A: Joel Tuch (consultant, 39):
Rules:

1) Masturbation is the only acceptable way to release sexual tension for the partner of a pregnant woman who rejects sexual activity.

2) You are allowed to ask her to join in and make it more than masturbation. If she isn't interested, see rule number 1.

"Natalie?"

"Sorry, let me try to remember," I said.

Nora had started asking me to recount each of my classes to her. She wanted so much detail about them that it felt as though she might also be a student, trying to learn without ever going to class or reading.

She liked to begin with me walking in and sitting down. It seemed impossible to bore her; in fact, she only complained when she felt that I was leaving too much out.

"Were other students already sitting?" she asked.

"Rachel was already there."

"Rachel and your professor, alone?"

"Yes, Rachel is usually early."

"What happened once everyone was seated?"

"The lesson started," I said. "Jones talked about the space within a poem. Space from line breaks, and from punctuation. She wanted us to think about how each affected the poem's meaning."

Nora nodded as though she could picture this quite clearly, and I felt slightly proud to have done a good job recounting.

"And did you read a poem today?" I told her I had. She asked, "What was your poem about?"

"It's nature poetry."

Nora rolled her eyes, said, "You've told me that before."

"I don't know. The poem was about nature." I didn't like talking about my own poems, mainly because they weren't very good and I thought that if Nora discovered this, she'd be disappointed.

"Will you read me a poem?" Nora asked.

I said, "I can't."

Nora looked let down. When I didn't change my mind, she let out a sigh and then picked the voter registration form off the table and looked down at it thoughtfully.

After a few minutes she turned to me again and asked, "Who are you going to vote for?"

My eyes hurt. Probably strain. The room was dark, but whenever I tried to turn the lights on, Nora said it felt sterile, it felt like she was about to have an operation.

"I'm not sure," I said.

Nora raised her eyes to meet mine. "Really?" Her voice flicked.

"I'm not sure what everyone stands for."

There was a quiz online that could help people decide, she said. "I should read it to you." She read to me from her phone.

How much money should the federal government be able to redistribute between provinces?

"What if I answer wrong?"

"There's no wrong," Nora said. "There are just different political parties."

How much should wealthier people pay in taxes?

"Umm, more?"

"Somewhat more, or much more?"

I looked at her face. I tried to guess what she wanted. She was somewhat wealthy. Would she want to be taxed somewhat more, or much more? I wondered about my parents. And then I wondered about Clara. And I wondered about the real difference between *somewhat* and *much*.

"Much more," I said.

How much should be done to accommodate religious minorities?

"What did you pick?"

She looked disapproving. "It's your quiz."

"I don't know enough," I said.

She looked at me. "Should I choose 'Don't know'?" She was trying to keep her face as blank as possible.

"Yeah. I don't know."

The disappointment of my answer made Nora press her lips together, and before she could ask another, I said, "I'm having trouble with my eyes."

She asked if I wanted eye drops. She got a bottle from the bathroom and passed it to me. I said, "I've never put them in myself before."

I laid my head back. Nora pressed her hand against my forehead and said, "Open."

I tried to keep my eyes open, but I couldn't stop their protective blink. Drops spilled on my cheek. I said sorry and then I held my eyelids apart with my fingers and Nora got the drops in. It burned so badly that I thought she'd mistaken eye drops for something else and I worried for a second that she'd tried to blind me, and then I thought, no, nothing bad on purpose. And she rubbed my cheek with the back of her hand.

At the beginning of March, I was added to a group chat that Clara called the House Hunters. All day there were listings sent back and forth. Four bedrooms, one bigger than the rest. Four bedrooms, no place for a couch.

"Natalie, are you in?"

There was a rising pressure to commit. Clara didn't like that I never sent any listings, and when she showed me the inspiration board she had for her bedroom and found that I didn't have one of my own, she looked deeply concerned.

"Do you not like the other girls?"

"No, I like them."

"Is it that you want to live further east?"

"No, it's fine."

"So, you're in, then?"

"Sure," I said.

She said, "Your tone is confusing."

"What do you mean?"

"Are you unsure?"

"All the time."

Clara stopped. I said that was a joke. She said, "Your jokes always sound serious."

"That's what makes them funny."

She asked if I was worried about rent and I said yeah, a bit.

"Natalie, that's valid."

She put her arm around my shoulder, and she said that we could both work part-time. Her cousin owned a restaurant in the city, and he would hire us as servers.

I said, "I don't have experience."

"Didn't you work at your parents' place?"

I was surprised that she had remembered this detail of my life. I wondered, if we were going to live together, if I would have to tell her about Nora.

I wondered, if I wasn't with Nora, if I would have a good time looking at the listings. I imagined Clara in her new bedroom—lights hung above a bulletin board, a new green cushion to back her desk chair—feeling grown, accomplished. The whole room would reverberate with selfhood, with a great and solid sense of being.

She withdrew her arm suddenly. "Wait, are you thinking of living with Paul? Is that what's stressing you out?"

"Oh—I don't know."

"Did he ask you?"

"Not really."

"He implied something?"

"Sort of," I said.

Clara looked at me seriously. A protectiveness made her eyes seem like deep caves. "If you're not feeling 100 percent about Paul, it's okay."

I watched her cautious face, the worried lines on her forehead, and felt a swing of appreciation for her, and then a hard lump in my throat. "Are you sure you'd even want me to live with you all?" I asked.

She looked startled. "Of course I do. Are you kidding? Why would you even question that?" She looked at me for a second, and then adjusted the usual tone of her speaking, to be therapeutically subdued. "If you're having doubts about Paul, it might be that those doubts are carrying over to everything." She tried to meet my eyes, but I looked away. "To your friendships," she said.

I imagined myself saying: *You know, Paul isn't really Paul.*

Would she be disappointed? Angry? I would tell her the story of being approached by Nora. The words *pregnant* and *baby*, how would they make Clara's face change? How would my saying them make them more fully born into my life?

I don't know if she loves me, I would have to confess. And I couldn't imagine staying solid. I would start to cry, and Clara would stand there and see me. I would become so crumpled, she would regard me the same way you might a used napkin. I would explain that I asked Nora if she loved me, and she didn't say that she did, but that doesn't mean that she could never, and maybe it doesn't even mean that she doesn't now, right? It just means that when I asked, at that moment, specifically, she couldn't say it?

"You know, maybe I should meet Paul," Clara said. "Does he ever ask to meet your friends? Have you ever met his friends? It's not a good sign if a guy doesn't have friends."

I said Paul was pretty busy right now, but maybe soon. I said not to worry, we were okay, and I would clear up the housing thing. Sorry for being weird, I said.

"Don't be sorry."

Her eyes lingered on mine. I tried harder to recover myself—a person making a show out of shuffling all the papers on their desk, trying to make a neat pile. I tried to steal one of Nora's expressions, a small and comfortable smile. But the way Clara touched my arm showed me that I hadn't done it right.

It snowed and melted, and then snowed again. It was so gray that a record was set. I told Nora that I was going to stay in the city for the summer. I told her I might live with Clara and some other girls, I wasn't sure. She said she'd forgotten how early everyone had to find housing. I tried to tell if she had any other feelings about my living with Clara and the others, any feelings that might turn into her asking me to stay with her instead. But her hand turned over a page on her lap. There was a textbook open on mine, which I glanced down at.

"Maybe I'll wait a bit before deciding," I said.

Nora turned over another page. "Do you not want to live with them?"

"Maybe I'll live alone."

She looked at me doubtfully.

"Or maybe I'll go back to Temagami."

She frowned. Stopped touching her papers.

"Maybe I won't even come back in the fall, for school."

"Are you teasing me, Natalie?"

"Did you read that article about the woman who had someone living in her attic and she didn't notice for six months?" I asked.

"In her attic?"

"They never caught the intruder."

"Was this a recent story?"

"Have you heard the story about the old woman who thought her dog was under the bed, but it was actually a man who kept licking her hand, pretending that—"

Nora shook her head. "Don't, don't, I'll have to check under everything."

"I'll check for you," I said.

She took my hand. She went back to her work, and I went back to mine. Later on, she kissed the side of my neck and asked if I would stay the night again. I told her yes. I asked if it was because of the attic, and she said no and I said, "So I'm not just for protection?" and she laughed easily, but I did check under the bed because I'd scared us both. She said, "Thank you, honey." And from the ground, I thought she might've said, *I love you, honey.* But when I got up from kneeling, she was arranging the pillows around her, and I thought, that's not how those words would look.

Before the end of the school year, everyone on our dorm floor decided that we should have one last group-affirming activity— we were going to play a game called Assassin. A few of the floors below us had played it in the fall. Clara had watched, enviously, lamenting a lost opportunity for fun.

"It's going to be even better now," Clara promised everyone. "We know each other, so we won't be timid."

In Assassin, everyone gets someone else's name, and a mock weapon. If you kill your target, you take their name, and you continue playing. The last one left standing wins. We picked our first targets from a big box in the common room. We weren't supposed to show each other.

There were rules: No killing each other in the dorm or the dining hall. After picking a name, Clara pulled my arm toward her and said, "My room." She showed me Annie's name on her piece of paper, and she said, "Switch with me?" I gave her Jessica. I didn't care about the game, I just didn't want to be surprised when I was killed. I wished that I could know who had me and make it easy for them. I would walk into their rubber sword, hand off my name.

The next morning, Clara killed Jessica after her first class. I asked her to promise that she would tell me if she got me.

I said, "Just tell me, and I'll let you do it."

Clara said, "Okay, okay. We'll be on the same team."

For the next few days, Clara and I walked each other to our classes. Clara said it was for protection—we'd be able to warn each other about potential attacks.

We walked through the park. I was on my way to Detective Fiction. Clara was looking for a girl named Maddie, who had a class about to start in the same building.

Clara looked around. Sometimes she did a quick spin so that she could assess our danger from all angles. She held her sword out, cautious, ready. Mine was looped through the side of my bag. "You should keep it out," Clara said. "After your class you could get Annie."

There hadn't been snow in a few weeks. The weather was wet, and the ground in the park was brown. The birds were back, but they blended in so well that you couldn't see them unless they started hopping.

"You need to at least kill Annie, because if I get through everyone except you, then I don't want to have to take her name from you."

As we neared the building, Clara went to hide behind a hot dog stand. "If I crouch here, I think she'll have to pass me," she said.

I said good luck.

She smiled, looking a little wicked. "Won't need it," she said.

At the beginning of the class, I looked down the rows of seats until I spotted Annie. I sat down, more difficult with the sword hanging by my legs. The guy beside me gestured at my weapon. "Assassin? I won at the beginning of the year."

I said, "I think my friend's going to win it." .

He said, "Oh yeah? Why not you?"

A TA stood at the front of the room and announced that Jones was going to be away, so they would lead us through the lecture.

I looked at the laptop of the guy beside me. He watched a video on mute called "Most Idiotic Drivers on Dashcam."

Clara texted, *got her. she had you next.*

I felt relieved. I wrote, *Please end it for me.*

you have to get annie first.

When class finished, I sat with my head down until Annie passed my row, and then I got up quickly to follow her. I paced my walking so that by the time we reached the park, I was only a few long strides back. Annie's sword was tucked behind her like mine, an afterthought between her body and backpack. She was walking slowly, so it wouldn't be hard to pass her and then crouch behind something and catch her with my sword. But was I really going to jump out at her? I wondered if I would have to shout while I jumped to get her attention.

I got ahead of her, and stepped out from behind the trees when she was close. I called out, "Annie?"

She turned to look at me.

I held up my sword. "I have you."

For a moment, my words felt suspended and then Annie's face changed quickly. A smile widened her cheeks, a deep breath fogged the air. She turned away from the place where she stood, and she ran.

Annie ran across the park. At the edge of the road, she got lucky: the light changed in time for her to cross. She was trying to get to the dorm so that she could be safe. I was surprised that she'd bothered to run, and I wondered if she actually cared about winning the game.

We both crossed the road. Annie turned her head over her shoulder and saw me, closer than she thought, and this made her laugh and speed up. We were faster on the pavement. No one on the street thought we were cute. They tried to move out of our way quickly. I clipped a woman's bag, and she yelled after me.

We were getting close to the dorm. I thought that I wouldn't catch her, but then she stumbled on a set of steps. I reached out and I touched the back of her leg with my sword. She slowed down and I jogged beside her.

"Nice one," she said, and she reached out. A small tap passed between our hands, like we were players subbing on and off a field.

Annie bent down, hands on her knees. It had felt good to be out running, and I realized how few moments I spent without thinking of Nora.

"I think there's only four of you left," Annie said.

"Three," I said. "Clara has me next."

"Really? I thought it was that other girl—"

"Which other girl?"

"She's the student who lives off-campus who's paired with our floor. I think her name is Rachel?"

"I didn't know that off-campus students were paired with floors."

"Yeah, she doesn't normally get involved in floor stuff. But I thought I saw her following you earlier."

I knew that Clara had me next, not Rachel. I looked around. There was more light than usual. The days were trying to drag themselves out of winter. The sky was so blue that I thought, if it were water, I wouldn't want to put my hand through it.

Annie looked at me curiously. She wore a pale-green raincoat. It had big brown buttons. I thought it suited her perfectly. It suited her so well that for a second it felt like she wasn't wearing any clothes.

"Do you want to pretend that I didn't get you?" I asked.

She pushed her hair away from her eyes, their curiosity deepened. "Did Clara tell you?"

I wondered if she could hear my heart pick up. "Tell me what?"

Her expression wasn't defensive, as Clara's had been. She didn't seem nervous that I might know Clara's side of things. "Never mind," she said. She gave me a confident glance, which I wasn't sure how to respond to.

"I should go," I said.

Annie looked up at the sky and then did up the buttons on her coat. "I hope you win," she said, and smiled. And as she stepped by, I found myself breathing deeply in.

Around the corner, only a minute from the dining hall door, Clara jumped out, both hands readied with swords.

"Natalie," she said when I yelled her name, upset. "It's all part of the fun." Then she pretended to slice me up with her swords.

We walked down the road, away from the dorms and from the school buildings. Clara wanted to eat out to celebrate her win. I told her she still had one name left, but she said, "I'm not worried about that."

On the street, the air smelled fried. Clara said, "I do want to eat something healthy. I don't want to eat something bad just because we're going out. What do you think?"

I said, "I don't mind."

Clara sighed at me, but I'd gotten distracted. Standing on the corner, Jones was glancing toward where the next bus should arrive. I was about to point her out to Clara, but then, abruptly, she left the stop and started heading in the opposite direction.

I held Clara's arm and she stopped walking. "What?"

"Wait a second, follow me." I tried to hold Jones in view. I had to break into a jog to keep her in sight.

"Why are we running?" Clara whined.

"I want to see something."

We followed Jones parallel down the road. She took brisk steps, and checked repeatedly over her shoulder. And then quickly, as though she'd practiced the trickery of such a disappearance, she stepped off the street into the doorway of a shop. I stopped and Clara bumped my shoulder. We looked down both ends of the road.

"If you tell me what you're looking for—"

"Oh," I said.

"What?" Clara looked around wildly.

"It's Rachel. Coming up the road, do you see her?"

Clara watched the opposite side of the street. She said, "To be honest, I don't think I've met her. She's not very social, is she—"

I pulled Clara in front of me so I could watch while hidden. Rachel looked through each of the shop windows searchingly. "She's following Jones," I said.

"Jones?" Clara asked. "What for?"

I said I wasn't sure.

"Do you think something's going on between them?"

Rachel continued walking down the road. Her steps were unassured, and I wondered what her plan had been if she'd caught up with Jones. Would she have feigned an accidental meeting? Did she not realize the way Jones had caught sight of her? How she'd hurried to move out of her path?

I thought of the conversation I'd overheard between them in Jones's office. And I wondered how many of those talks they'd had. I told Clara that I'd heard Jones tell Rachel something about setting up more boundaries.

"Really?" Clara asked. "Then there's something going on."

We got poke bowls. Clara asked for extra cucumber.

"Does Jones look uncomfortable when Rachel goes up to talk to her?"

I thought of Rachel always waiting around after class. But I couldn't imagine Jones's movement in response. I thought she didn't usually hurry to clear her things away. I told Clara I wasn't sure.

Clara said, "Well, if she knows Rachel's following her around, then that's really bad."

"When I overheard them, it sounded as though Rachel was crying—"

Clara widened her eyes. "Do you think something is *going on* going on—"

"Romantically?"

She said, "It could be—sexual—"

I shook my head reflexively, but I didn't know.

"And if she was crying, well—"

I said, "She could've been crying about poetry."

Clara looked at me as though I were quite naive. She said, "Natalie, no one cares that much about poems."

That night I stayed in Clara's room until eight thirty while she got ready to meet up with a guy she'd been talking to. I watched her get ready, turning side to side in her mirror, patting her face with blotting paper.

She said, "I feel bad," and she meant for leaving me. She said, "I figured you'd be going to Paul's anyway."

I said I needed to do some studying. And then, when she left, I went to my room.

I called Nora. She'd gone to spend the night in Kitchener. I asked her how she was, and she said, "I didn't feel as well today."

"You didn't?" I asked. I imagined that Nora had asked me one night, in her room, about having a baby. Instead of having her own private desires, I imagined her kissing my stomach, laying her hand against it, talking about how she wanted our lives to intertwine. A baby because she loved me.

Nora was quiet on the line. And then she said, "You know, it won't be long now until they'll be able to yawn."

I imagined the twitching growth of pink skin, of cells. I felt grossed out. "Really?" I asked, trying to sound curious.

Nora said, "Isn't that incredible?"

"How does it breathe?"

Nora said, "They don't breathe. They get all their oxygen from me."

"So then it won't yawn the way you or I yawn."

"I guess not," Nora said.

And then there was an unsatisfied quiet between us. Nora had had another doctor's appointment that afternoon while I was in class. I asked her how it went, and she said it was good, everything was fine. I hadn't gone to any of the appointments with her. I'd wanted to miss class, but Nora had insisted that I didn't.

"You know, I think I saw you earlier today?"

"Saw me where?"

"Running through the park."

I felt my whole life flush with the heat of Nora's eyes on me. "Oh," I said.

"You looked like you were having fun."

"I was playing a game."

There was quiet. I wanted to explain to Nora that I didn't even want to play it, and that I hadn't chased Annie for that long before catching her. Nora didn't say anything more, but it felt like some point had been made. She asked if she would see me tomorrow. And then she told me that she was going to make something I liked.

I said, "You don't have to."

And then she said, as though trying to disarm me, "Natalie, I take you seriously."

I felt a lump in my throat. I wondered why she would say that. Did she think I didn't take her seriously? Did she think I wasn't taking myself seriously?

"I didn't want to play Assassin, it was mandatory."

She said, "You're not in trouble, Natalie."

I tried to imagine the way Nora felt. I wondered if she'd watched me running through the park and felt embarrassed. Maybe I hadn't looked like someone whose partner was having a baby.

"Nora?"

She responded with quiet.

I asked, "Do you miss your wife?"

I thought, if they had only stayed together how many more months, Nora would have been with her instead of me, and she would have said to her, *This is ours,* and those words would have rung with such certainty.

She said, "I miss *you,* Natalie."

I closed my eyes. I saw a vision of responsibility, of parenthood. I thought of a farmer tending to his land with the persistent worry of weather—uncontrollable heat, too many days without rain. One more and the whole year would be ruined. I felt how a baby would cause this strain.

I told Nora I should go. I had to write a poem for class.

She said, "Read a poem to us." I felt the inevitability of this plurality.

"I haven't written—"

"Then just off the cuff."

I had nothing, so I said, "Roses are red—"

A small Nora laugh.

"Violets are blue." A million ways of ending, but I said, "Sugar is sweet, and so are you."

Nora said, "There's a version of that poem in *Les Misérables*." I asked how it went. She recited, "Violets are blue, roses are red, violets are blue, I love my loves."

I frowned. "Does it rhyme in French?"

Slight exasperation. "It sounds better in French," Nora said.

Before I tried to write anything, I decided to google Jones's name. I read a sample page from her new book. The first poem was called "no evidence of a fight." It was gentle and ribbing and good. Furtively sad. I read reviews, which repetitively called the collection smart and deft. Then I watched an interview with Jones for one of her very first books.

The interviewer lowered his voice, and he asked a muddled question about "queering the genre of Canadian nature poetry." His smile afterward was contrived and self-satisfied, as though this question alone impressed a keen understanding of Jones and of poetry.

Jones didn't smile back, she spoke assuredly:

"A lot of contemporary poets are moving away from the traditional language and themes that have been used in nature poetry. Do you mean queering as in different from the norm? Or do you mean queer as in my identity?"

INTERVIEWER: I suppose both might be good questions. His voice became lower and lower.

JONES: I guess it might be queering nature to not think about the city as pure or impure. To not think of it as less a part of nature than a rural space.

On his back foot, the interviewer: Yes, yes.

Jones laughed. I guess you meant that all along?

I typed her name and then I added, *queer?* There was her author picture again. And another interview: "Kate Jones and Queer Ecology."

The interviewer spends some time describing her: We meet at a coffee shop in the west end where Jones lives nearby. She is reluctant to talk about her personal life and mentions, almost by accident, that she will get married this summer, but of course she provides no other details.

INTERVIEWER: You have a clear fascination with flowers and plants.

JONES: There's a lot going on with flowers and plants.

They go back and forth a little. I think of flirting, I think of tennis.

JONES: There's a tendency to see the word *nature* and think, in a panic, that you're about to suffer through something dull.

I thought of Jones's first lecture to us. Thought of how everything could be used as practice for something else.

INTERVIEWER: Your poems gesture to some of the ways flowers are used symbolically.

JONES: Yes. That's one intriguing way I think ecology has intersected with the queer. Historically, queer figures have used flowers as identity markers—green carnations, like the story of Oscar Wilde, for instance.

INTERVIEWER: I don't know the story.

JONES: Wilde told a handful of his friends to wear them to the opening night of his comedy *Lady Windermere's Fan*. From then on it was considered a subtle hint—green carnation on your lapel, a man that loved other men—

INTERVIEWER: Wow, really?

JONES: See! Nature poetry!

INTERVIEWER: Can you speak a little bit on your concerns with the male/female binary in ecology?

JONES: You know, the reproductive system of plants is hardly binary, and really, nature can't be fully understood if animals or particles or plants are considered stagnant, fixed. My question is, how can this influence our human perspective?

INTERVIEWER: On reproduction?

JONES: On everything.

I closed my eyes. I thought of Jones and I wondered if her life could be something like the one that I wanted. I wondered what she did at the end of the day, and who she spoke to, and what she ate. Was that what Rachel was trying to see? I wondered if I might start following Jones around too. But then I thought, how could I follow Jones and also *be* Jones? There must be some dichotomy there, some extrication of one from the other.

I shuffled far into bed, rested my computer on its side. I watched a time-lapse video of flowers opening, and then I looked up *a woman giving birth* and watched one titled "Woman Gives Birth Only 30 Minutes after Finding Out She's Pregnant."

First comment: *LOL now the search begins on who the father is.*

I watched a video called "Straight Girls Kiss Another Girl for the First Time (social experiment)." Bent necks, hands holding each other's faces, the kissing was quite vigorous.

My eyes felt tired, and I thought of how, if I fell asleep, the videos would continue to play. If it ran all night without the suggestion of my clicking, each video would lead itself on, and I would wake up in a very different place than I was in the beginning.

eighteen

I woke up earlier than usual. I was tired, but I couldn't go back to sleep, and I felt as though I'd spent all night trying to solve a problem that itself wasn't fully formed. The dorm was quiet. There were empty cans in the common room, which I decided to pick up and throw away. I wiped the table clean, and the sink. There was food in the drain. Noodles, wet crackers, remnants of a chunky salsa. I decided to reach in and scoop all of this out.

I imagined that these small actions would be hardly noticed, and I was sure people would argue that they didn't really help anyone. Who cared if there was food in the drain or cans on the table, or if the spills were never wiped away? But as I stood in the hazy light, I couldn't help feeling that I'd helped everyone be a little more taken care of, and I wondered if this was how it felt to be a mother. Awake while everyone else is still asleep.

Outside, it felt like it might rain. The cold wasn't so bad, and the air was beginning to smell more like earth, more like spring.

At corner stores, there were buckets filled with tulips. The price of strawberries was lowering.

I passed by a coffee shop, where I got a green tea and a sprouted muffin, which I ate as I walked. I wondered if this moment was a clear demarcation of adulthood. I was drinking a tea, and eating a muffin that was not sweet, which was actually a bit sour, save for a few raisins and cranberries. I was watching an early work crowd go by. Blouses and ties, firm, clip-clopping shoes. I walked with them until I was drawn to a display in the window of a florist's shop. I went in, thinking of a gift, thinking of Nora.

The florist asked me if she could help. I said yes, maybe.

"Is it for a special occasion?"

I said not really. She asked if there were colors that I liked.

I said, "I think I'm looking for something mature, and put-together."

"Is it for a professional environment?" she asked. "For a co-worker, or—"

I tried to imagine what a man wearing slacks, coming here from work, would buy his girlfriend who was waiting for him in his apartment, which was very modern and neat and had a fireplace full of round pebbles. Their relationship had its problems. He was very busy, and she was often fed up, not because she wasn't also very busy, but because she was always smiling at him, and arranging plans, and his expressions of happiness were so monotone. And so, he was buying her flowers to show her that he thought of her, and that he really liked her, and that he would like them to stay together to see how things went. He was buying her flowers to say that he was happy without having to change much about how he behaved.

I said it wasn't for a co-worker. The florist suggested some peonies, some sweet peas. I said that seemed good. She said, anything else?

I told her, "Whatever you think goes."

And so, at the end, she added a small cream rose.

When I got to Nora's house, I knocked but there was no answer. I sent her a text, which said *hey I'm at your door.*

I felt conscious, as I stood on Nora's doorstep with the bouquet, that everyone around could see me holding it. I lowered the flowers by my hip.

Nora? Are you home?

I looked up to the windows of Nora's bedroom. They were dark. I thought maybe she wasn't back yet from Kitchener, so I rested the flowers on her doormat, and I texted, *I left something at the door for you. I'm sorry you felt sick last night. I'll see you later.* And then I took the streetcar back to campus, where my first class was beginning.

As the day passed, I felt my usual nervousness build until it was time for poetry.

In the hall, I saw Rachel approaching from the opposite way. She was looking down, her thumbs tucked into the straps of her backpack. I wondered if she knew that I'd seen her following Jones. But it was hard to tell if her eyes were downcast because she was embarrassed or if she would even be embarrassed if she knew what I'd seen. Maybe she would look at me as always, as though I were miles behind, say, *You aren't following her too?* As though I were missing the ambition needed to gain crucial knowledge.

We met at the door, and Rachel said, "Go ahead." And I did. We sat down beside each other, like always. She took out her usual notebook and pen and, without speaking, opened it and began marking up the page. I took out my own things: a printed page with my poem, and then a few blank sheets of paper where I would write notes.

Rachel looked at me from the corner of her eye. "Don't you find it hard to keep track of loose pages?"

"Not really," I said.

She made a *hmming* sound, and then the door opened and the rest of the class filtered in.

While other students read their poems, Rachel sipped water and moved her mouth silently over the words of her own poem. When it was her turn, she cleared her throat and made purposeful eye contact with Jones.

I could tell that Rachel's poem was memorized even though she looked down at her page like it wasn't. She projected her voice as though we were sitting in a bigger room and she used a bit of a poem-accent, a theatrical flourish that made it seem sometimes like she was trying to be British.

When Rachel finished reading, the class didn't speak. At the beginning of the school year, hands had raised, and other students had given her compliments. Rachel received compliments by nodding her head, as though each point of praise acknowledged a success she had already deeply considered. Now, no one's hand went up. We all knew Rachel was good, and the consistency of that goodness had led to quiet tension in the room. Now, after she finished reading, the pause that followed hung open, a mouth unhinged. For others, we were more generous. We would try not to wait too long, would try to say something generous, *Yes, I like that line very much*. And the student would smile gratefully, feeling like at least part of their poem had won. I tried not to look at Rachel while she read. And actually, I wrote quick and uninterrupted notes, thinking that if she looked over, she might think I was abound with criticism, or completely distracted. She might let in a small, subduing doubt.

Jones raised her head. "Rachel, have you considered making this one continuous verse?"

Rachel said yes, she had considered it. In fact, it was only yesterday that she'd broken it up every third line.

"Have you ever read Alice Oswald? Yes? Have you read 'Wedding'? Okay, think of her syntax, yes?" Rachel said yes. "The repetition in your poem follows more of a generative order. The next word is the expected word. Oswald uses broken syntax, so that her meaning moves forward and back."

Rachel nodded and wrote. Jones didn't slow her speaking to accommodate her note taking, and I wondered if she didn't want Rachel to write down everything she said exactly. I watched the side of Rachel's face and tried to sense some disappointment at Jones's suggestions, but found none. The kind of feedback Jones gave her was often more technical and more specific than the comments she offered to the rest of us. And I thought Rachel must have taken this as its own kind of compliment. Unlike the rest of us, she might actually be good.

"Natalie, are you ready?"

Jones looked at me. I felt nervousness rise to my throat. I told myself, *No, you're exhausted and bored,* and I hoped that repeating this as a mantra would make my voice sound still and self-assured.

"Sure," I said.

Before I started reading, my mouth got so dry that my lips stuck together and I had to lick them free. I kept my page on my desk, my hands in my lap. I wondered if everyone thought of me as unbearably nervous, if each week they dreaded the sound of my voice, aware of the possible shaking. I looked up, imagined all twenty people thinking, *Come on, just get through it.* When Rachel read, it would have been all right if she'd stumbled. A hesitation, a flaw in her confidence, we would have loved that. Sweat had started to run down my side, I held my arms in more tightly. I felt like announcing that I was not myself, except that I was myself. And then, the poem began.

My lines were shorter than Rachel's. At the end of each sentence a cleaver disjointed one word from the next. I heard my voice settling over the words, and I found that it clung when it needed to and then, in relief, it carried on. When I finished reading, I looked up. A couple of people nodded their heads at me. I turned to Jones, who was mouthing some of the words to herself thoughtfully.

"Natalie, you move from using *her* to using *you.*"

I looked down at the poem.

"You might choose between them. *You* is more directive. *Her* is passive. You might ask yourself if you're writing from a place of passivity. Or if you're writing from a place of control, of direct address."

I nodded at Jones, understanding.

And then she said, "At the end of your poem, you introduce another entity, which now you refer to as *them*. It might be effective if you gave *them* a name. You communicate this entity as some intrusive force, yes?"

My lips felt numb. I wondered what had been communicated accidentally.

Jones frowned. "Did I misunderstand?"

I looked down at my poem. "I'm not sure."

"Sometimes writing is clarified at the same time as your feelings." Jones smiled at me. Rachel looked hard at the table.

After Jones finished speaking, a few other people raised their hands to tell me what they liked. My inability to take compliments well undermined my desire to receive them. I ran my finger along the side of the desk and tried not to look at anybody. A few times I smiled and brought my eyes up halfway. Rachel pressed her fingers into her temples. We moved to the next poem, she brought her pen back to her page, ink spreading out in a single place.

After class, Rachel walked straight to the front of the room. I took my time packing my bag. I tried hard to listen. Rachel said, "Can we arrange a meeting—"

There was a line set on Jones's face. I watched her eyes follow the backs of students leaving. I wondered if she was wishful, wanting badly to be able to pack up her things, to avoid Rachel, whose presence was a demand. I got up from my seat. I pretended to be looking for something in my bag. And then I pretended that I'd noticed something lost. I looked underneath the table, and beside the chair. And then I looked once more in my bag, but the imaginary item was still not there, and Rachel was still speaking.

"Are you going to your office now?" Rachel asked.

I thought of Jones on the street, sidestepping into a shop. I wondered if there was an official way these matters were handled, but then also wondered what making these matters official did. Did they exacerbate the rumors of what went on between Jones and her students? Would Rachel be punished and then in her embarrassment never become a poet? Did Jones think about that?

I put my bag over my shoulder, tried to carry a look of perturbed misplacement.

I heard Jones say, "Rachel, actually—"

And, as I glanced at her, halfway to the door, her eyes fell heavily on me and she said, "I have an appointment now with Natalie."

I stopped walking. Felt the command of her turned attention. Rachel looked over her shoulder at me. I nodded because I was confused, and Jones had spoken so assuredly that I thought we might actually have a plan that I'd forgotten about.

Rachel said, "Okay, definitely. Another time, then." And as she turned to leave, we switched places. Jones faced me and opened her mouth to speak. Rachel's bag caught the handle of the door on her way out, and she had to stop to unhook it.

"Natalie," Jones said.

She glanced toward the door. Rachel was now gone. She crossed her arms over her chest. Her neck was red, eyebrows furrowed.

I said, unsure, "I don't remember making an appointment—"

Jones said, "No, no, we didn't."

"Oh," I said.

She looked down at her arms. She seemed disturbed, and I wondered if it was because she had so easily made me question the reality of my day. A slight insistence and my mind could have completely rearranged. I thought it must be strange to have so much sway.

"I'm sorry, Natalie," Jones said. "I shouldn't have handled things this way—"

I shook my head, not sure exactly what she'd handled but aware that I had been an excuse for her not to see Rachel.

Jones sighed to herself. She said, "You wrote a good poem today."

I smiled at her, and then looked down.

Jones said, "You have discretion."

I wondered if she meant in my poem. Or if she meant right now, in regard to what had happened with Rachel. I thought of telling her that I'd seen Rachel following her around. But then I thought, looking at her eyes, that I would only be telling her something she knew.

Instead, I asked, "Are you all right?" And I surprised myself, hearing that I sounded quite like an adult. That my tone was almost as silken as Nora's. Almost convincing enough for Jones to feel like she could actually confide—

"Of course, yes, I'm fine." She began to adjust the strap on her bag. And then she asked, "Don't I seem all right?" And I saw for a moment the impossible dissolution of her demeanor. I could see the skeleton of her lessons, the thought and practice and rigor that were behind them. I could see the troubled face and tone that she had concealed during those interviews I'd seen online. I could hear her private discontentment, see how she might take things personally, see how she might be hurt, or upset. I could see the fear that lingered now after Rachel left, the alarm that had caused her to say, *I have an appointment now with Natalie.*

I looked at Jones, and I opened my mouth but didn't answer. She gave a smile, and a retroactive laugh to conceal the real asking of her question. And then her feelings were hidden again, behind the bounds of some perimeter.

Nora had put her flowers in a vase on the kitchen counter. She kissed me in the hallway, and said, "That was such a surprise."

There was a bowl of apples beside the vase. She said she wanted to bake a pie.

I said, "You've been baking a lot lately."

She took a peeler from a drawer. The roundness of her stomach meant that she had to hold her arms almost straight out in front of her to reach the apples on the cutting board. The same roundness hadn't reached her face. I remembered to ask her about her appointment. She told me that it had been okay and seemed happy that I'd asked.

"I took a video, in case you wanted to see."

"You did?"

"Do you want to see?"

I stood by her shoulder, and she showed it to me. The baby was gray. When it moved its arms and legs, the world around it moved slightly too.

"Does it hurt?" I asked.

"When they move?"

I nodded.

She said, "It can."

I wanted to take the flowers out of her vase and give them to her again. Explain that the bouquet had been a kind of vision, a dream—the flowers were about me taking care of her. Had she ever heard of queer ecology?

Nora said, "Are you all right?"

"I'm sorry I didn't go with you."

"You had class."

"How many appointments are left?"

Nora said it would depend, but there would be at least one more ultrasound. I told her I would go to the next one.

I asked, "If I go with you, what will you tell the doctor—about who I am?"

"I'll tell her you're Natalie."

"Won't she wonder who I am in relation to you?"

"I'll tell her you're my partner," she said. She began to peel an apple.

"You would?"

"I don't think she'll ask," Nora said.

"Right, but if she did—"

"Then I would say that you were my partner."

"Right," I said. Trying to sound casual, and matter-of-fact. *Partner.* The word made me feel fastened to her.

"You had poetry today, didn't you?"

I was still thinking of how I partnered her. And I was thinking of how I would make sure to go to the next test, and I would try to make sure that the doctor asked who I was. I would have to make my identity a must-know.

"I think the poem I read today was good." My lips twitched involuntarily, and I found myself smiling.

"Oh?" Nora said. "Well, it can't have been the first time."

"I think it was. I felt like it was the first time the poem didn't disappear immediately after I'd finished reading it."

"Is that the difference between a bad and good poem?"

I said, "I think it's part of it."

The spirals of apple peel began to fall flat on the counter. Nora used her nails to pick them up and drop them into the garbage.

"Why don't you read me this poem?"

I felt my stomach clench. And with surprising conviction, I said, "No, I can't."

She looked disappointed. "Why? You said it was a good one."

I looked at Nora's stomach again. My poem was about her. Was it flattering? I thought of Jones instructing me: Did I want to be passive, or direct? Should I name the entity, the intrusive force? Nora might see it clearly.

I said, "It needs to be edited."

"You know, I might be able to help you." Her voice sounded indignant.

"Jones said—"

Nora slammed her fist down. An apple rolled off the counter and fell. She lowered her foot onto it, and it crunched The spit of it all across the floor. I stepped back. Nora gripped the counter so hard that I thought she might try to tear it away.

"You trust your professor more than you trust me?"

I looked at her, bewildered. I opened my mouth but didn't know what to say.

"Wouldn't I have useful advice?" Her eyes cornered me.

I looked away, toward the apple on the ground. I thought of how it would never become a pie. It had been whole just a second ago.

"Isn't my opinion valuable?"

"Nora—that's not what I meant."

"What did you mean, then?"

I tried hard not to look at her stomach. I tried not to look at her foot, which stepped in the mess.

"I get nervous to show you," I said. "Because I care about what you think."

She looked at me, jaw set. "Writers are selfish, and arrogant. I can be interesting. I have my own thoughts and feelings."

The room was quiet. I thought at any moment Nora might break apples again.

I said, "I'm not a writer."

She glared at me. "You don't know who you'll be yet."

I felt myself hunch, helplessly. I wanted to show her that I wasn't trying to argue, and that if I was accidentally, then I wanted to lose. I wanted her to win.

Nora turned to the sink and wet a cloth. Her mouth trembled. She bent to a knee.

I said, "I can do that."

She didn't answer.

"Nora, stop."

I knelt beside her and took the cloth from her. She used the counter to pull herself up. I picked up the pieces of apple and then wiped the floor until the cloth was sticky. She watched me, her breathing softening slowly. I wanted to wipe the floor until her breathing was so quiet and deep that I might mistake it for the sound of her sleeping. But Nora said, "I think it's clean, Natalie," and I stood up.

I washed my hands in the sink. Nora walked up behind me. She said, "I didn't mean it." I washed my hands some more. The smell of the soap was strangely bright, like a different day and place.

Her hand touched my arm. I said, "I don't mean to be selfish. Or arrogant." These words bubbled in my throat, and I thought of how froth might spill out of a sick mouth.

I looked back at the cutting board full of apples. Nora said, "Never mind, I didn't mean it."

I asked if we should finish baking. She said she didn't want to. She said, why don't we do something relaxing?

For a few moments, we sat on the couch in silence. And then Nora asked if I wanted to watch something. I told her i should probably study. I took my books out of my bag. She turned on the TV, volume low. She kept adjusting it and asking, "Is this too loud for you to concentrate?" And I told her no, it was okay.

Nora looked toward the screen. I held a book in my lap, working on the illusion of study. Nora poured mixed nuts into a bowl and put them between us.

"Cashew?"

I shook my head.

"Walnut?"

"No, thank you."

I watched her from the corner of my eye. In front of me, there was a late-night host nodding toward a handsome man on his couch.

"Who is that?" Nora asked.

"I don't know."

"Is he from a Marvel movie?"

"I don't know."

"He looks like he could be."

"Maybe."

"There are a lot of those movies."

She shook her head a little when the famous man laughed and said, *A very tight costume.* A glimmer of judgment sharpened her eyes and I felt comforted by how it seemed to compose her. I liked seeing the Marvel man cross one leg over his thigh, the tight cut of his pant riding up his ankle, his forehead creasing when he drank a raw egg instead of answering which of his co-stars he liked the least.

So, what was your workout routine like?

Nora rolled her eyes toward me, and I smiled back at her. The side of her face was blue with the TV light.

"Pistachio?"

I said no. And then I thought, the worst man alive probably has a wife. And she might think of leaving. And she might not think of leaving.

"Are you still watching?" Nora asked me.

"Not really," I said.

She turned off the TV and we walked up to her bedroom.

Nora folded the covers back. When we lay down, we faced each other and looked silently. Nora's head rested on her arm. Her stomach almost touched me. I thought about forcing my own to grow. I thought, what if every day I gathered the ribbon of my own desire and I forced it into a ball. What if that ball lived inside me and fed off me and, without any air, was able to yawn.

Nora spoke. "What are you thinking, Natalie?" Her voice was tired. I wondered if we were still fighting, or if that had ended as we watched TV. And then I wondered if Nora and her ex-wife had fought a lot. Maybe lying exactly as we were.

I asked her, "Do you remember the moment you first met your wife?" And I watched her face.

Inadvertently, she smiled. She said, "I remember."

"Will you tell me how it went?"

She looked at me, as though trying to imagine if her story would make me upset. "We met in an English class. She would always offer to read when the professor asked. And not only would she read the passages, but she would always get up and stand."

"She would stand?"

"She would clear her throat and look out over us all. She would read the passage so loud and clear and well that it was hard to really make fun of her. She made it sound just how it was written to sound." Nora's smile looked private. "And then one day I asked her why she always stood up. Why didn't she just read sitting down."

"And what did she say?"

"She looked at me as though I didn't know anything." Nora smiled again. "She said, it would compromise the material."

The tone of reminiscence sounded like a candy left in your pocket. A restaurant mint that has gotten hot and cold again, and when you find it, it's still a restaurant mint, but it's gotten soft, the taste not as sharp.

I felt the ribbon that collected around me. It was red and raw, and I was dying to swallow it. My stomach pressed against Nora's stomach. I felt my own pulse between us.

"What happened?" I asked.

"Between her and me?" Nora asked. "I think I told you."

"You said she didn't think it was meant to be anymore—having a baby."

Nora said yes. "We had started to imagine different futures."

I looked at her. Saw her mouth open and then close and then open again and say, "And she had an affair."

"Really?" I asked.

Nora said yes.

And then we were quiet. I thought of what to say. I thought of apologizing to her. And then I thought of saying something moral, like, *That was wrong.* Or punitive, like, *That's unforgivable.*

But before I could decide, Nora said, "Remind me of that girl in your class—from poetry."

"Rachel?"

Nora nodded.

"What about her?"

"Do you dislike her?"

I wondered why she would ask me about her now. I felt reluctant to say too much, not wanting Nora to start to find her interesting.

"She's just intense."

Nora asked, "Does your professor like her?"

I decided to answer carefully. "I think Jones thinks she's a good writer. And I think she wants to help her with her writing."

"You're being very diplomatic with me."

I said, "No," very quickly, as though being diplomatic were the same as lying. "It's just, at the beginning of the year, I heard this rumor."

"A rumor?"

I felt very weak. That somehow I betrayed Jones by repeating something which might be untrue. Even to Nora. Even in privacy.

"I feel bad saying," I said.

"Oh? I won't spread it."

I looked at my hands. I worried that if I told her the rumor, she would accuse me again of trying to seek Jones out intentionally. Maybe she would try to probe the true nature of all my feelings. And what if that true nature was uglier than she, or I, expected it to be?

I said, "Last year, some people say that Jones slept with a student."

Nora raised her eyebrows. "Do you believe that?"

"I don't know," I said. "I understand how it might happen—"

Nora frowned hard at me. "You do?"

I shrugged, not wanting anything I said to *mean* anything about me.

"Do you meet with Jones often?" she asked more sharply.

I said no, only that once to get my bag.

There was a pause and then Nora said, more delicately, "It's all right if you like her—"

"What do you mean?"

"If you *like* her—"

"Oh," I said. "No—"

"Is she ever—sexual toward you?"

I felt a terrible shock, and I realized how upset I would be if the rumors about Jones turned out to be true. I stuttered, I said no, never. "She isn't like that."

"She isn't?"

"She isn't," I said. But the way Nora looked at me made me feel like I was being naive.

"Are you tired?" Nora asked.

I nodded.

"Do you want to sleep?" she asked.

I said I did. I turned over. Nora reached over me and held my hand in hers.

"You won't leave, will you?" Nora asked.

"What do you mean?"

"You won't leave during the night?" Her voice was unusually wanting. I wondered why I didn't feel flattered.

"Of course not."

I lay very still. I looked toward the street light that shone faintly through the blinds on her window. I imagined being down in the road, looking up at the house, never having met Nora. She began to sleep, her fingers let go of my hand. Her body was warm.

Was the air outside cold? I remembered the sight of her across the park, and thought, what if we had only looked at each other? If she'd not gotten up and walked over? Would I have thought, from time to time, of her eyes tipping their brim toward me?

Nora shifted. Her knee rested against the back of mine and I resented the thought of never-meeting. The heat of her stomach against my back, of her arm on my chest, wasn't it love?

Nora moved again, pushing the duvet down and then, mostly asleep, put her arm over me. I watched her elbow bend over my hip. And her hand, realizing its emptiness, closed over the sheets.

nineteen

The next morning, Clara was in her room. I knocked on her door, remembering that she'd had a date the night before.

She looked more tired than usual, which made me think it had gone well, but when I asked her how it had went, she looked down at her hands.

"Well—"

"Well?"

She twisted her fingers together and tried to crack them. "Well, we went back to his house," she said. "His room was really neat, like he'd just cleaned it." She was pulling her fingers, but they weren't popping. I told her to stop, and she said, "But it feels like they need to."

I asked, "So, then, the date was good?"

She put away the makeup that she'd left on her desk. Put a curling iron back in its drawer. Her jeans were hanging over the back of her desk chair. Without answering me, she took her bra off underneath her shirt and pulled it out of her sleeve.

"It was okay?" I asked again.

"Yeah," Clara said. She wiped her nose with the back of her hand. "Definitely nothing bad." She stared at her duvet cover.

I hesitated—it was unusual for her not to be forthcoming. "Clara?"

"Yeah?"

I considered how I should be. A question that would be coaxing. A question that would make confession feel simple and possible.

"Did you guys—you know. Since you went to his house . . ." Clara looked at me but didn't speak, so I said, "Did you have sex?"

Her eyes lingered away from mine for a second. And at first it seemed like she might act too embarrassed to talk about it. But then she looked up and she nodded at me.

"Did something—"

"I told you nothing bad happened," she said.

I said, "No, I know. We're just talking."

She scratched her neck, nervously. "The kissing was fine," she said. "No, the kissing was good, actually."

I asked how things had been at the bar. She told me that she'd drunk, but not much, same with him. She told me that he was good at making conversation, easy to make laugh.

"That's good," I told her.

"And then we went to his place."

She said that his room had been painted a very dark blue. I said okay. She said, "The blue was a little unsettling."

I said, oh?

She told me the blue was so dark that it had almost been black, and it was strange how much the blue might've actually been black. She said, "Maybe that shouldn't have bothered me."

I told her it was fine that it had.

"And you know. It's always weird at first." She waited for me to agree, and I did. "So we started out just talking, and then just kissing, everything normal." Clara looked at me. "It's not the first time I've done it, so it wasn't that big of a deal. There didn't have to be any pressure." She looked up toward the ceiling. "And then I suggested something stupid."

"What?" I asked. Clara paused, and I worried about her stopping. "What?"

She asked, "Are you going to judge me?"

I told her no, I wouldn't.

"Okay. Well. I told him, if he wanted, we could—watch something together."

"Watch something," I repeated.

"Okay, look, I'm going to write down what happened and then we can talk about it." I said okay. Clara ripped a page out of her notebook and wrote, *I told him that we should watch porn.*

I looked at her. "You said this during?"

"Yeah, we were having sex. But he said he wanted to."

"How did you choose what kind to watch?"

"He told me to pick."

"What did you pick?"

"I just picked something normal."

"Okay," I said. I wanted to know what it was.

"And then, after we watched, I told him that I wanted to blindfold him." Clara covered her face with her hands. She asked, "Are you judging?"

"No," I said, so she pulled them back.

"But then he said he wanted to blindfold me too."

I nodded as though this made sense.

"So we both blindfolded each other, and we decided to start again, at opposite ends of the room."

"How was that?" I asked her.

"I liked it at first, not being able to see each other." A teary-ness had started to redden her face. "I know that blindfolding is really normal. It's really common, I think everyone does it." Clara was quiet for a second. And then she said, "I peeked when he wasn't looking."

"What do you mean?"

"Midway through, I took my blindfold off. And then I was just watching him."

"He didn't realize?"

Clara shook her head. "No."

"Did you tell him after?"

"No. Is that bad?"

"It's not bad, Clara."

"I think it is bad," she said. "He only agreed to be blind-folded because I'd agreed to be blindfolded and he hadn't expected me to see him."

"It's not bad, Clara, it's okay."

"I know it's bad," she said. I sat closer to her. She said, "And I can't make it up to him because he can never know what happened."

"Why did you take your blindfold off?" I tried to imagine Clara in the blue-black bedroom, arms out ahead of her.

"Because I didn't want to be blindfolded. I wanted *him* to be blindfolded." Her eyes were half-full. "I know, it's messed up."

"Clara—"

"Should I tell him?"

"No, don't tell him."

"Are you sure?"

"No—I don't know. Do you think he'd be upset?"

"I don't know. I'd be upset. Wouldn't you be upset?"

I tried to think of Clara's problem in terms of Nora. I tried to imagine that we were having sex and that in the middle I stopped her and said, *Do you want to watch something?* I wondered how Nora's face would look. Would her eyes dig in curiously, would she open her mouth, say, *Like what?*

"I don't know," I said.

"Wouldn't you want to know?"

"I don't know."

We sat for a moment without saying anything. And then Clara said, "I didn't sleep there. And I cried on the bus home. I know people cry on the bus a lot. But I'd never cried on the bus before."

"I'm sorry you had to cry on the bus."

"It's fine," Clara said. She crossed her arms.

"If this is the worst thing you've ever done, then you're all right."

Clara said, "Yeah. I guess it's fine."

She picked up her phone, so I swiped at mine. When I looked back up at her, her face had relaxed a little.

"What are you looking at?"

She turned her screen toward me and pressed play on a video. One hand held a kitchen knife, and the other, a bar of orange soap. The knife cut horizontal lines and then vertical lines, and then it began shaving off identical cubed pieces.

"Satisfying, right?"

"Turn the volume on," I said.

It was the same sensation as holding on to a smooth rock, or getting someone to stop tapping their pen. The soap was scraped away thinly, the sound against the blade like a quick stutter. Clara and I watched the video loop. And then we found another that was almost exactly the same. Pink soap. After pink, I said, "Blue soap." And then Clara scrolled to find other kinds. Purple soap, and then green soap.

twenty

In December, before Christmas break, Nora and I had put up her tree together. It was a real tree. It had been wrapped in rope, and when Nora and I cut it free, all the branches sprung out and pine needles scattered all over her living room. I could remember all of Nora's ornaments wrapped in paper, kept in a neat box. Delicate and glass, we hung each ball gently, making sure each branch could bear the weight. When we were almost finished, I stood by the window and I looked at Nora, her back to me, her arm stretched toward the top of the tree. I caught my own feeling of wonder, my own long look toward the room, which I thought would never again contain so much beautiful light. I asked, "Does it look like this every year?"

Nora's smile was unrelenting. She walked over and kissed me, and I held on to the open sides of her housecoat.

I said, "You know when you go to a diner, and there are things that are good to order, like eggs and pancakes and a hamburger?"

Nora laughed. "Okay?"

"It's disappointing if you go and you feel like something else. Like if you just feel like yogurt or oatmeal."

Nora's eyes shone as she said nothing.

I said, "But it's amazing when you go and you feel like ordering the exact thing they're famous for."

"Like eggs, and pancakes, and a hamburger?"

I nodded at her. Nora shook her head at me as though what I'd said was some kind of wonder. And then she held my face to her lips and she kissed it all over.

Clara said she was worried about me. I looked at her, annoyed. I asked her why.

She said, "I don't know if this Paul is good for you anymore."

An hour ago, I'd sat in Nora's living room. The dark sky had made the whole day feel late. Nora's legs were stretched onto my lap. She was reading a book called *Becoming Attached*. I stared at the title and the picture on the cover, a child being thrown into the air, arms beneath it, blurred like wings.

"What does it say?" I asked.

Nora looked at me. "I'm at a strange part."

"Read it to me?"

"'Much of the child's psychic suffering—arising from its own innate, oral-sadistic impulses projected onto the environment— consists of fears of being devoured, or cut up, or torn to pieces, or its terror of being surrounded and pursued by menacing figures.'"

"Why is there psychic suffering?" I asked.

"It's just a theory," Nora said. She closed the book. "There are other books over here, did you want to read?"

I rubbed my eyes.

Nora asked, "Are they still bothering you?"

I nodded.

She said, "Maybe you need glasses."

I told her it was because of the small font in my book. She asked which book and I said *Atlas Shrugged*.

"Why are you reading *Atlas Shrugged*?" she asked.

Because I'd found it in the library and because on the cover there's a muscled gold statue with his head in his hands and a city leaning away from him.

"Well, do you agree with her?"

"Agree with who?"

"Ayn Rand."

"About what?" I asked.

"Her whole philosophy. Objectivism."

"I don't know," I said. "I didn't realize that's what it was about."

I didn't look at Nora for a moment. She stopped speaking and returned to her book. I looked up Ayn Rand on my phone. I looked up the meaning of objectivism.

I turned to Nora and said as confidently as I could, "You know, Rand says that the book is about the *role of man's mind in existence*."

Nora didn't look up. She said, "It's about capitalism."

"What about John Galt?" I asked.

Nora paused as though she might not answer, but then she said, "I didn't actually read it. So I don't know all the names."

"You didn't read it?" My stomach felt hot, my voice became louder. "Then you don't know what it's really about."

Nora's eyes rested over me. I felt her observing. "I think I get the gist," she said.

"It's mainly about trains."

"Natalie, it's about more than trains."

We stared in opposite ways. Sometimes my eyes were brought forcefully to her stomach. Nora looked at the wall as though there might appear a figure to take care of us both. But nothing appeared, and when Nora looked back at me, it felt obvious that she couldn't believe I was the person beside her. I turned my eyes back to my phone, where Ayn Rand quotes continued as I scrolled:

She did not know the nature of her loneliness. The only words that named it were: This is not the world I expected.

Clara asked, "Does he cheer you up?"

"Cheer me up?"

"When you're down, does he listen to you?"

I looked at Clara. And she looked back at me, concerned.

"What's the nicest thing he's ever done for you?"

"It's not all about me," I said.

"Your relationship is about you, Natalie," Clara said, and then shook her head at me.

I stood on Nora's front step, about to leave. We'd stopped talking about books, and instead had eaten a shepherd's pie she'd made several days before.

"Where will you go tonight?"

I told her a bar on Queen Street.

She told me it was good that I was going to celebrate. My last class of the semester had passed that morning, and now I only had my exams left. She looked at me.

"Are you upset about our disagreement?"

"No."

She said, "I don't like to argue."

I said, "I didn't think of it as an argument."

Nora said, "In relationships, you can get in the habit of having disagreements which revolve—"

She looked pretty standing in the door frame. I noticed the effort she made for her voice to be soft, and realizing the effort made me want to kiss her. Nora's hand rested on her chest, her fingers up toward her neck. It reminded me of seeing her in the grocery store, how she'd covered her mouth with her fingers, eating shortbread cookies. I smiled to myself.

Nora stopped speaking. "What is it?"

I said, "Nothing. You just . . . look nice."

Nora looked disappointed. "Were you listening to what I was saying?"

"You were saying that disagreements revolve."

"I'm thinking of the future—"

I thought, how funny, I'd been thinking of the past.

Nora cut herself off. I leaned close to her, and she brushed her hand along my forehead. "Have fun," she said.

"I'm sorry," I said. "I was listening."

She said not to worry. She said, "Go on."

I stepped back. I met her eyes, which gave me a long and distant look. I gave her a smile, which she returned. But I felt it as it slipped from my face, walking down the road.

It was nine thirty. Clara's door was propped open, and so were others on the floor. Clara turned her music off because someone was playing theirs louder. She pressed a drink into my hand. She said, "You look good," to me. My clothes felt tight, and the taste of my drink burned down my throat. Clara kept redrawing her eyeliner. I watched her for a while but then decided to walk up and down the hallway.

The door of Annie's room was open. I looked in and saw her standing there with a few people. She looked over them and waved at me. I waved back and then kept walking up and down, trying to feel my legs underneath me.

"Natalie?"

I turned around and saw Clara had stuck her head out. I went back to her room. She asked if she should change again, did I like her shirt? I said I did, and she said, "Oh all right." And then she folded her coat over her arm, and we walked down the stairs.

We rode the subway south. She gave me an ID, which she'd bought off an older student. My hands felt sweaty. Clara told me I should undo a button. "It'll just make you seem more comfortable." I smiled at her, but I didn't undo any buttons.

The street was busy. Through the windows of each bar front there were incandescent bulbs that glowed popularly. When we stepped inside, I became very aware that we hadn't gone to a student bar. Around us were real adults. I turned to Clara. "Are you sure you want to stay here?"

A jeweled chandelier hung over the bar. A group of men let out hard laughter. Collars were loose on everyone's throats. I felt my top button tighten.

"Yeah, it's great," Clara said. She looked around. Her eyes looked like the bulbs. Filaments burning.

There were low tables on one side of the room where people were eating, and on the other side there were high-tops for standing. The bar was in the center of the room. We walked over to it. A few people standing near looked pointedly at us, and I wondered if they thought we were too young. Looking around, I had the impression that everyone else had just come from important jobs.

The bartender wore a black sleeveless top. I noticed her arms because they were muscled, and she had tattoos on her shoulder. They were too cursive to read. Behind us, I saw more girls from our floor walk in. Annie and a group got a table, which meant they would have to order something to eat. I asked Clara if we should sit down with them, and she said, "Just wait a minute, Natalie." And looked a bit annoyed.

The bartender slid four shots forward. I watched her face. Dark eyebrows that could have also been tattoos. I thought, maybe I won't have sex with anyone except Nora for my whole life, and then the bartender looked at me and I almost smiled but felt a reprimanding pang of guilt.

Clara spoke to a different bartender. A guy also wearing black. He told Clara that if she ordered a certain kind of beer, her next one would be half the price. She said, "I'll do that, then."

I drank two of the shots. They tasted bad. Clara ordered more. I wondered how old the bartender was. And I wondered what it was like to be thirty, because in my head I thought, *He looks thirty.* He had a shaven face, but a lot of hair on his forearms and hands. His arms reminded me of a fisherman. I could imagine them wrapped up in a net, his thumb stuck in the mouth of a fish, showing it off to us after he'd caught it. He'd say something disgusting like, *What will you do if I eat its head?* And even though we wouldn't answer, he'd bite down on its fish-flesh, and he'd impress himself with his own ability to forget what he was doing while he was doing it.

Clara was still talking. I felt light-headed. I wondered if it was the shots already. I felt inclined to do more, but Clara had switched to beer, and I'd taken the glass she'd offered me. I tried to drink it quickly, and halfway through I did start to feel more dizzy. I walked with it until I found myself bumping into Annie's table. Her arm pulled me to sit down. "Maybe you should eat something."

There were fries in the middle of the table. I put one in my mouth.

"What was your last class of the year?" Annie asked me.

I said something about poetry and then I asked her what hers had been. She asked me if I was sad that first year was over. I felt a heaviness stifle my reply. I wondered if Annie had ever googled whether or not someone loved her. I wanted to ask her if she'd kissed Clara or not. I wanted to tell her that I felt like she was less likely to lie than Clara. Did that make me a bad friend?

I wondered if I should go to the bathroom and call Nora and ask her again, one last time, would she ever love me?

"Natalie?" I refocused on Annie. She put a few more fries onto a plate and she set it in front of me. I ate one after another after another. I started to hear the conversation around me better. Annie said that she was excited to live off-campus, and the girl beside her agreed but also said she was worried about how to split the cost of groceries.

After a few minutes of listening, Annie elbowed me. "Hey, isn't that Jones?"

I looked up from my empty plate over to where Annie gestured and saw, sitting not too far from us, Jones. She was dressed the same way as she dressed for class. She wore a thin black blazer. She was talking to a woman with short dark hair and a drink so orange that it seemed like a light.

"How do you know her? You're not in her class."

Annie said, "I like her poetry. It's weird to see her here. Do you think she's on a date?"

I watched Jones's hand move across her chin. She listened, nodding. She kept her elbows on the table, hands gesturing as though she was trying to explain something. I wondered if she ever got tired of explaining everything.

"What's her poetry class like?"

I turned back to Annie. "She's smart," I said.

"Oh, yeah?" she said, smiling. Which sounded like teasing, which sounded also like saying, *Obviously.*

"Very smart," I said.

"Do you believe the rumors?"

I wondered why everyone asked me if I believed the rumors. I shrugged at Annie.

She said, "You're above the rumors."

I said, "I'm not. I just don't know."

My hand started to feel too heavy to reach out for another fry. I wondered if I could ask Annie to feed them to me.

"Did you ever get to the bottom of that?" Annie asked. She was looking at the bar.

"Of what?" I wondered if she was asking about her and Clara. But she pointed.

"Rachel," she said. "Did she ever have you in Assassin?"

I blinked heavily. The room felt like it was slipping, so I focused on the sight of Rachel, sitting on a stool.

Annie put her hand on my shoulder. "You should drink water."

"She's looking right at her," I said. Annie didn't understand. "She's not even trying to pretend." I pressed my hand against my forehead.

I thought about how unfair Rachel was being to Jones. I thought there should be repercussions, and I imagined being called into a hearing where Jones would say, *Natalie, can you corroborate that Rachel was following me?* And I would stand and say, *Yes, I can.*

And she would ask, *Do you believe the rumors about me?*

And I would say?

"I have to go," I told Annie.

"Where?"

Standing was difficult, unsteady. My words warbled and I found myself saying, "Confront her."

Walking, I bumped the back of a stranger, which caused their head to turn, but I ignored them. I thought only about the kind of justice that would be possible when I reached Rachel. I would tell her right then, I knew what she was doing, and that it was wrong. I would force some kind of reckoning.

"Rachel."

She had been angled toward Jones. When she turned and saw me, her eyes narrowed immediately. "Why are you following me?" Rachel asked.

She tapped her fingers on the bar top. The unexpectedness of her accusation made me forget my pursuit of justice. I wondered if this was the point where I would find out that Rachel did not exist—that she was actually me, or that I was actually her, and—

"Come on, Natalie," she said. "We both know what's going on."

For a moment she seemed very certain and calm. And I wondered if I'd been wrong about her—*had* she been following Jones? I felt the pressure of a headache pull my vision in two. I wondered what would happen if I collapsed. I wondered if someone would pick up my feet and drag me to the back of the bar. Maybe they would shout out like they do in movie-restaurants, *Is there a doctor in the house?* But I could feel it, there weren't any doctors in that room. Anyway, the next thing they would ask was, *Are there any poets?* And then Jones would have to stand, take responsibility, say, *Yes, I know the words for this.*

Rachel said, "I'm talking to you."

I said, "What are you talking about?"

She said, "I'm not going to do anything, I just want to know."

Clara came over. I tried to give her an assured look. A look that showed her I was about to take care of things, that I was about to tell Rachel how wrong she had been. But as I tried to focus on Clara's face, heat pulsed through my head. I stumbled, but Clara put her hand on my back and I remained standing.

"Natalie? Are you all right?"

A glass fell off one of the tables near us. It smashed and drew all our eyes toward it. Rachel said, "Look, I won't do anything, just tell me."

Clara said, "What are you asking her? She's too drunk."

Rachel said, "I'm asking about her and Jones."

"Jones?"

Was I too drunk? Why couldn't Jones come over and say she had an appointment with me, hadn't I done that for her?

Rachel looked at me. "Are you sleeping with her?"

Clara laughed and then looked at me as though I should start too. When I didn't, she lowered her voice and said, "Are you serious?"

Rachel said, "I've seen you."

"Seen me what?"

"Go into that house."

I didn't understand. "I've never been to Jones's house," I said. "I don't even know where she lives."

"Don't lie. I've seen you go inside. And I've seen her go inside."

"You've seen them go into a house together?" Clara asked.

Rachel hesitated.

Clara said, "I think you've made a mistake."

Rachel looked at me more pressingly. She said, "Why do you go there?"

I felt the edges of my mind ebb.

She said, "84 Sunder Street, you've never been?"

"84 Sunder—"

Rachel nodded, her voice digging, almost there. "I've seen you go in."

84 Sunder—the address became a door. A glass door surrounded by brick. Yellow light in the windows, my body made of a million moths. The tall hallway, footprints wearing out the carpet, water running in the kitchen, 84 Sunder.

I said, "That's not Jones's house."

"Who do you think lives there?"

"You've seen Jones go inside?"

Rachel said, "A few times." And then, more cautiously, "I don't go there often."

Clara shook my shoulder. "Natalie?"

Rachel met my eyes. "Are you sleeping with her?"

I could see Jones's face over Rachel's shoulder. Her hands still moved through the air, her hair was growing out, almost touching the tops of her shoulders. Clara tried to pull at me, but I moved her arm off. I felt my body begin to rush. Winded lungs. My heart, flightless, but still trying to flutter. I looked at Rachel.

"What was Jones's last book called?"

"Why?" she demanded.

"Please—what was it called?"

She frowned at me. "You don't know?"

I searched on my phone. I thought, *Nora, please.*

Clara said, "What are you doing?" They both leaned over my screen.

The House Plants. I could see the first few pages online.

"Why does this matter?"

"Who is it written for?" I asked.

"What?"

"Who is it *for*—"

"It's not dedicated," Rachel said.

"What about her other books? Her earliest books?"

Rachel shook her head. "What does this have to do with anything?"

I tried to lean away so that Rachel and Clara couldn't see, but they craned their necks.

Rachel said, "That's an early one." *The Red Fern Poem.* I pressed on the cover. There was a page left blank. And then another page.

Clara said, "It might not show in a preview." And then she said, "We can go to the library tomorrow. Or we can go and buy the book, and you can look through it all you want." She put her hand on my wrist. I worried she might try to take the phone, so I pulled my arm away from her. She let go.

I scrolled and scrolled. Two more blanks and then the words. So certain, and so written that they threatened to erase me.

For Nora—
All of it.

twenty-one

There were two hands that kept me from falling. And there was a voice that I sometimes answered. I said, "I need a taxi." I said, "84 Sunder Street."

The windows of the taxi rolled down and I leaned my head out. There was someone pulling the back of my jacket, keeping me from going too far. I looked down at Nora's name, saw 12:45 a.m. I called, but there was no answer.

The taxi stopped outside Nora's house. I was followed out. I walked over the sidewalk and I stood leaning against the tree in her yard.

"You know who lives here?"

I said, "Nora lives here."

"Is she going to let you in?"

I knocked on her front door, but she was sleeping. I looked toward the upstairs windows and I started to yell, but a hand covered my mouth and a voice said, "We'll get in trouble."

"I need to speak to her."

"Let's sit on the sidewalk."

I sat down beside the tree. I pulled up some of the ground. Wet seeds. Thin grass. I imagined Jones walking by the yard, watching the winter turn to spring. She might write about that.

"What are you doing? That's dirt."

"I want it," I said.

"Try and sit still."

I said, "I think I'm about to die."

She asked why.

I said, "I just think I'm about to."

The road looked damp. A street light shone above us. I felt as though we were sitting at the bottom of a well, with flashlights shining down, people trying to recover us. Rain fell very light.

She said, "I still don't understand."

I rested my forehead on my knees. We were like circus performers waiting for the tents to be pulled down.

"Do you see that?"

"See what?"

"You have to look up."

I lifted my eyes and saw that, ahead of us, there was a small deer. I watched its legs, gray and thin. Cloven hooves, soundless.

She said, "Keep still. I don't want to scare it."

I said, "That's a deer."

She said, "I know."

The deer walked with its head up. In Temagami, I imagined the sounds of hunting. Deep snow and gunshots, and all the birds taking off. The thought of Temagami felt particularly painful.

Like thinking of yourself when you're first born. Like thinking of yourself when you are not yourself at all.

"Is it sick?"

"Why would it be sick?"

"It looks thin."

"There's less to eat in the winter."

The deer walked by us. It looked over once. Its head turned and I thought, *You're about to run,* but it didn't. It looked over us passively and then it turned away and carried on down the road. I tried to stand to follow it, but she pulled me back down.

"I don't want to scare it," she said.

I still held a bit of dirt in my hand. I opened my fist and I saw small white roots, flowers that might've sprung. I ran my finger through them. I thought, to make things right I would need to come to Nora's yard every day and take a new handful of dirt. I would need to dig a hole so deep that there would be explorations of it. And these explorations would need to be as serious and demanding as the kind that launch people into space.

"If you put those back, the roots might still grow."

"I don't want them to grow," I said. I stared down at the dirt, the excavation. I imagined a wife telling her husband not to go down into the hole. Imagined him being lowered into the earth, held by a brown rope. A headlamp bobbing light as he looked around.

The wife had said, *If you love me, then you wouldn't,* and then the husband had said, *If you loved me, then you wouldn't.*

"I think it's gone."

"The deer?"

"I don't see it anymore."

"Was it real?"

"We both saw it," she said.

I said, "I hope I'm not awake."

She said, "We're both awake."

"I hope I'm asleep."

A moment passed.

"Who is Nora?"

I thought I heard a shot. I thought I heard the deer running back toward us, dripping blood, asking us for shelter. But when I looked around, I saw that the neighborhood was silent. Nora's neighborhood. I looked behind me at her house. I wondered why she hadn't told me when she'd first realized. How long had she known? I thought of Clara and her blindfold. I felt the betrayal of being seen unknowingly. My mind, smiling a gap-toothed knowledge. Can you look at someone, half in darkness, leave them there, and still love them?

"Are you together?"

Once, I remember Nora saying, *It feels like you're always going to poetry.*

Had she been disappointed that Jones and I hadn't recognized her between us? I thought, maybe if I had read more of Jones's poems, or if mine had been better, or if I'd looked at her hands for longer—they were always moving, if they had only once been still—we might've seen the way we were similarly bound. I thought, the hole needs to be bottomless. It needs to never end. The ground needs to part between my hands, it needs to sink, just like the feeling of her.

"You can't do that, stop."

I had started digging again. I tried to pry the earth out.

"Natalie, Natalie."

I felt the dirt underneath my nails. The ground was wet and soft. She tried to pull my arms, but I broke free. I dug and dug, but I couldn't get away, the ground was still the ground and Nora's house still the place in front of me.

"Natalie, stop."

I looked over my shoulder toward the street. I said, "Rachel?"

I rubbed dirt on my face, trying to wipe my eyes. She held her hands up as though she might try to stop me, but she never did.

"She didn't tell me."

"Nora?" Rachel asked. "What didn't she tell you?"

"That she was married to Jones."

I looked up toward Nora's bedroom. No lights on.

I said, "I love her."

Rachel looked at me. And then she looked up toward the windows, and then up toward the sky.

I asked, "You've really seen Jones go in?"

She nodded.

I said, "Who let her in?"

"She let herself in." Rachel's eyes returned. "You really didn't know? This whole time?"

I gave her a look that made her quiet. My hands were so dirty that I thought they might start to crawl away from me. I looked toward the door.

Rachel asked, "What does it look like inside?"

I could see the kitchen counter. Nora saying, *Do you want to order a pizza?* She smiled at me, wearing her robe.

"Natalie?"

I looked at Rachel and I felt tears rising against my eyes. "Why didn't she tell me?" I asked.

Rachel looked toward the bedroom windows. There was stillness. Not even the possibility of a shadow. She asked, "How did you meet?"

I said, "She came up to me in the park."

Rachel paused, thinking. "So, then, did she know the whole time?"

"What do you mean?"

"Is that why she chose to talk to you? Because you were in Jones's class?"

"No," I said. And I shook my head. I didn't believe that.

"Why not?"

"Because that isn't why she talked to me."

"Then why?" I paused. Rachel said, "I think—"

I said, "It doesn't matter what you think."

She looked at the ground, and then at me. A small point of pity in her eyes—

"What about you?" My voice had gotten louder. "Following Jones around all the time. She was afraid—"

Rachel pushed me hard. And I pushed her back. And then I'd been pinned to the ground and Rachel's arm was digging into my neck. I struggled for a minute, but my hair was in the mud and the side of my cheek began to sink, so I said, "Get off," and she did. She flattened the dirt, which had been scuffled, with her hands.

I asked, "What did you think was going to happen when you caught up to her?"

Rachel stared at the ground. And then, after a moment, she said, "Why don't we read the poem?"

I shook my head. "Which poem?"

"'The Red Fern Poem,'" she said.

"No, don't read it."

Rachel took out her phone, and I saw her pull up the poem. My hands reached toward her, but she moved her phone out of the way and she stood up, brushing dirt off her lap. I was shaking. I thought of Nora asking, *Have you ever written a poem about me?* And I thought of the countless words Jones had written about her. I thought of Jones, and I felt my own lack, no comparison. Rachel was right, why else would Nora have chosen me? I felt the embarrassment of being younger, of being inexperienced. My unknowingness, an awful juxtaposition.

Rachel said, "What if we've ruined the garden?"

"We haven't ruined it."

She asked if I was going to knock on the door, and I said no. And then she said we should leave. I tried to stand up, but felt dizzy. Rachel reached down and pulled my hand, and then once I reached my feet, she kept her arm around me.

We walked out of the neighborhood. There was no one on the road. The ground shuddered underneath us, a subway passing.

I read a book once about a very long road.

I asked, "Who wrote *The Road*?"

Rachel looked at me strangely, but said, "Cormac McCarthy."

Soon, we'd have to start lighting fires and trying to heat cans without burning our fingers. We would have to suck water from the tap and talk about the coast, we would say, *We have to get to the coast.* And everyone would understand what that meant. The quiet deepened. If everything went black, all we would have to do was try to close our circles. Fit everyone in a room. Maybe I should go back to Nora. Back to her garden.

We could make her front yard like a field and grow so much wheat that it would put us in danger of thieves. Other people wanting to make bread. We could spend all day moving worms away from tomatoes, patting flies off our backs. But maybe I wasn't imagining the end of the world correctly. I think Cormac said it would be cold.

"No," Rachel said. "There was ash and fire."

"I remember," I said. "But there was also snow."

Should I go back to Nora? I turned to tell Rachel, but before I spoke, she looked at me and said, "'The Red Fern Poem.'"

I said, "I don't want to hear it."

I looked back toward the distance between myself and Nora. Short enough that it could be walked.

I looked over at Rachel. "Are you reading the poem?"

"I'm not speaking."

There's an episode of a TV show where two people in a train accident have a metal rail pushed through their chests. They have to sit together on the operating table and the doctors have to decide who's in the best physical position to be saved. The actors' stomachs have to be covered in red glue. It had to be painted on them to look like a terrible injury. Afterward, they stand beside each other in the bathroom, and they lift their shirts up. They look at the mess that's been made, and they're surprised that it can be rubbed clean.

"I think I've seen that episode."

There's an episode where a whole family is in prison and the son's arm is infected but there's no anesthetic because all the hospitals have already been pillaged and the prison is actually their home. The cells aren't locked, they're open.

"A different show?"

They tie a belt around his arm. The belt used to be around the father's waist. The father is so thin now that you expect, without the belt, his pants would just fall down.

"How did the world end?"

"I can't tell you," I said. "That's what the whole show is about."

Rachel looked up at the street sign. "Come to my place? It's closer."

I stumbled, my chin hit her shoulder. She held tighter to my arm.

We walked around the side of a narrow white house. Rachel lived in a basement apartment where the sink was right beside her bed. The stove only had one burner, and there was no oven, only a microwave. She filled the sink with warm water, and she told me to wash my face in it. I washed my hands too, and the dirt that had flecked up my forearms.

She sat on her bed, and I sat on her floor leaning against the wall.

"Are you going to throw up?" she asked me.

"I don't know," I said.

She said, "So, Nora—"

I said, "Don't, my stomach."

She said, "I don't think Jones visited that often."

I said, "It's not about how often."

Rachel reached down. She handed me a shirt from a drawer built into the side of her bed. "Change. You'll feel better."

I held her shirt in my hand. The room smelled like a cellar. Concrete and cold. But it also smelled like candles, which were placed on almost every possible surface. On the wall beside her bed there was a watercolor poster of all the women who had been to space.

"Do you need help?" she asked.

I was holding her shirt, I wasn't moving. I wasn't sure how to undress in front of her. It felt as uncertain as beginning to read one of my poems in class. I imagined her eyes boring in, the fury of her ambition, a constant search for her own betterness—

"Natalie?"

But she wasn't looking at me the way she looked at me in poetry. Maybe she was concerned about my drunkenness. Or maybe it made her sad to see my body still covered in dirt, my face not really that clean. "Okay," I said.

She came forward, stood over me. "Are you going to stay there?"

"Yeah."

She leaned down. I lifted my arms, and she pulled my shirt over my head. I had a bra on. Rachel didn't tell me to take it off, although for a moment she paused, and I thought she might try to see what it felt like to say something like that. She fit her shirt over my head, guided my arms through. I pulled it down.

"Bottoms?" she asked.

I nodded and she handed some to me. I put them on myself. She looked at the wall. Her hair tangled at the back.

"This is where you live," I said.

She had a small table by her bed that was made of books stacked uniformly. Jones's book was on top, closest to her hand.

I asked, "Why did you follow her?"

"I don't know."

"Do you want to be with her?"

She said, "I don't know." And pressed her hands into her eyes.

I wondered what Jones had looked like when she was our age. I wondered if she had started out like either of us.

"You should stay here," Rachel said. I was already dressed in her clothes, already leaning against her wall.

I said, "Okay."

I thought of Jones and Nora meeting for the first time—the red fern poem. I wondered at what point they had decided, *Yes, this.* Had it been after a joke that one of them had told? A fit of laughter that devolved into a vision of life together, a long lane of grass, a place to get married. I imagined Nora standing. And I imagined Jones. The yellow wash of ceremony.

Rachel said, "Are you going to be sick? If I fall asleep—"

"I'll be fine," I said.

"You can try to fit next to me," she said. "I'm going to lie down now."

"I'll lie down here." I pushed my back against the wall, and I lowered my face onto my hand.

Rachel said one more time, "'The Red Fern Poem.'"

I imagined the red fern. I imagined Jones. I'd felt before the desire to write a poem of just one word. Just Nora's name in the middle of the page. Had Jones felt that too?

"Please, no," I said.

Rachel said, "No, I won't. I was just going to tell you, it's not her best one. She has much better poems."

Lying on the ground hurt. "Really?"

She said, "Yes."

I thought of Nora's pregnancy, and for the first time I imagined the softness of a baby. Nora's hands on the side of my face, her nose crooked to mine. My hands reaching forward, Nora passing the baby to me. I look down at their face and I see the possibility. I see the way life moves forward.

Rachel said, "Natalie, sleep here with me."

My dirty clothes were on the floor. I wondered if there were ants inside them and I watched for a moment before I stood up. My knee hit the edge of Rachel's bed, and she moved over for me. We breathed up at the ceiling.

"Okay, read it to me," I said.

I wondered if in the poem there would be all the words that Nora should have told me. I wondered if her pervasive *I have something to tell you* would expand to be more. But then I remembered this was Jones's poem, and not Nora's.

I thought more now about Nora's reason for being with me. The rumor of Jones and one of her students, which Nora firmly believed to have been an affair—the crux of her curiosity? Me in the park, on a bench, young, maybe a student of Jones's. Now, did Nora understand her wife better?

Rachel turned her head. Our arms touched. The blanket was hot, but I didn't move it off me.

She said, "My phone's beside you."

The Red Fern Poem.

I imagined holding a baby's small hand and foot. My fingers keeping their neck up. I think, *It's all right,* but they're crying and then I'm crying and Nora is facing away. Nora says, *I'll show you what to do,* and I say, *You lied to me,* and she says, *Only in the beginning,* and I think, *No, I can't live that way.*

I felt sweat running down my neck, but there was nothing there when my hand reached back to wipe it.

Nora asks, *Where have you gone?* I say, *I'm right here,* but I see her pick up the phone to try to call me. A baby is crying. I say, *It's okay,* but that doesn't comfort them. Nora says, *Come over.* And I think that I never left, but then realize that Nora's right, I'm not there.

Rachel's fingers accidentally touched my hand. I moved away quickly.

She said, "Sorry, I didn't mean that."

I said, "You stopped reading."

And then Rachel looked at me as though I'd annoyed her, and she said, "No, Natalie. I just got to the end."

twenty-two

It was summertime. The grass was hot and sweet and the tops of my shoulders were already red. In the middle of the park there were swings and a climbing frame. Small children ran back and forth. Underneath a tree, a group of women sat with their babies, just crawling.

"Natalie?"

A little farther ahead of me there was a woman pushing a stroller. I wondered who she might be if she just turned her head. If she chose, once among the trees, to sit on a nearby bench—

◆

I live in a house without air conditioning. There's a fan in my room that blows the dead leaves off a plant that has been there since the first day I moved in.

There are five rooms in the house. It began as a house full of friends, but all but one friend had moved away, so now it's the one friend and a revolving group of others. When I moved in, the girl living in the room above me came downstairs and shook my hand and said, "I'm Jubilee, but you can call me Lee." And I'd liked that she'd told me the whole story right away. Once Jubilee, now Lee. She asked me to tell her if her feet were too noisy. She said she'd lived underneath a lot of people, she knew how that could be annoying. And then she asked with her hands stuck into her pockets if I wanted to watch some TV.

◆

The summer was so hot that the wooden floors always felt like they were dripping. I liked keeping my window open. The house opposite ours had a statue of an owl perched on their window ledge. Pigeons landed there anyway. I watched them flapping around each other. Sometimes they tried to fight the owl with their wings, but mostly they just stood there, bobbing their heads toward the edge.

"Do you want to sit somewhere?"

"A bench?"

"Sure, a bench."

Rachel and I sat down. She looked at me. Her face was not as tired as I remembered. There were times, even, when it seemed that she was at rest.

She asked, "How are you, Natalie?"

I looked at her. I felt that I must no longer look my age, my mouth felt old as a shell, I could barely break it open to say, "I'm fine."

She said, "It's been a while." And I didn't say anything back.

I spent another moment watching the back of the woman and her stroller pushing farther away. I saw another woman pass, not pushing a stroller.

Rachel said, "It's not her."

"Not who?"

Rachel smiled, and I traded her back.

We looked out across the other benches and the trees. And I thought about how, a little less than a year ago, I'd seen Nora looking over. That day had been much more overcast.

"I wanted to show you something." Rachel pulled a page from her bag and rested it on my lap. I felt that if I kept looking out at the benches, I would feel the full force of memory, a reel spinning me back.

My eyes tracked down. I saw that there was a poem printed, and I began to shake my head. But Rachel said, "It's short." And then she said, "Just look at it. I want to fill you in."

◆

After I left Rachel's house, in the morning after the terrible night, I walked back to my dorm room. Nora had tried to return my calls twice already before I'd woken up. And she'd sent me messages, repeated, *Are you all right?* But I hadn't answered her yet.

The door to Clara's room was closed. I knocked on it, and when there was no answer, I knocked again. She called and asked who it was, and I said, Natalie.

She opened the door. Her eyes were defiant and red. "What?"

"Can I talk to you?"

"About?"

"About last night."

She looked in my direction, but her eyes didn't touch mine; they landed on my jacket and then on my shoes. "Who's Nora?"

I said, "Clara, please."

She said, "Who is she?"

I struggled. "She's someone I was seeing—"

"What about Paul?" She met my eyes.

I looked at her with resignation.

She said, "Seriously?"

I said, "I didn't know how to tell you . . ." A rag of a sentence. Too used.

Her voice rose, shakily. "Go away."

"Clara."

"I'm serious, Natalie." And I could hear this seriousness, so I nodded at her, and she closed her door quickly.

I stared at it for a moment. I felt my hands so empty, my pockets so empty. I thought about retreating. Really retreating. I thought of going very far. All the way back to Temagami? Somewhere that I could be shut in and non-existent. I looked down at my phone. Nora had sent so many messages now. She'd sent so many that my chest ached and for a moment I could smell the cream walk of her hall, fruit baking in the oven.

I ran from the dorm room. Across a courtyard where grass was growing, down the street, until I found myself inside a faculty building, sitting outside Jones's office. The door was closed. I sat alone in the hallway, thinking that if anyone saw me, I would be removed. I was still wearing Rachel's shirt, and some of the dirt from Nora's garden.

"Natalie?" I looked up. "Are you here to meet me?"

Jones walked down the hall. She was wearing a sweater that was loose on her throat. She took out her keys and gave me a receptive smile. I thought of telling her right then about me and Nora. Wouldn't that be an unbelievable turn of events? And wouldn't that be what I wanted? The windfall that would sweep through her eyes, an understanding that would capture me eternally—I would not only be the Natalie she taught, I would be the Natalie who slept with her wife, the Natalie she imagined when she thought of the untenable parts of her life.

"Are you all right?"

I felt afraid to look at her face. Felt certain that Nora's betrayal would feel infinite, especially acute looking directly at her. But she continued to stand there quietly, and when my eyes fell on her face, the expression she held was so still that I felt a crush of recognition—finally, her author photo. She opened her mouth, and I shook my head. I didn't know what retribution should feel like, or how it could be enacted here. And then I wondered if this wasn't my fantasy of revenge, but Nora's. I wondered if this might be her moment. Wondered whether, if I said to Jones, *I know your wife,* Nora would somehow feel relief, satisfaction at last, the clash of composite actions doing away with each other.

"Natalie?"

I tried to speak, but immediately my throat curdled over the sound I meant to make, and I found myself gasping. Jones stepped forward and I bent over my knees. I didn't feel embarrassed, I felt terrible. Jones knelt down beside me. Her hand pressed on my shoulder. I reached up and I touched her fingers. Forgetting for a moment who I was, and who she was supposed to be. I only thought that it had felt merciful to be touched that way. Jones didn't remove her hand. I thought sadly of her lectures. Thought of the long desk we'd all sat around. I thought of reading poems, trying hard, and failing. I realized how all the months had gone, blurring past. Had something been accomplished here?

"Natalie," Jones said. And this time, my name was a word used for soothing, for shushing. For placing between the teeth of a person who might need to bite down.

I managed to breathe, and I managed to say, "I'm really sorry." I wondered if Jones found it strange how many of her students she encountered crying.

She said, "You don't have to apologize."

"I'm not being appropriate."

Jones tilted her head, expression furrowing. She said, "Can I help you, Natalie? Has something happened?"

I felt more tears fill my eyes, and my breathing labored again.

Jones moved her hand off my shoulder and stood upright. "Do you drink coffee?"

I had to breathe two hard breaths in to get a longer, even breath out. I nodded at her.

She said, "Do you want me to go and get you one?"

I looked at her standing there and talking to me, and I tried to imagine the way she might look and stand and talk to Nora. I shook my head slowly. I felt that I wanted to be alone with her and so I couldn't be alone with her. Thought, if she got me coffee, and then told me to sit and drink it in her office, I would curl up again, and then she might put her hand on my shoulder, and I might reach up and touch her fingers, and I might not let go.

"I can't—"

I stood up. My body felt slick. Under my nails there was still dirt from the garden. Still the feeling of digging furiously into the ground. I thought for a moment that Jones might notice and say, *Oh, I know what you've done.* But instead, she met my eyes, said, "You'll be okay?"

And I nodded. And I realized, to my surprise, that we were the same height.

◆

The poem Rachel passed to me was only five lines long. I began reading, annoyed and skeptical, but then quickly, and without any of my own generosity, the poem applied the same pressure as all good art, and the words began to bubble like something ready. I licked my lips. I felt the satisfaction of reading something that felt necessary and irrepressible. I looked at Rachel.

"Okay," I said.

She said, "It's good, right?"

I said, yeah, and then I asked, "Did you write it?"

And Rachel said no, but looked pleased. She said, "It's written by Laura Robins."

"Who is that?"

She smiled. She said, "She's *the* student. The student of Jones's rumor. I found her."

"You found her?"

Rachel said yes. She and Laura had both been at a poetry reading and they'd started talking afterward.

I said, "Oh, so you weren't out searching for her?"

Rachel frowned. She said, "I guess not exactly."

I felt some relief. "You made it sound like you'd tracked her down."

She said, "No, it was coincidental." Then, impatiently, "Do you want to know what she said?"

I said yes, I wanted to know.

◆

Okay, this is wrong now, Natalie. You have to tell me what's the matter, or what—have you just left me?

I remember standing underneath the awnings of storefronts to avoid the rain, which had gone on for days. I started carrying an umbrella with me, though I never opened it. I let the rain fall on my head.

I knocked on Clara's door again several times, but there was no answer. When I tried to approach her in the dining hall, the girls sitting beside her tapped the table, and then they all got up and left quickly. Birds flying suddenly out of a tree.

Natalie, I feel that you're being unfair, and I think if you're upset about something we should talk about it properly.
Natalie, it's been three days and this isn't like you—I'm wondering if I should call the police, report a missing person?
If you're getting these messages give me a sign, or I'll call tonight. I'm worried.

I wrote her back: *don't call.* And then I stared at the appearance of her writing. Ellipses, and ellipses, and then—

Natalie, don't you realize how worried I've been?
Call me now.

I called her then.

"Natalie, what's happened?"

Had she never imagined that I would find out about Jones? Did she think that we would live all our lives in some private shell? That we would never go out for fear of meeting someone she knew? Or did she expect that I would find out, but that, because I loved her, I would forgive her. And my forgiveness would become just another unevenness in our lives.

I wondered if Nora cared if I had any other relationships. Did she care what my parents might think about her? Or what they might think of me? Did she care if I grew up well, or happily, or did she just see me as in her sight, and out of her sight? By her side, and wherever else I might go—less consequential without her.

When I spoke, I used a voice more still and cold than my own. And I felt as though I raised a sword. A bony finger from out of a cloak. I said, "I know about Kate Jones."

She breathed in, a brisk intake that meant I had said something she did not expect. I felt relieved that there was not silence. That I had provoked something to occur.

I waited, feeling my accusation in hand, wondering what I wanted now, after speaking. Would she apologize? Would the world between us ever mend? Once, we had stood in the grocery store together. And she had smiled at me with such allure, and I didn't understand. My eyes hadn't been wide enough. I should have opened them wider. I had been much younger then, hadn't I?

Nora cleared her throat.

I spoke again. "Why didn't you tell me?"

"I was going to."

"When?"

She was quiet.

"Why did you come up to me in the park?"

"Because I wanted to."

"I must've seemed so stupid."

She didn't say.

"And you always said I was smart."

I thought, I might've started off like a young boy—at first the young boy is thin and when you look at him you think of saplings, you think of milk and bread. But then the boy is handed off to harder men to be made a harder man. He lives away from his family. He runs in the sand. His chest grows and his hair grows. And when you see him next, you cannot mistake his adulthood. It is so quick and sudden that it seems time may have skipped.

I thought of my own incremental knowledge. Had I become any different?

"You lied to me," I said. How quiet I was.

Nora spoke finitely. "I thought in a few months she wouldn't be your teacher, and I would tell you about her after that. I didn't want to upset you while you were in her class."

I wondered if that was true, and I thought about how I'd perpetuated the lie of Paul. Not for Clara's benefit, but for my own. Hadn't I planned on telling her the truth? Had I planned on telling Clara the truth the same way that Nora had planned on telling me? Had we both realized moments for disclosure, and ignored them, even while knowing how this neglect would one day bleed?

"We spoke about her so many times."

"And it was difficult not to tell you," Nora said. "But think about how that would have affected your life."

I held a hand over my mouth, my nose was stinging, my eyes burned. "Were you just trying to get back at her? Was that why you came up to me?"

Nora said, "Natalie, how could you—"

"You believed she was seeing one of her students last year, so you thought you would see what that might be like? You thought you would see if you could understand—"

"No," Nora said. "You're trying to make a neat story."

"I'm trying to understand what happened. And Rachel said—"

"And Rachel said?" Her voice twisted, I could hear in her breath, the stomp of apples.

I looked down at my hand. I remembered dully that once, in Nora's arms, I had felt taken care of. And I wondered if that memory could still be real. Or did everything have to change—a light flooding backward from this conversation?

"Natalie, why don't you come and see me?"

"I can't."

"Natalie, really?"

"No."

She breathed in. "I thought you loved me."

I put my head down into one hand. I opened my mouth and then closed it, felt tears between my fingers, the rough sound of my crying breath.

Nora didn't comfort me. Her voice hardened as though years and weather had passed through it. And she said without giving in, "I really thought you did."

◆

Laura Robins was American, and she was a few years older than we were. Rachel explained that she'd grown up on a ranch in Albuquerque, and I asked Rachel if that was really important for me to know, and she said, "Yes. It adds texture."

Rachel told me that she had asked Laura if she could buy her a drink after the poetry reading. She said that Laura had smiled and said okay. Rachel paused after recounting this far. As though it were important for me to take a moment and recognize that, if she chose, she could approach people in a way that was quite charming.

Rachel said she told Laura that she'd taken Jones's class. She said that this had made Laura lower her eyes, but then she had said, *I guess we have that in common.*

"I asked how she'd liked Jones's class. And she ordered one of those red beers ..."

Rachel shook her head fondly. I wondered if she was appreciating the cool casualness of their conversation, or if Laura was a person who, thinking back, made you feel partial.

Rachel said, "We were talking about Jones's teaching. We both agreed that she was excellent." I thought that was an exciting way to describe something—as excellent. "And then I mentioned the rumor that had gone around." Rachel raised her eyebrows at me, as though she were about to start showing off. "Laura said that it was a pointless rumor, but I told her that in our class Jones would go out of her way to take a particular interest in certain students—"

"That's not really true—"

"It isn't untrue," Rachel said. "Jones was willing to spend extra time with certain students. Like me."

"You were kind of insistent."

Rachel looked at me blandly. "She took you aside."

"Not in *that* way," I said.

Rachel shooed this conversation away. "It doesn't matter. I was just saying it so that she might tell me what happened with her and Jones." Rachel paused briefly, then continued, "So I just ended up asking her if anything had ever *happened.*"

I said, "But how did you know that she was even the right person? The rumor could have been about anyone in the class."

Rachel shook her head. She said, "You didn't meet her. You didn't hear her read her poem." I started to speak again, but then Rachel said, "Laura asked what I meant. She asked what it meant for something to *happen.*"

I paused and I listened more carefully.

"I told her the rumor was that Jones had been sleeping with one of her students. And Laura said that she hadn't slept with Jones—"

I felt relief, and embarrassingly it showed.

Rachel looked at me as though she understood, but then she said, "But she did say that she and Jones were very close. Closer than you would expect, and closer than what, by rules, might have been allowed."

"What do you mean?" I asked.

"She said that she'd been to Jones's house."

My face felt suddenly very dirty. I felt oil slick on my eyelids. My ears rang and I thought they might be full. I thought, *No, not her house. Not Nora's house.*

"Why did she agree to go?" I heard my voice, quite accusing.

Rachel looked at me disapprovingly. She didn't like questions that were basically rhetorical. "Laura said that they read poems. She said that she used to be nervous to read out loud and so Jones taught her some things to help with her confidence."

I asked what kind of things, and Rachel ignored me.

She looked into my eyes as though they were a river she were about to fish, and then she said, "And Jones showed her some of her books. And Laura said that she'd met Jones's wife once."

I felt the expected impact of this. Rachel watched me. I felt my chest begin to swell, and I tried to imagine the ways that these kinds of feelings could be managed. In real life there are dams. There are locks. There are mechanisms that stop overflow, which hold and then let. I spoke. "And did she—" I broke off. "Did she like her?"

Rachel said, "Laura said she'd been quiet. She said their house was very particular. That the decorations changed from room to room."

I wanted each of Rachel's words to be a plate that might shatter. I wanted to find myself on the starting line of a race and hear the gun go off, then find that I'd been mistakenly shot, and that the race had gone on and I'd lost by default. I'd stepped over the line, but then I'd lain down when everyone else had started to run, and the referee had come over and touched my shoulder, and I'd said, *I've been shot, why don't you help me?* And he said, *You haven't been shot,* though his small, wavering eyes had searched me.

Should I tell Rachel all this?

"She said that Jones confided in her. Told her there were problems between her and her wife."

"What kind of problems?"

"There seemed to be a lot." But I sensed something particular that Rachel hadn't said. "She said that Nora had just miscarried. She said they were waiting awhile before trying again—"

I felt crushed by my own inability. Time had passed and now Nora and I weren't together and I couldn't say anything to her. Why hadn't she told me? Was there something I could have done to make her feel I was someone she could be honest with?

"Why would Jones tell Laura all of that?"

"I think sometimes you must meet people and be filled with such strong affinity that you think differently about rules, and boundaries," Rachel said. "I think Jones was afraid of doing that again."

"Doing what?"

"Treating students like they might be friends."

I thought of Jones's hand on my shoulder. I thought also of how Rachel had been toward her, a pursuant. And then I thought of how Laura had sat in Jones's home, privy to how the rooms were arranged, looking at Nora with knowledge I'd never had.

"So, nothing more happened between them? It was all talking?"

Rachel smoothed the hair at the front of her head. "Laura said the thing she misses the most about Albuquerque are all of the horses." I looked at her, awaiting the answer to my question. But Rachel said, "She must have had a strange upbringing for her to say all she missed was the horses."

"But—that was all she said?"

Rachel looked at me with some care. I saw a glimpse of how we'd been outside Nora's house, underneath the street light. Two shadows in the garden.

"Jones is still a good teacher. And not a bad person." Her eyes reminded me of lilies because of how the petals curled back, as though overripe, as though begging. "And I don't think I'm a bad person either, and neither is Laura."

I wondered if she sounded hopeful, or if she'd decided.

"And neither are you, Natalie."

I looked at her. Mouth closed over the words she'd just spoken. And I found myself resting for a moment on the kind arc of her intention.

◆

Lee doesn't go to school. She works in a bar, and she bets on sports online. She asks what I plan on being, and then she says, "Don't worry, you can always change what you decide."

I got a job writing people's essays for their summer courses. They meet me in front of the library, and they look at me with desperation, and I say, *Don't worry, when do you need this by?* I write their papers late at night. The plugging of words into their essays makes me feel like I'm draining electricity from the lights. When I'm done, the room is dimmer, and the next day, when I hand them back their papers, they look at me relieved.

Lee explains the rules of basketball to me, and I watch some of the games with her. She wins her bets a lot. When she loses, she stares at the screen for a minute and she braids a strand of her hair. I watch her fingers, and I feel like I'm watching a spider climb the wall. After a minute she pulls the braid loose and she says, "Well, never mind."

I say, "That was a tough one." And she smiles, closing her eyes.

In my room, I think about Nora and her baby. What day was it born? I look up women giving birth. For a moment, I can't imagine Nora's face. I watch a woman lower herself into a bathtub. A man reaches between her legs, the woman holds her face toward the ceiling, I stare at her neck. Every muscle is strained, all the effort is red.

I look up *lesbian sex*. And then I look up *real lesbian sex*. And then *lesbian couples having sex*. The camera is in the corner of the room. Not a good view, but I watch their backs. I think, *Nora has never taken a photo of me.* They kiss. I can remember the feeling of Nora's hand underneath my chin. Shuffling between her legs, holding her hips. I remember her warm skin against my face, a laugh in her breath as I tried to push my tongue inside her. One of the women moans, I feel an elevator rush from my throat to the bottom of my stomach. And I turn it off. I sit alone.

School is about to begin again. Lee sits with me. She asks, "Have you ever watched baseball?"

I say, "It's kind of boring."

She says, "Yeah, it is. Watch it with me."

In the middle of the game, I ask, "What's an inning?"

Her team is losing. She asks, "Why are you so nervous for school?"

I show her the books in my bag. She skims the pages with her thumb. She says, "Think about how smart you're going to be."

When the baseball game ends, Lee looks at me and she says, "You know—" And then she gives me a serious smile that I don't know how to take.

I hold my hands in my lap. "What?" I say, and I try to smile at her.

Through the window, the failing light reminds me of Nora. The bluish dark that has the day not completely over with. The baseball game is done. I lie down on Lee's bed. It feels like the first time I've really seen Lee. In the seconds it takes for me to reach over and hold her shoulders between my hands, I notice her face, her lips, her skin. When I kiss her, I realize that people are different from each other, and I feel like an idiot, and I feel like, if I stop moving my lips, I'll cry.

She feels long. Her hair is brown between my fingers, and I brush it out of her face. I undo my jeans and take them off. She kisses my knee earnestly. I feel my nose tingle, so I pull her toward me and lift her shirt over her head.

Lee holds one arm underneath my waist. I feel the certainty of her pressing into me. I breathe out. She looks up. "Am I hurting you?"

I shake my head at her. It feels good, but I don't say anything.

She says my name as though she's reminding me that she's there. "Natalie?"

I say, "I'm okay."

She is very still. Her elbow bent, I hold her wrist. I say, "Please."

She says, "Yeah?"

I lead her hand. I can't feel how I surround her, she breathes out as though it's a pleasure, my lips held against her mouth.

◆

I went to a reading downtown in a bookstore filled with chairs. Jones thanked everyone for coming. She adjusted her glasses and looked around graciously. I stood at the back of the room. When it was over, everyone left their seats and gently clapped, and then I noticed Nora in the very front row. I could only see her shoulders, I could only see where her hair moved to reveal the side of her neck. Jones smiled down at her. A man walked up to the microphone and said, "If anyone wants their book signed—"

Jones made a gesture to Nora, and I watched as she walked up to her side. Jones leaned forward and said something close to

Nora's ear. I saw Nora smile, and she said something back, which Jones nodded at. And between them, I could not see where I might've fit.

The audience made a line toward the desk where Jones would sit and sign books. I found myself standing at the back of the queue without meaning to. I watched Nora's mouth open and say again words that I couldn't hear. Were they good words? Strong and complimentary? Jones laughed, and I thought they must've been. And then, as her laughter became a conversation with the first person in line, I heard the sound of a baby beginning to cry. Nora looked over to the side, and from where I stood, I couldn't believe that at one time I'd lain next to her. That she'd wanted me to stay, that she'd asked me what I was thinking of. A baby cried. Nora moved. I watched Jones become distracted and turn her head. Her lips were still upturned, leaning toward a smile. And her eyes were soft. I thought of caramel, the endless chew of possession, the spit in your cheek that you swallow, as though it is also a good part of the candy.

The crying stopped. Jones leaned back toward her books. Nora looked over Jones's shoulder for a while and then lifted her eyes to the rest of the room. They wandered and wandered, and then, as though meeting an unexpected step, they fell onto me.

Her lips broke their polite, deferential smile. They parted into a small oh. And I saw her face brace with worry. I saw myself—a tension in her jaw, a furtive look to both of her sides, as though I might dash forward suddenly, and start taking. I tried to concentrate everything I felt into some external fact of my being. I hoped that my face, my body, the clothes I wore, the way they hung on to me, would show her not exactly what I looked like, but exactly how I felt. Like a person who, not that long ago, had told her how I loved her. These words were still a strong part of me, these words and the time that had passed after them.

I wanted to show Nora that I wasn't going to ruin anything for her, so that she could look at me without that worry. I wondered what gesture would be most conciliatory, but didn't think I could pull anything off, so I just looked at her and hoped she understood me.

Jones spoke to Nora. She looked away from me, and I felt the bones of our relationship aching. Overtop my real bones, buried in the air that stretched between us. When Jones stopped speaking, Nora's eyes returned to mine. There was talking all around us. Jones to the next person in line. Friends to each other. I waited. Nora's eyes stayed. I wondered if she was trying to appeal to me silently. If she was also hoping to be understood, not as the person she appeared to be, but as the person she felt that she was. Her eyes didn't say if this was right. But I thought I saw in them a heavy bend. The impression that I had meant something.

I got out of the line. I walked out of the store, trying to drag my sweaty hands against my clothes. I wondered how long I'd think of Nora and feel this blown stretch of my life. What was the curing ability of time?

◆

The sidewalk is wet. The rain feels warm; it is fast-soaking. In a park near my house, a birthday party is being moved inside. Pale pink balloons are untied from benches, and a girl being pushed on a swing is lifted out. The children look up toward the sky, yelling, "Rain, rain, rain," as though it is a song.

I pass a house that reminds me of Nora's house. In the windows, the persistent glow of light, and the shadows of people in their lives. I am always passing this house. I am always turning my head to the side.

On the street, Lee holds my hand and I'm not used to the feeling of someone holding my hand in public. We share a popsicle sitting on a park bench.

We don't run into Nora, but I imagine that we do. I imagine that she appears in front of us. I say, *Hello.*

Nora looks as close as she ever has to the day that I met her. Her coat is closed, but it threatens to open.

Nora says, *I'm about to make dinner.*

I ask, *What are you going to make?*

She says, *I remember once we had an argument about that.*

I say, *I don't remember having an argument.*

She says, *We did, we had an argument.*

Lee pulls my arm, says, "Look—I always see them."

I expect her to be pointing toward my fantasy, but she is pointing toward a man lugging a huge dog in a wagon. He has to pull with both arms. The dog is very old. All of his hair looks like gray whiskers. His eyes don't have the usual dogness that suggests a happiness to just be. His eyes look like an old man's eyes. He seems a bit frightened, a bit fed up.

"He must really love him," Lee says.

I nod at her. And then, in a second, ask, "Do you mean the dog, or the man pulling?"

In the dark, when I'm back in my room, I see Nora by the window. She has collected where the blinds let in light.

I say, *We never argued about what to make.*

She says, *I'm sorry, I thought we did.*

I say, *You shouldn't show up like this.*

She tries to come over and sit on the side of my bed, but when she moves into the dark, she starts to disappear. I tell her to stay where she is. She says, *I want to come closer,* and I tell her no, I can't see. The vision breaks. There is a crack in the wall, but it's always been there. It's a line that follows through to the ceiling. I think, maybe, the building will fall down. But then, it hasn't yet, so why now?

Nora has gone. Back to bed? I hear the drift of her breathing. I'm reminded of the way that lakes deepen—uneven from the shore. I should be asleep. I still feel some panic in being awake in the middle of the night. When the morning comes, it doesn't matter how you are, the day starts, and then you find yourself in it.

I imagine that Nora has left my room and that she has reappeared in her own house. Jones asks her what's wrong and Nora says, *Nothing, I ran into somebody.* Jones goes over to her, sits down gently, and she says, *A bad memory?* Nora starts to stutter because I don't want her to say yes, so instead she turns over Jones's hand and she says, *Did you enjoy the book signing?*

Lee asks me if I've ever had a girlfriend before, and I tell her that I spent last year with a woman.

Lee holds her thumb against my hand. I say, "She's gone back to her wife. They have a baby."

When I said those words, I felt my separation from them. I am not Jones. I am not with Nora. Lee holds her hand against her chest.

"I'm sorry," Lee says.

"Oh, don't be sorry."

Lee nods and it's quiet while she thinks. And then she looks at me and she puts her hat on my head. I look at her from underneath the wide brim.

"Excellent hat," she says.

I smile at her, I can tell that I still look sad.

"You wear it excellently," she says.

I try harder to smile.

"I guess you're a Blue Jays fan," Lee says.

I nod at her. The running of Lee's joke gives me time. It gives me a chance to make the thread of her voice, her hat, the main subject of my mind. I try to make the way I feel like cloth. I imagine a stitching that can be undone.

Lee says, "I'm also a big fan." She still grins, even as she reaches. I see her wanting to make me feel better, a determination that she doesn't hide. I realize that I must have my own determination.

I touch her hat. I say, "It actually isn't mine." I force a wobbled smile, but it doesn't matter. Lee's doesn't diminish at all.

She says, "Oh? Whose is it?"

And I say, "It's my girlfriend's." And I feel my own mouth, without volition, open wide.

The early evening is my favorite time. I sit on a fold-out chair in the small square of grass outside of our house. I smell smoke blowing off a barbecue.

I lean my head back. The smoke lifts underneath me, and the breeze is cool. I can see legs—the people who are gathered in their backyard. All shorts. I picture smooth shins, their sweat looks like oil as it runs down. I want to sit on their patio furniture. I picture glass tables, wiped compulsively. Black mulch, their children watching a caterpillar moving across a brick. I see myself. I am the man with the spatula turning food over twice. And then I'm his wife, sitting underneath a wide umbrella having a sip from his beer, seeing if this time I like it. I'm tempted to believe that if I were them, I would be happier. But I know it isn't true.

If I stood there, I would breathe in too much smoke. I would stare into the barbecue and I would want to leave. I would want to be one of the coals caught on fire. The joke that caused the most laughter.

I open the book in my hand.

Above me, there are a hundred green leaves all on one branch. In the grass, the ants have found something rotten. I watch them. Trying, together, to carry the thing away. The air is so blue that I expect it to chime. I feel tired thinking about all the effort it takes to try to make your life better. I turn back to my book, Richard Hugo. I flip a page.

He says, *Say your life broke down. And the last good kiss you had was years ago.*

I say, *Okay, let's say that.*

Let's say you live in a town where there are only churches and a jail.

Only churches and a jail?

You're the jail's only prisoner, and the town would like you to leave. They'd like to be a town where everyone is free.

Then I'll leave.

You'll leave?

I will.

Are you sure you will?

I don't answer. I put the poem aside. I wonder if I'm okay. I ask myself, and I feel that I might smile.

I have not thought of Nora for the last time, but as I sit, I'm not looking for her apparition. I'm not wondering how I will go on.

The afternoon is later than it feels. The sky becomes a sun-setting yellow. The kind of color a cowboy would have to walk toward. The window above my head opens, and Lee calls out to me that some game is on. I look toward the door where, always one second ahead, there is the possibility of myself. I think, *Don't hurry.* I stand slow. *But don't wait.* I avoid the carrying ants. I pick my books up off the ground. There are soft petaled flowers planted along the street. My eyes drag the pink and purple across the path. I push open the door and then I close it against the sight of my long shadow. I think, everywhere, there is a hint of who you are becoming. I touch the wooden railing. I feel the blue pull of memory wanting to drag me back. I think I smell pine. I think I feel hands pulling my hair back. But I hear my feet against the floor, and coming down the winding stairs is the sound of Lee's TV, a play-by-play. And I think as I walk that there is no finality, there is only each stair up. The light from the window, firming the air. All the things I will and will not have.

acknowledgments

I would like to thank the Canada Council for the Arts for their support, which helped me to write later drafts of *The Adult*. I am extremely grateful.

Thank you to my agent, Sam Hiyate, for your early belief and then, for exercising years of patience. Thank you to Diane Terrana, for your honest and challenging feedback, it was integral. Thank you to the University of Guelph's MFA program, and especially to Catherine Bush for your support and for your shrewd senses which led me to work with Kate Cayley and Souvankham Thammavongsa.

Sou, thank you for your generosity, for your guiding questions, and for your confidence, which have made me better and more thoughtful.

Kate, thank you for being my ideal reader. Thank you for your willingness to be in this process with me. Your editorial guidance, and your friendship have meant so much.

I am so grateful to Sarah Jackson and Abby Muller. I couldn't have hoped for more thoughtful editors. Thank you also to Madeline Jones and Mae Zhang McCauley. I feel lucky to have been able to work with you all.

Hannah, Eric, Heather, and Ally, thank you for reading an early version of this book, and for being so generous with it. Most of all, thank you for being my friends.

Thank you to my parents, Gail and Chris. Mom, your inexhaustible interest, and unfailing belief have been so crucial. Dad, I think I first wanted to write a poem because I saw you do it. Thank you for your deep care and love.

Emma, you are a saving influence. Thank you for sharing your life with me. Thank you for reading this book almost as many times as I have. Thank you for promising that it would work out—you are the person I didn't have the heart to let down.

© KEVIN WORKMAN

BRONWYN FISCHER is a graduate of the University of Guelph's MFA program in creative writing. She also holds a bachelor of arts from the University of Toronto. Born in Bahrain, Fischer now lives in Toronto with her wife, Emma.